THE HALO FOLD

THE FOLD SERIES BOOK 7

NICK ADAMS

Elliptical
Publishing

PROLOGUE

Converted warehouse, Bristol, United Kingdom, Earth

As soon as it materialised in the darkness, it fell over and cursed silently, partly for its clumsiness and partly from the intense heat it found itself subjected too. The temperature was expected however, but it didn't make it any less shocking. Before picking itself back up, it remained completely motionless, waiting and feeling for vibration. Its acute sense of movement only detected the faint gnawing of unknown indigenous lifeforms within the fabric of the peculiar above-ground dwelling. After a few moments, and suitably convinced its intrusion had gone undetected, it rose and inspected its immediate surroundings with its two forward-facing mandibles and pair of inefficacious eyes.

The almost complete absence of light was of no consequence to this particular species, as on its home world they inhabited deep underground tunnels, only emerging up into the planetoid's permanent twilight to collect water ice as and when necessary.

It had deliberately chosen this time during the darker period as reconnaissance had shown these warm-blooded humanoid creatures seemed to shut down and remain motionless during most of it – a strange concept it couldn't quite comprehend, but it did make this important incursion considerably easier.

The space it had chosen to arrive in was rectangular, rarely used and thankfully a little cooler than the rest of the dwelling. It scuttled towards the blocked opening into the next room and sniffed the obstruction. It realised with amazement the initial scans had been correct, this partic-ular species actually do construct their dwellings partly out of food.

Resisting the urge to have a nibble and extending one of six legs from its thorax, it pressed down on the metallic handle and dragged the obstruction inwards. The space beyond was larger, hotter, with more food, this time covering the floor, and rows of thick spars across the ceil-ing. It combatted the hunger impulse once again and selected a particular module from its armoured suits menu. It scanned the space, already knowing the alien artefact it wanted would most likely be here. It was. On the far side of the space, sitting on a platform of yet more food.

A series of vibrating clicks emitted a warning, some-thing else was present in the space. Some form of motion detection beam was present. It cursed again, the beam's existence should've been logged long before now.

Luckily, the detector was in a corner up above the

obstruction facing into the room and hadn't registered the movement directly below. It scanned through its menu of jamming frequencies and selected what the system recommended to counter the device.

A faintly shimmering field enveloped the arthropod. It had to shield its eyes as a bright white light flicked past a row of large transparent panels on one wall. It paused again as the vibration of the passing land vehicle rose and gradually faded outside.

Once satisfied it was safe to recommence its advance into the room it did just that, slowly, heading directly towards the electronic alien artefact. With its pair of long mandibles wafting around out front, it was relieved to find the jammer succeeded in concealing its progress, as nothing untoward occurred as it crept forward.

It was very conscious of its six feet vibrating on the hard floor. It knew the humanoids were able to detect sound waves, so it elevated the front of its thorax and moved forward slowly on four.

This aided it on arrival at the artefact, as it was able to snatch it up with its front legs and secrete it inside its armour. What it hadn't expected or planned for was the artefact having an alarm all of its own. It began vibrating at a high frequency, causing the arthropod to panic as it knew the sound waves would be loud too.

It spun around and made for the aperture it had entered through, unfortunately catching a leg on an indoor plant that shook only slightly, but enough to be detected by the motion detector. A second and even louder vibration shrieked out. The arthropod quickly activated its return to hive function in the panic, forgetting it had to be as stationary as possible to utilise this. It realised what had happened and skidded to a halt to reactivate the system. It spun around as a new lower frequency vibrated behind, to come face to face with the humanoid standing in a second open portal staring straight at it.

The vacuum snap as it jumped knocked the humanoid back into the bedroom and rearranged the smaller items around the lounge.

1

Converted warehouse, Bristol, United Kingdom, Earth

EDWARD VIRR STARED at the video footage in amazement.

'See what I mean,' said Phil, an unsettled tone to his voice. 'It was a fucking insect.'

'You have a termite problem,' replied a grinning Andy, as he peered over their shoulders. 'You need an extermi-nator guy, a big one.'

'Yeah, one who can cope with four-foot-tall arthropods with a penchant for stealing personal computers and utilises bloody *Star Trek* technology,' said Ed, shaking his head in bewilderment. 'That's just bizarre.'

'You sure it wasn't just a hologram,' said Andy, peering around the ceiling.

'You know very well I've only recently moved in here,' said Phil. 'I haven't had any emitters installed yet.'

'What was on the tablet?' Ed asked.

'Everything,' replied Phil.

'It was encrypted though wasn't it?' Andy asked.

'Triple encrypted,' said Phil.

Ed pulled out his personal tablet and laid it on the table.

'Cleo, have there been any strange ships in the vicinity overnight?' he asked.

A twelve-inch hologram of Cleo wearing a white and gold robe appeared on the tablet's surface.

'All ships are strange to me, but if you're referring to any crewed by giant termites, then the answer is no,' she said. 'Nothing out of place, well, except for the weird comet of course.'

'Weird comet?' said Ed. 'What weird comet?'

'I saw that, it was on breakfast news this morning,' said Andy. 'It's passing through our system at the moment. They say no one saw it coming and it just appeared at the last moment from behind the sun.'

'That's a load of bollocks,' said Ed.

'That's exactly what the experts are saying,' chuckled Andy. 'Although they didn't word it quite like that.'

They both turned to Phil, eyebrows raised.

'Let's just suppose that's where it came from,' said Ed. 'What would a race of sentient insects want with your tablet'

'Search me,' Phil replied, shrugging. 'They'd need a quantum computer to decrypt it anyway.'

'If they have the technology to jump a comet around the galaxy, chances are they do,' admitted Ed, rubbing his chin thoughtfully.

'It's certainly been a night for strange things being

stolen,' said Andy, glancing down at Ed's tablet now displaying its default screen that included a rolling feed of international news reports.

'What d'you mean?' Ed asked, following his gaze.

'Hang on a sec, it'll roll around again in a minute,' said Andy, pointing at the scrolling feed. 'There,' he said, after a moment. 'Dozens of human embryos stolen overnight from a fertility clinic in California.'

'And that one too,' called Phil, indicating another report. 'Six cryonic chambers missing from a depository in Germany.'

'With bodies inside?' Ed asked.

'Yes,' said Cleo, appearing again. 'All died very young from acute terminal cancers. None of them were over twenty-six. In fact, they were the six youngest in the facility of over four thousand.'

'Is it just me, or is there a picture building here?' Ed asked, walking to the window and staring out at the plethora of dockside bars and restaurants below.

Andy continued looking at Phil, a quizzical expression washing over his face.

'Phil, was all the Theo technology on your tablet?' he asked.

Phil stared back and shrugged again.

'Yeah, some of it,' he admitted.

'What about the Theo birthing chamber stuff?' Ed asked.

'Oh, yeah, for sure,' he said, looking between the two of them. 'That's old technology for us now. You think they're wanting to produce human bodies to experiment on?'

'If that was the case, they could've just snatched a few loners who wouldn't be missed,' said Ed. 'No, it's something more than that. It has to be.'

'Like what?' Andy asked.

'Beats me,' said Ed. 'But I'll lay a bet the answer's on that comet.'

'Road trip?' Andy quizzed, raising his eyebrows.

Ed smiled and nodded.

'Ooh goody, road trip,' said Cleo, appearing again. 'I'll stoke the boilers and put the kettle on.'

'Can't we leave tomorrow?' moaned Andy, joining Ed at the row of windows. 'I was looking forward to blowing the froth off a few down there in some of Bristol's famous pubs and bars tonight.'

A grin worked its way across Ed's face.

'So was I to be honest,' he said, glancing back at his tablet. 'Cleo, can you keep an eye on that comet? We'll be up in the morning, it'll give the others time to get up to the ship anyway.'

'I'll have the *Gabriel* and paracetamol ready to rock, boss,' she said, giving him a mock salute and disappearing again.

2

The starship Gabriel*'s bridge, high Earth orbit*

CALLON BEAMED as Ed zipped up onto the bridge on the tube lift. She'd been given Rayl's seat and had spent some of the last few months with Pol learning to operate some of the *Gabriel*'s systems.

'I understand from Pol you're becoming quite an array wizard?' he said, sliding into his couch and returning the smile.

'It's amazing,' she said. 'The stuff this ship can do is just mind-blowing.'

'You haven't moved on to defensive measures yet have you?'

'A bit awkward,' said Pol, rolling her eyes. 'The new Earth defensive platforms still get a bit peevish if we acti-vate any weapons systems.'

'Haven't they sorted that out yet?' Ed asked.

'The software designers are trying,' Callon replied. 'But the *Gabriel*'s registered as a civilian yacht and shouldn't be full of battleship-class armaments.'

'We'll be out of their range in a while,' he said. 'You'll be able to play to your heart's content once we're beyond the jump zones.'

'Callon's been using her newfound skills to track the comet,' said Pol. 'You're right about it behaving strangely.'

'In what way?'

'Well, they were right about it suddenly appearing from behind the sun, it then tracked across the system getting to within five point two million kilometres of Earth and then continuing on a path towards Jupiter.'

'Where is it now?'

'That's just the thing,' said Callon. 'A couple of hours ago, it tracked in behind Jupiter and never reappeared.'

'Jupiter's big,' he said. 'Lots of gravitational forces there. Perhaps it just got pulled in.'

'Too far out,' said Pol. 'Its speed and trajectory would've seen it pass by without much deviation.'

Ed nodded and glanced up at the holomap.

'Are Andy, Phil and Linda far away? We need to get after it.'

'On their way,' said Callon, pointing and highlighting a shuttle rising up through the upper atmosphere. 'Linda's already here.'

'*Gabriel* all good to go, Cleo?' he asked.

'All shipshape and tickety-boo, boss,' she said, appearing this time dressed in her favourite black ninja suit. 'I understand we're going to be galactic bug exterminators.'

'Don't jump the gun,' said Ed. 'They might prove friendly yet.'

'Have you forgotten *Starship Troopers*?' said Andy, appearing on the bridge with Phil.

Ed sighed and rolled his eyes.

'That's a sixty-year-old movie, Andrew, and an even older book, it's fiction.'

'Seemed pretty real to me when my dad put it on when I was seven.'

'You still are,' said Linda, closely following and dressed in a ship suit and slippers.

'I take it you came up yesterday?' said Ed.

'Somebody has to help Cleo with the housework,' she said, retaining a deadpan expression. 'While you two were poisoning yourselves in Bristol's dens of iniquity, I was mopping floors and polishing the brass.'

The other six just stared at her.

'Okay, I might have had a couple of mojitos,' she admitted, shrugging.

'Or six, followed by a bottle of burgundy and half a packet of paracetamol this morning,' said Cleo.

'Shut up, you,' she groaned. 'Can't a girl bullshit just a little round here?'

'Did you get any reply from Bache?' Andy asked, changing the subject and glancing over at Ed.

The others all looked over to regard Ed with interest, much to Linda's obvious relief.

'He says the GDA have come across large insects many times, but there's no record of any sentient, spacefaring species. The expert he spoke to thought he was joking and scoffed at the very idea. He also thought the video footage from Phil's apartment was faked.'

'Seemed pretty real to me,' said Phil. 'It disappeared with my bloody tablet, a brand new one too.'

Linda piloted the five-hundred-metre starship out of orbit and headed towards the nearest designated jump zone.

'Take us over to Jupiter,' said Ed. 'I want to see if that so-called comet's still around or if it just used the planet as a cover to jump away.'

'Do we need to be cloaked when we get there?' Andy asked.

'Probably best,' Ed replied. 'They appear to have some pretty remarkable technology. If they do have aggressive tendencies, we don't want to make it easy for them.'

Twenty-two minutes later the *Gabriel* reached the jump out zone, a couple of milliseconds after that it materialised five million kilometres from Jupiter and immediately cloaked.

'Okay, Callon,' said Ed, leaning back into his seat. 'Time to put your newfound skills to the test. Wadda we got?'

Callon, her head buried in the floating displays, paused before replying.

'A dispersing trail of water ice along the comet's last known trajectory, ending in a rather noisy jump signature,' she said.

'Embedded?' Ed asked.

'No.'

'Emergent location?'

'Erm—A system seventy-one thousand, five hundred and sixty-seven light years away,' she said nervously, glancing up at Pol.

'No way,' said Linda.

'That's bollocks,' said Andy. 'Nobody can jump that far.'

'Sorry, Callon,' said Ed. 'I'm afraid they're right, the margin for error when jumping even a tenth of that distance is just too enormous. It'd be suicide.'

'Callon's evaluation is correct,' said Cleo. 'I've just run the same analysis. It's a system on the galaxies fringe in the very edge of the Milky Way's halo.'

The bridge was hushed for a moment, until Andy broke the silence.

'The halo? That's just outrageous,' he blurted. 'It'd take us days to get there, even with the latest long-distance jump technology.'

'Eight days and seventeen hours,' said Linda, shaking her head as her navigation hologram phased into definition.

Again, they all turned to stare at Ed. He was craning his neck up at the main holomap above as the same course parameters hove into view.

'Well, we'd better make a start then,' he said, scanning the circle of faces. 'Is everyone cool with that? It probably means we'll be away for at least three weeks and eight-hour shifts on the bridge.

Getting a round of shrugs and nods, he turned to Linda.

'Don't say it,' she said, pointing at him accusingly.

'Say what?' he asked, his face a picture of innocence.

'You know, "engage" while extending a hand and

looking into the middle distance with a brooding expression. It's getting a bit wearisome now,' she said, her finger continuing to point.

'Oh, right, okay,' he replied, rubbing his chin and dropping his voice an octave. 'I'll make it so.'

Everybody laughed except Callon, who didn't have a clue what the joke was about and Linda, who closed her eyes, gritted her teeth and began counting to ten out loud.

'Clear the bridge, she's going to blow,' said Andy, making for the tube lift, closely followed by the others.

3

___

The starship Gabriel*'s bridge, non-system space*

THE EIGHT DAYS had dragged interminably and everyone aboard the *Gabriel* breathed a sigh of relief when finally they were summoned to the bridge for the last jump. Their destination was an unclassified and unexplored system in the galaxy's halo which contains some of the oldest stars in the Milky Way. Formed around fourteen billion years ago, they sit outside the clusters normally grouped within the spiral arms and, according to the GDA, just too distant and spread out to be of any economic value. It seemed even the Ancients hadn't bothered with these regions, only seeding the human genome into the more densely grouped spiral arms of the Milky Way. No known bi-pedal races had ever been recorded originating in the vast depths of the halo.

'Is that it?' grumbled Andy, as the system in question

revealed itself on the holomap. 'We've come all this way for that pile of rocks?'

'Hmm,' grunted Ed. 'Doesn't look much of a holiday hotspot does it?'

'Nothing habitable in there at all,' said Pol. 'Not for us anyway.'

Ed looked over at Phil, who was piloting the ship on this occasion.

'Can you jump just outside the system and then navigate in?' he asked.

'Sure,' replied Phil, quickly replotting the jump co-ordinates.

'I want to have a good look around before they have any idea we're here,' Ed continued.

'That's if they're here at all,' mumbled Andy.

'They're here all right,' said Pol, glancing across from her floating screens. 'There's movement almost everywhere.'

'But they're just rocks,' said Callon. 'I can't detect any ships at all.'

'Yes, but they're navigated rocks, just like the comet we saw,' said Pol. 'There's thousands of big ones, small ones, all sizes really and all being piloted, mostly around the planet-sized bodies.'

'There's no movement around that planet though,' said Callon, highlighting one of the bigger darker spheres. 'Why are they ignoring that one?'

Phil gunned the cloaked ship into the system, and while Pol concentrated her powerful array on the rock traffic, Callon was able to get a much better survey of the dead world. The closer they got, the better her resolution.

'Oh,' she exclaimed, sending the latest image across to Ed's display.

'Well, well,' he murmured, his eyes widening.

'What is it?' asked Linda, craning her neck to see.

'Evidence of oceans and rivers,' he said. 'This planet used to have an atmosphere.'

'What, like Mars?' she replied.

'Yeah, but a lot older and…fuck!'

Everyone glanced up from what they were doing as Ed didn't use that word very often.

'Is that what I think it is?' Callon asked.

'Shit,' said Andy. 'Is that the remains of a city?'

'Well it certainly ain't a natural formation,' said Ed, excitedly.

'There's another one,' said Callon, putting the image up on the main holomap and pointing. 'And another, a really big one.'

'We need to go there,' said Ed, glancing at Phil.

'On the way, boss.'

They all watched transfixed during the journey into the system as more detail became available. This had been a very densely populated world a long time ago. Although over the vast spread of time, the cities had crumbled virtually to dust, the outlines from space were still quite unmistakable.

'There's nothing left standing in any of the cities,' said Callon. 'Just the shadow of the layout.'

'Except for that,' said Andy, pointing at something sticking up in the centre of the largest one.

As the resolution improved, it quickly became apparent it was a low stone arch.

'Anything paying us any attention?' Ed asked.

'No unusual movements,' said Pol. 'Well, no more unusual than thousands of flying rocks already is.'

'Locating the comet will be virtually impossible amongst that lot, especially after all this time,' said Linda.

'What are we going to call these bugs?' asked Andy. 'We're not going to be able to ask them are we?'

'Halopods,' said Phil, without looking up from his flight screen.

Everyone glanced at Phil, before turning their attention to Ed.

'Sounds pretty good to me,' he said.

'Could be an old Wyndham novel,' said Andy. 'The Day of the Halopods.'

He laughed at his own joke, immediately realising he was the only one doing so and quickly shut up.

'Are we planning on landing on that thing?' he said, quickly changing the subject.

Ed raised his eyebrows and turned to Pol.

'It doesn't have an atmosphere anymore, gravity's point six two Earth, so you could,' she said. 'So long as the surface can take the weight and you would obviously need to wear suits.'

'Or take one of the shuttles down,' said Phil.

Ed rubbed his chin in thought.

'I really want to know who used to live here and what happened to them. It might be pertinent considering these bugs are taking an interest in us,' he said.

'We could take the *Cartella* down there,' said Andy. 'It's the lightest ship we have and there's half a dozen Theo suits in its lockers.'

Ed stood and turned to Phil.

'Slip the *Gabriel* into a low orbit and have an embedded emergency jump programmed just in case we're rumbled,' he said.

'No heroics or wandering too far,' said Linda, giving Ed one of her don't argue stares. 'You get whatever evidence you need and you get the hell back here, is that clear?'

'Absolutely,' he said, a little enthusiastically, giving Andy a wide-eyed expression that Linda couldn't see. 'Andrew, fancy a stroll on a dead planet?'

'Do you think they had any pubs down there?' Andy asked, standing.

'If they did, I think the beer might be a little bit past its sell by date now,' said Phil, not looking up from the helm icons as he slotted the cloaked five-hundred-metre starship into orbit.

'The same goes for you, Andrew Faux,' growled Linda, watching him steely-eyed as he walked to the tube lift.

'Mister trustworthy, me,' Andy replied.

'Hmm,' she grunted. 'Rayl might still be here if you were.'

Andy froze with his back to Linda, a wide-eyed expression on his face and his fists clenching and unclenching.

'What the hell is that supposed to…?'

Ed leant forward, grabbed Andy by the belt and dragged him into the lift. Both disappeared down towards the hangars in the blink of an eye.

'Don't let her rile you,' Ed said calmly. 'Linda and Rayl were very close and she misses her.'

'Not as fucking much as me,' Andy snapped, kicking the side of the lift.

'We all know that,' Ed replied. 'We also know you didn't do anything to warrant what she did. She's the one with the issues. They most probably stem from the horrors she witnessed on her father's ship shortly before we found her.'

They arrived at the hangar deck and strode left towards the port hangar.

'D'you think she'll ever be at peace with that?' Andy asked.

Ed shrugged.

'I'm no psychologist, but I do know PTSD can rear its ugly head in many forms and sometimes take a lot of counselling.'

They entered the port hangar and made straight towards the *Cartella* parked backing onto the right-hand wall.

'She's never had any and would never talk about it, well, not with me anyway,' said Andy, as he opened the side airlock.

'Perhaps she'll get the medical help she needs in the navy,' said Ed. 'Although knowing her she'll just hide it away again.'

'Am I piloting?' Andy asked.

'Yeah, okay, it'll give you something to concentrate on instead of dwelling in the past,' said Ed, slapping Andy on the back.

'Do I do that?'

'Just a bit. It's been a year now, Andrew.'

'Yeah, I know.'

'Right, come on, take me to that archway, let's see what happened to this planet.'

4

The Cartella, *approaching uncharted planet in the halo*

THERE WAS STILL the thinnest of atmospheres around the dead world, as Andy piloted the *Cartella* down towards the site of one of the larger cities. It barely warmed the heat shield at all, enabling him to keep the nose down and their destination in sight.

'It gets bigger and bigger doesn't it,' said Andy, as they approached and watched the vast sprawling and crumbled metropolis stretch away to the horizon in every direction.

'That was a big river,' said Ed, pointing out the now dry and wide winding channel snaking its way through the ruins.

Andy stretched forward in his seat and peered downwards.

'Anywhere in particular you'd like to me to park?' he asked.

'There's a bit of a building with an arch still standing over there,' said Ed, pointing over to the right. 'Let's give that a try. But keep the motor running for a few moments after you land, just in case it collapses downwards. I don't want us to end up upside-down in someone's basement.'

'Don't worry,' said Andy. 'I've been upside-down in this ship before and it's not something I plan on repeating.'

Ed sat gripping the sides of his seat as Andy flared the ship and turned through three hundred and sixty degrees while checking below. Seemingly satisfied, he dropped the ship, creating clouds of dust that completely obscured the view. The landing was so soft, it took Andy a few moments to actually confirm they were down.

'Hmm,' he grunted. 'It seems we're down.'

He did as Ed had suggested and kept the antigravs spinning for a few seconds. Nothing moved, no tilting, no sudden drops. They glanced at each other, before Ed spoke.

'Shut her down,' he said, peering unimpressed at the billowing dust storm outside. 'We need to let all this crap settle before venturing out.'

It took twenty minutes with the low gravity for visibility outside the front screen to return.

'Any movement upstairs, Cleo?' Ed asked.

'No unusual insect movement detected,' replied Cleo. 'Although, I do have the exterminators' number on speed dial just in case.'

'I imagine even the commercial sprays would struggle with four-foot bugs in fucking body armour,' grinned Andy. 'Forgive me for being a cynic, but I'll stick to my marine issue laser pulse rifle thanks.'

'Talking of rifles,' said Ed, standing and pulling two weapons off the rack behind them. 'Best we take a couple with us.'

The Theo suits were next. Ed never could get used to the way they swept up from a pad under your feet and enclosed around you. He swore it was like being suddenly wrapped in black cling-wrap. There was that worrying second or two before the oxygen began to flow and the systems came online that unnerved him every time.

'Ready?' he asked Andy.

'Ready,' came the reply over the suit intercom.

Dust enveloped them as soon as the outer airlock opened, but soon cleared as Ed went first and made his way down the steps. He peered under the ship to see how far the struts had penetrated the surface and was encouraged to see it was only a few inches.

Extending his right leg, he let his foot fall onto the surface. It crunched like fine gravel and he wondered if James Dewey had felt so apprehensive when he first set foot on Mars some thirty years ago. The small cloud of dust around his boot soon settled and he turned and nodded at Andy, still standing in the airlock.

'One small step for a...'

'Shut up, Andrew, and get down here,' said Ed, taking a few paces away from the ship.

'Buzz Aldrin never got that kind of abuse,' Andy moaned, following in Ed's footsteps.

Ed ignored him and walked carefully across the crunching regolith towards the structure he'd spotted earlier. It was peculiar in the fact that the entire city had crumbled into dust probably many millennia before and yet this archway was so well built, it was seemingly one of the only things standing proud of the regolith for kilometres around.

It was about six metres tall and constructed of half-metre rectangular dark stone blocks. It was bigger than it had seemed from above and although some of the building around it had collapsed, this section was remarkably intact. The archway had geometric patterns carved into it and Ed ran his hand around its curvature, removing the thick layer of dust and marvelling at the intricacy of the design.

'Wow,' said Andy, looking over Ed's shoulder. 'Someone was a bit handy with a hammer and chisel.'

Ed peered through the arch and into the darkness beyond to discover a steep slope leading downwards. When he illuminated his rifle light, the beam revealed a tunnel going down about fifteen metres and turning right. Scuffing the dusty slope with one foot, he found it wasn't a slope at all, but a step completely filled with the gritty regolith.

Andy did the same to Ed's left and cleared enough away to enable him to step down and repeat the process.

'It's a staircase,' he said, his boot sweeping enough off each step to enable him to descend.

'Enable your personal shield,' said Ed, following behind. 'We don't know what's down here, our scans couldn't penetrate below the surface.'

Once they reached the right-hand corner, they realised the staircase turned back on itself and continued down. It did this eight times before Andy spoke.

'How deep d'you think we are now?' he asked, flashing his light down the next flight.

'Gotta be around fifty, perhaps sixty metres,' said Ed, shining his beam downwards too. 'Hang on,' he said, squinting into the gloom. 'There's no turn, it goes straight on at the bottom of this one.'

'There was a door here,' said Andy, illuminating the broken remains on the ground and pointing out a recess in the walls where the frame had been.

'It looks like there was a second one just a bit further up,' said Ed, walking up the now level corridor. 'There's a lot less dust here, just a couple of centimetres and completely undisturbed.'

'No one's been down here for a while,' Andy murmured. 'Hundreds, perhaps thousands of years.'

'Holy moly!' exclaimed Ed, shining his light past where the second door had been.

Andy spun his light around and aimed it in the same direction.

'Shit, how big is it?' he asked, walking over and staring into a room so big, their lights, although powerful, failed to illuminate the far wall.

The ceiling was about thirty metres above them, and glancing left and right Ed couldn't make out a side wall in those directions either. Regimental rows of square pillars held up the roof, spaced about every twenty or so metres. Ed walked up to one of them and brushed it with his glove. More of the intricate carvings similar to the archway above adorned every flat surface of the pillar.

'Stonemasons must've made a good living in this

town,' said Andy, shining his light on all the surrounding pillars and finding them equally and similarly decorated.

Ed stood and stared at the designs for a few moments.

'D'you know, I'm sure I've seen something similar to this before,' he said.

'Bollocks, how could you have?'

'I don't know, they just seem familiar.'

'Could be something you saw in the Valley of the Kings that time we went to Egypt, maybe?'

'Hmm, I'm not so sure,' Ed mumbled.

'Let's not blunder out into this sea of pillars and get disorientated,' said Andy, jabbing his thumb back at the door. 'Let's follow the wall around and see how big this room really is.'

Ed nodded, turned back to the entrance and headed off to the left. He counted the pillars on his right as he went, the light beams creating eerie and slightly disconcerting shadows as they passed each row.

'This is all carved out of solid rock down here,' said Andy, running his glove along the wall. 'See how flat and perfect the walls are. Whoever dug this out had some quality equipment.'

'It all seems so human too,' said Ed. 'The shape of the doors, the carvings. I just don't understand how an age-old human race could've evolved independently and this remotely in the halo.'

'Perhaps the Ancients did come here,' said Andy.

Ed stopped suddenly, causing Andy to bump into him, their personal shields fluorescing as they touched.

'That's it!' exclaimed Ed, shining his light on the

nearest pillar. 'That's where I've seen these markings before.'

'Where?'

'Around the doorways into the Ancients' remote gateway control rooms.'

'Holy crap,' said Andy. 'So they were here too?'

5

____

Underground chamber, uncharted planet in the halo

THEY BOTH STOOD in silence for a moment and considered the fact that this chamber might have been constructed by the Ancients.

'The three moons are missing above the planet,' said Andy. 'So there wasn't a gateway here.'

'But there might have been a hundred thousand years ago,' Ed replied. 'Remember all the rocks and debris the halopods have utilised.'

Andy shone his light around the wall to his left.

'So there might be a control room somewhere here?' he said.

'Big place to build deep underground for no reason,' said Ed, striding on with renewed purpose and lighting up the wall again, this time with added scrutiny.

The corner of the chamber appeared out of the gloom, with a mirror-smooth wall continuing off to the right.

'Twenty-six pillars to the corner,' said Ed. 'Twenty-two metres apart, that's way over one point one kilometres across this chamber if it goes as far the other way.'

'And you felt you had to tell me that, because?'

'Just trying to get a scale of the place.'

'Well, I'm trying not to think about how far underground we are, or how far away the ship is,' Andy moaned. 'And this suits chafing me around my gentleman's area.'

'Anything else?'

'No, I think that's about it.'

'Good, now shut the fuck up and find me a control room.'

They plodded on in silence for a few minutes until the next corner came into view.

'It might not be in this building,' said Andy, dejectedly. 'It could be anywhere on the entire planet, or never have existed at all.'

'You really are in a glass half empty mood aren't you?'

'I'm just bored trudging around this big empty hole in a suit that's trying to prevent me ever having children.'

'I tell you what,' said Ed, as they turned the corner. 'If we haven't found anything when we get to the middle, we'll turn and walk down the line of pillars to the entrance and return to the ship. We can have something to eat, recharge the suits, you can find one that fits better and we'll come back and check the other side of this chamber. How does that sound?'

'Deal. Can I have ice cream?'

At the twenty-sixth pillar they turned in towards the

centre and began following the line of pillars. Ed counted them again and a few minutes later when they again reached number twenty-six, he stopped.

'This is the centre of the chamber,' he said, peering around.

'Forgive me for not jumping up and down with glee,' mumbled Andy, pointing onwards. 'But I believe the raspberry ripple is in that direction.'

'Yeah, I know,' replied Ed, sighing. 'I was kinda hoping there might be something here other than just a circle on the floor.'

'Well, there isn't, can we go on to…oh, bloody hell!'

'Bloody hell, what?' Ed asked, following Andy's gaze upwards.

'That's the first mistake I've seen the stonemasons make.'

'Mistake? The Ancients don't make mistakes. What are you looking at?'

'There's a lump missing out of that pillar about eight foot up.'

Ed stood back and looking up he followed Andy's finger. The carvings were normal all the way up, but at one point, on one side, it looked like a small section was missing or damaged.

'Lift me up there,' said Ed, putting his gloves either side of the pillar and raising a boot.

Andy cupped his hands under the boot and hoisted Ed up until he could run a glove around the slight flaw. Andy ducked his head as dust rained down on him.

'Don't mind me,' he said, shaking the worst off his helmet.

'You're not going to believe this,' said Ed, through gritted teeth as he struggled with something.

'Stop wriggling about,' moaned Andy from below. 'Or I'll drop you.'

'Got it!' Ed exclaimed, dropping back down.

'Got what?'

Ed didn't answer as a rumble from below had them both staring at their feet. A triangular section of the circle on the floor sunk down, followed by another and another and so on.

'It's a spiral staircase,' said Andy, then he turned to glance up again. 'Was that another recessed handle like at the other control rooms?'

'Yep.'

'Wow, well, I'm sorry for doubting you.'

'Accepted.'

They waited until the clunking and rasping of stone had stopped before venturing down the newly arrived staircase.

'I hope it's not too deep,' said Andy. 'I hate these things.'

Ed went first, taking the outside route around where the treads were widest. He was pleased to see Andy had got his wish, as it only went down about four metres before opening out into a control room he was quite familiar with. It wasn't identical, but the basic layout and equipment he had seen before was all present.

He stopped suddenly causing Andy to bump into him and their shields once again fluoresced.

'I wish you'd stop doing that,' said Andy.

Ed just pointed to something in the corner.

'Oh!' grunted Andy, as he too saw the skeleton lying in a pile. 'That's put me off my ice cream that has.'

'I'll give some to him,' said Ed. 'He could do with a little fattening up.'

'Hey, listen to you cracking the jokes now.'

'I do have a sense of humour you know?'

'What's that on the skull?' Andy asked.

'Some sort of helmet,' said Ed, leaning over the remains and peering at it. 'It's wired into that unit beside you.'

'D'you think it's one of the Ancients?' Andy asked. 'I thought they were all in that omnipresent gaseous form now.'

'Well, Neferuptah said there'd been twelve of them originally and not all of them had computerised themselves. A couple had wanted to remain in human form, but utilising their own life-expanding technology.'

'What, like our autonurse?'

'I suppose so.'

'I'm sure Cleo will be able to carbon date one of the bones,' said Andy.

'You can pick one up if you like,' said Ed. 'It might invoke a curse, disturbing the grave of a god and all that.'

'Ah, don't say that. I have enough nightmares as it is.'

Ed ignored the dead eye sockets following him across the small room and stood in front of the main control panel.

'You're going to press the top right-hand button again, aren't you?' said Andy, watching Ed wipe the panel clean with a glove.

'Well, there's no gateway up there this time is there? So, at least this time we won't lose the *Gabriel*.'

'You're not worried everything might explode then?'

'Nah, but I would like to know what they are?' he asked, pointing to several oval protuberances sticking out high on the walls around them. 'Didn't have them before.'

'Camera system perhaps?' Andy speculated.

'Why would you need eight of them?' replied Ed.

'Fair point.'

Ed shrugged and touched the icon he knew to be the power up button.

6

The gateway control room, uncharted planet in the halo

THEY BOTH EMITTED a sigh of relief when nothing went bang. There were only the recognisable hums and whirring noises of the system coming online that were to be expected. Wall panel lights illuminated the room in a dull yellow wash that enabled them to extinguish their rifle lamps.

'Where does the power for this come from after all this time?' Andy mused. 'It could be tens of thousands of years since it's been activated.'

'Buggered if I know,' said Ed. 'Must be coming from underground somewhere. There's nothing on the surface showing any power signatures.'

'Lithosphere thermal generator,' said a sudden deep resonating voice.

They both jumped out of their skins at the suddenness and volume of the unexpected answer to Andy's question.

'What the fuck?' Andy blurted, taking an unintended step back, his eyes darting around the room nervously, but finding no one.

Ed took a deep breath and allowed his heart rate to recover before speaking.

'Hello—who are you?' he asked, realising the voice came from the equipment.

'My name is Pyriaeus the Fourteen,' the voice stated.

Ed thought about the name for a second.

'Are you one of the Ancients?' he asked.

'Ancients? I'm not that old, I am one of the twelve, unless—how long have I been in stasis?'

'We don't know,' said Andy. 'But I have a feeling you're going to be surprised.'

'You're humanoid and speak Ellinika, so you survived the arthropoda emergence?'

Ed and Andy glanced at each other and winced.

'Erm, if you mean this planet? We have bad news,' said Ed.

'This planet died a long time ago,' said Andy.

'Ah, I wondered why I couldn't communicate with any of my surface systems or satellites,' he said. 'So where are you from?'

'A long way across the galaxy in one of the spiral arms,' said Ed.

'If that's the case, what brought you here?' he asked. 'I deliberately chose this location for a new human society because of its remote location and almost impossible to find by accident.'

'The bugs or arthropods as you call them. They paid us a visit and we tracked them back to here,' said Ed.

'They're still here then?'

'Oh, yes,' said Andy. 'Hordes of them.'

'Where did they come from?' Ed asked.

'Stand back by the entrance,' he said.

Ed moved over to the doorway, closely followed by Andy. Ed shrugged as their eyes met, but were then attracted by the oval objects high on the walls they'd pondered over earlier. They began to glow a deep mauve and as they watched, a man appeared where they'd been standing a moment ago. He shimmered for a moment before becoming slightly more solid in appearance, but it was obvious by the vagueness of the projection, something wasn't quite as it should be. Pyriaeus glanced down at himself and groaned.

He wasn't tall, but had a high golden headdress that made him seem bigger. A black goatee and long Roman-style robes with gold edging finished the Ancient's weak holographic image.

'Hang on,' said Andy, looking up at the glowing projectors. 'I think we need to do a bit of housework.'

He approached one of the emitters, stood on tiptoe and wiped a thick coating of dust off its lens. It glowed brighter and the Ancient's hologram improved in clarity. After he'd cleaned all the other lenses, the hologram had become crisp and as if the man was real and standing before them.

Pyriaeus smiled and bowed his head. They did the same as it just seemed the natural thing to do. He glanced down at himself again, straightened his robe and peered over at the pile of bones on the floor in the corner adopting a philosophical expression.

'I haven't aged well then,' he said, turning back to them. 'Must've given you a fright when you came in.'

'Not as much as your sudden voice,' blurted Andy. 'I nearly peed myself.'

Ed winced and gave Pyriaeus an apologetic look.

Pyriaeus smirked in return.

'You asked me where the bugs came from,' he said, sighing, his expression turning back to one of consternation. 'I had just completed the gateway and dialled in another nearby galaxy to test the system. A bunch of rocks sailed through before I could shut it down. They got caught in the planet's gravity well and the bugs, as you call them, that were deep inside survived the entry. The fight to eradicate them went on for a couple of hundred rotations, but they were incredibly quick-learning and industrious. They could reverse engineer anything and improve on it. We soon found ourselves facing our own weapons and losing vast swathes of the planet. They can breed at an alarming rate too, so you can kill thousands of them and next day they come back at you ten-fold.'

'They must've stripped this planet of everything they wanted, because they're out in the rest of the system now and they have rocks with jump drives,' said Ed.

'So, if we could eradicate them from out there, we could recolonise Tessamaine,' Pyriaeus said, his face brightening.

Ed's awkward expression didn't go unnoticed.

'You look sceptical.'

'There's no atmosphere anymore,' said Andy. 'It's just a dead rock now.'

'Ah, that explains your suits,' the Ancient said, his face dropping again. 'The cities?'

Ed shook his head.

'Sorry, all dust I'm afraid.'

'You have the same tailor as Neferuptah,' said Andy, suddenly changing the subject.

Pyriaeus blanched, his eyes wide as he turned to stare at Andy.

'Neferuptah!' he exclaimed. 'You know of her? She's still alive?'

'In her own way, yes,' said Ed. 'I talked to her recently.'

'Omnipresent cloud of gas is the best explanation,' said Andy.

'She can manifest herself as anything, anywhere in an entire system,' said Ed. 'Move planets with just a thought.'

'We're always very polite to her,' said Andy, adopting a phlegmatic expression and rolling his eyes.

Pyriaeus gazed into space for a moment.

'She always was the clever one,' he admitted.

'You were close?' Ed asked.

He turned back to Ed with a tentative smile.

'She was, is, my wife,' he said.

'Wow,' said Andy, turning to Ed. 'What would be the element for an anniversary that long?'

An alarm went off in Ed's suit shortly before the same insistent siren sounded in Andy's.

'Two-hour warning,' said Ed. 'We need to get back to our ship before the suits run out of energy. Pyriaeus, would you like to come with us? Is there something portable you can download yourself into?'

'It doesn't appear there's any reason for me to remain,' he said, dolefully.

He stooped down and pointed at the cabinet under the control panel.

'Open that and pick out the big data core top right. That's the complete back-up of my civilisation here from start to finish. Then open that one there beside you and take both the cores from in there.'

'That's everything is it?' asked Ed.

'Yes.'

'Before you turn yourself off,' said Andy, glancing at the pile of bones in the corner, 'would you mind if I brought one of your bones with us? We could have it dated and you'll find out how long you've been in stasis.'

Pyriaeus shrugged.

'Of course,' he said. 'They're no use to me anymore.'

'Back yourself up and you'll become a guest of honour on our starship,' said Ed.

'Thank you. Do you have holographic capabilities for me there?' he asked.

'Absolutely,' said Ed. 'I think you'll be quite impressed.'

A rattling sound coming from the doorway caught their attention.

'They're here,' Pyriaeus said. 'I thought you said this planet was clear of them?'

'It was,' said Ed, turning and bringing his rifle up to cover the doorway.

Andy, who was closer, leant against the stone doorframe and peered around and up the spiral stairway, his rifle in the shoulder.

It was only a couple of seconds before his weapon fired and a four-foot insect crashed down the last few steps and lay twitching just inside the door. Some thick grey goo seeped out from its torso and began pooling around Andy's boots.

'Fuck's sake, that stinks,' he moaned, as a rumble from the stairway had him involuntarily taking a step back.

The stairs began moving quickly up, with the sound of crackling and more grey goo dribbling from the top of the now blocked doorway.

'Now we're trapped down here,' said Ed, turning to Pyriaeus. 'I take it you did that?'

'They would've overwhelmed the two of you in seconds,' he replied. 'Their numbers are limitless.'

Andy stepped back again to avoid the growing pool of stinking goo.

'Ah, shit,' he cried. 'I think I got some in my boot.'

'How did they know we were here?' Ed asked.

'You probably alerted them when you activated me,' said Pyriaeus. 'One thing they do well is detect electronic signatures. You can turn on the smallest electronic device and somehow they'll feel it thousands of kilometres away.'

'I wish I'd known that earlier,' said Ed, slumping down onto the control room seat. 'Now we're as good as trapped down here like you were.'

'Not necessarily,' said Pyriaeus, turning and regarding the back wall with interest.

7

The Gabriel*'s bridge, orbiting dead planet, halo region*

'WOAH!' exclaimed Phil. 'What just happened?'

The holomap had lit up with two large detonations a hundred thousand kilometres away amongst the rocks inhabited by the halopods.

'Shit,' muttered Linda, as the resulting rock shrapnel expanded outwards, causing absolute chaos with the rock traffic. It smashed its way through everything big and small until it was difficult to determine what was shrapnel and what was still controlled vehicles.

'Did they do that?' asked Callon. 'Or are they under attack?'

'Or was it Ed?' Phil asked.

'Ed and Andy are still underground,' said Pol. 'The *Cartella*'s still parked down there.'

'Whatever it was, they weren't expecting it,' said Linda.

'I've got a weak power signature on the planet now,' said Pol. 'Down near where Ed and Andy went in.'

'Bloody hell,' said Linda, watching a sudden swarm of smaller rocks pour from a contingent of the much larger ones that weren't near the explosions. 'They're all heading here.'

'They must've detected someone turning the lights on too,' said Phil. 'How do we warn Ed?'

'We can't unless he sticks his head out,' said Linda.

'What happens if they discover the *Cartella*?' asked Callon.

It went quiet for a moment while everybody looked nervously at each other.

'I can make sure they don't,' said Cleo, materialising in the centre of the bridge. 'I'll lift it off the surface and keep it cloaked and out the way.'

'Don't you take it too far,' said Linda. 'I envisage they're going to need it in a hurry.'

'I promise it'll be close,' she replied, vanishing again.

The holomap displayed what looked like a swarm of bees descending towards the planet.

'I think we should back off a little,' said Phil. 'If just one of those hits our shields, they'll know we're here.'

'I agree,' said Linda. 'Bring all the weapons online too, we may need to provide covering fire.'

Phil quietly lifted the cloaked starship into a higher orbit, then held position matching the turn of the planet again. The floating displays in front of each station changed to a red glow as the weapon pods motored out from the ship's hull and the *Gabriel* went onto a war footing.

The peculiar and rather sinister horde of rocks approached, passed the *Gabriel* and descended down to the surface. There was no longer any debate about why they'd come, as they swarmed down and landed in close proximity to the power signature.

The *Gabriel*'s powerful cameras watched as dozens of halopods scuttled out from each vehicle as they touched down. The ever-burgeoning sea of insects made straight for the arch and swirled through and down, like water circling down a plughole.

'Shit,' muttered Pol. 'Can't we do anything?'

'They're not wearing any suits or anything,' said Phil. 'The buggers are able to survive in space.'

'Let's just hope they're hiding down there,' said Linda, her face a picture of worry.

'Or there's another way out,' said Callon.

'The power source has just disappeared again,' said Pol.

'That's a good sign, I hope,' muttered Phil. 'Perhaps they'll all bugger off again now.'

Unfortunately on the surface nothing changed. A few dozen halopods that had remained above ground, milling around the vicinity of the arch, continued doing just that.

8

———————

The gateway control room, uncharted planet in the halo

'YOU HAVE A BACK DOOR?' Ed asked, turning to follow Pyriaeus's gaze.

'Call me paranoid,' he said. 'Because I remained mortal, I always ensured I had a means of escape. Unlike some of my colleagues, I couldn't just download myself somewhere else if things got a bit dangerous.'

'Well, why didn't you use it at the time?' asked Andy, pointing to the pile of bones.

'I did, but the whole region was overrun with them. They were coming that way too. I had to backtrack into here again and seal myself in. I only had enough supplies to last a few days in here, so I came to the inevitable conclusion I had to upload myself like some of the others and wait until one or more of them came looking for me.'

'Only they didn't,' said Andy.

'No, but you did,' he said, glancing at the pile of bones on the floor again. 'Eventually.'

Ed walked over to the main console, opened the cabinet beneath and removed the larger data node, secreting it in a suit pocket.

'Can we open that exit, or do you have to do it?' Andy asked, while opening the other cabinet and nodding towards the back wall.

Pyriaeus turned and pointed at his skeleton.

'Under me is a small hatch. Open it and turn the handle. Follow the passageway right to the end. You will find a blank wall. Again, in the floor there's another similar hatch and handle. It operates a second spiral stairway, a much longer one as it takes you up to the basement of one of the main government buildings.'

'There are no buildings left,' said Ed.

'Then we need to hope it's not blocked,' Pyriaeus admitted, ensuring deliberate eye contact with both of them.

Ed and Andy both nodded to recognise they both understood the situation.

He went on to say, 'I hope they haven't found your lander either.'

'Cleo will have kept it safe,' said Andy, giving Ed an optimistic glance.

'She would have,' Ed replied, moving over and bending down to peer into the cabinet that Andy had opened. 'Are you ready, Pyriaeus?'

'I am, good luck gentlemen,' the Ancient replied, his hologram fading away.

Ed removed the two nodes and secured them safely

within his suit. Andy picked up one of the bones as he pushed the rest of the skeleton to one side with his boot. The skull, still with some sort of weird helmet attached, rolled away and bumped into the wall with a crack.

'Oops, sorry,' muttered Andy, glancing back to where Pyriaeus had been only seconds ago.

Ed stooped down and brushed the dust away from the small hatch with a glove. It was jammed shut, so he stomped on it a couple of times and managed to prise it open with his rifle.

The handle turned clockwise smoothly. At first nothing happened until a deep rumble within the wall caused them to step back. Six of the large stone blocks sank inwards before swinging away like a door. They both brought their rifles up and peered through, reigniting the weapon lights. Sure enough, just as Pyriaeus had promised, a narrow corridor led away into complete darkness.

Squeezing through the small gap, they crouched down and began down the low claustrophobic passage. It went on and on, bullet straight into the black. The air smelt ancient and stale, reminding Ed of castle visits in his childhood.

'I don't like this much,' murmured Andy, close behind him.

'I agree,' said Ed, gloomily. 'I've had more enjoyable nightmares.'

'What do we do if it's blocked or the staircase fails?'

'Buggered if I know,' replied Ed. 'Perhaps wait and see if the bugs get bored and piss off I suppose.'

'Hopefully before we suffocate to death.'

'You really are all gloom and doom today aren't you?'

'Of all the recognised outdoor pursuits, potholing is decidedly bottom of my list. After all, you're already buried.'

The end of the passage appeared suddenly ahead.

This time Ed could see the little hatch, it opened easily and the handle turned, albeit reluctantly. The end wall dropped downwards without warning, causing them both to jump back in surprise.

'Fuck's sake!' exclaimed Andy. 'Couldn't he have put a warning sign up or something?'

Ed wasn't listening, he was already moving forward and shining his light up the curving stairway beyond.

'You coming or staying to bellyache some more?' Ed asked.

'Show me the way, illustrious leader,' Andy replied, as he pushed up close behind. 'It's well past beer o'clock anyway.'

Ed glanced back, putting his finger against his visor in a shushing gesture. He listened first and, once satisfied there were no bugs rattling around just above, he began the climb back towards the surface.

As they climbed, Ed noticed the dust got thicker and thicker, until, as they had done on the descent earlier, they had to scrape the treads clear for each foothold. The dust was extremely powdery and puffed up around them, restricting visibility even more in the darkness.

Finally, after climbing for several minutes a glimmer of light above raised their spirits. Underfoot the dust gradually became gravelly and then lumps of rock increasing in size, before becoming small boulders. They began climbing over ever bigger debris that was now discernible as building detritus.

'The remains of the government building,' said Ed, squinting in the half light. 'Turn your light off, we don't want to make it easy for them.'

It had got dark while they were underground, but the glimmer of light available piercing the rubble was just enough to see by. When Ed finally scrambled up into clear space, he realised the illumination was from one of the planet's moons hanging overhead. He watched and noticed it was visibly moving across the sky.

'We need to get a wriggle on,' he said. 'That moon's going to be over the horizon in minutes and then it'll be pitch black.'

'Edward, don't move,' said a familiar voice in his ear.

'Hello, Cleo,' he replied. 'Are there bugs about?'

'Just a few,' she said.

No sooner had she said it, when the muffled clatter of bug feet in dust reached his ears. His eyes were becoming more accustomed to the low light now and he realised they were actually about four metres above the surface. The building had collapsed and they'd climbed up to the top of the remaining pile. He slowly moved his head to the left as movement in his peripheral vision caught his attention.

'Oh, shit,' Andy whispered, as he too witnessed the sea of bugs swarming around below them. 'They must've found the ship, they're everywhere.'

'I got it up and out the way,' said Cleo. 'Hold fire while I get it over to you. Be ready to jump.'

They did as they were told and kept their heads down. A minute later the sound of antigravs had them scouring the heavens above. They knew Cleo would keep the *Cartella* cloaked and its shields up until the last minute. Bracing themselves, they both prepared to jump up on top of the rubble as the scream of the motors neared.

The *Cartella* materialised about fifty metres away on their right-hand side. It began side-slipping in towards them, its airlock powering open. Ed stood and clambered out, closely followed by Andy.

Suddenly, something low and fast zipped past them and hit the ship near the open airlock. Cleo had already dropped the shields to allow them entry, so the projectile pierced the hull and as they looked on in complete shock the *Cartella* exploded.

Ed could see the expression of horror on Andy's face and knew his wouldn't be any different. They had to duck back down as hot debris showered down around them. Due to the lack of oxygen there was no fire, but Ed could feel the heat of the blast as it swept over them. The main hulk of the ship was luckily blown away from them and crashed down amongst the sea of bugs below who instantly began swarming over it.

9

Ruins of an unnamed city, uncharted planet in the halo

ED GRABBED Andy's arm and yanked him back down into the rubble. It stopped him staring and swearing and woke him up to the fact they really needed to hide back below.

Some of the closer bugs were standing up on their hind legs and were scouring the vicinity, knowing that ship had most likely come down to pick someone up.

'Back down to the stairs,' Ed hissed, beginning to backpedal the way they'd come as fast as he could.

Andy got the hint and quickly followed. Ed didn't turn around, but he could hear Andy huffing and puffing close behind as they descended through the ruins.

The gradual increasing rattle of insect feet provided them with a further injection of adrenaline as they reached the stone spiral stairway. Using the same cleared footfalls from before, they thundered down and down, pushing off the outer wall with their left arm as they descended at breakneck speed.

The rattle of bugs was becoming louder and Ed knew if they fell, they'd be in trouble. The report of Andy's laser rifle made him jump with the realisation that the bugs had caught up with them. He looked around as a dead bug brushed the back of his leg as it clattered down past him on the inside.

'Keep going,' Andy shouted, as he fired over his shoulder again.

Ed had to jump over the body of the dead bug that had come to rest on the outside of the staircase right over the sunken door to the long corridor. As he leapt through he turned to aim his weapon back over Andy's head. Andy quickly realised what Ed was doing and after negotiating the body himself, dropped down to flip open the small hatch and turn the handle.

He wrinkled his nose from the smell emanating from the dead bug and flattened himself to the floor as a barrage of laser fire from Ed lit the tunnel up like daylight. A pile of bodies and grey goo slammed into the floor and wall only a few feet from his head, just as he operated the handle.

The door slammed up just as quickly as it had opened. The sickening crunch of crushed bug echoed down the corridor, followed by the stomach-turning stink of grey goo that dribbled down the face of the door.

They both slumped down to catch their breath and as their eyes met, Andy spoke.

'We've lost the *Cartella*,' he said, sounding almost tearful.

'If we get out of here, I'll build us a new even better one,' said Ed, hoping he sounded confident enough.

Andy managed a half smile, went quiet again and stared at the floor, a tear running down his face.

'Thinking of her, aren't you?' Ed said quietly.

'Every minute of every day,' Andy replied, glancing disconsolately at his friend. 'We had our first kiss in the *Cartella*.'

The sound of a heavy thump against the stone door brought them back to the present.

'We need to move,' said Ed. 'If they breach this door we're in the shit.'

Andy nodded and they both dragged themselves to their feet and began running back towards the control room.

It didn't take them so long to navigate the tunnel this time, partly because they knew it was clear and there was nothing to fall over and partly because if the bugs did get through that door, they would be able to rip down this passage faster than they could.

Ed turned the handle as soon as they were through and watched as it swung closed and rolled forward, becoming flush with the wall again.

'Wadda we do now?' Andy asked, kicking the wall. 'We're trapped in both bloody directions.'

'Well, I seem to remember something I learnt as a kid,' said Ed, tapping his chin with his fist. 'When you disturbed an ants' nest, they'd all swarm towards the threat. Especially the soldier ants, which is what these buggers all seem to be.'

'Yeah, and?'

'When the ship crashed I'm hoping they all went there. It's the hive mentality that all insects have.'

'So you think they won't be above here anymore?'

'I'm banking on it.'

'Okay, say they have gone. We have no ship up there now.'

'Do you really think Linda and the others will have been sitting on their hands since we lost the *Cartella*?'

'No, I suppose not.'

'They'll have one of the shuttles on the way. It might be already here and this time we know not to drop the shields until the last second.'

Andy turned towards the blocked stairway and grimaced.

'Is there a turny handle for this one too?' he asked, surveying the floor.

'There must be somewhere,' said Ed.

'Plug his lordship back in and ask,' Andy quipped, as he scuffed around in the dust with his boot. 'There's no handle hatch down here and the walls are bare too.'

'Hold on,' said Ed, turning to face the still glowing control panel. 'He activated the stairs electronically, so perhaps there's a button for it on here.'

He wiped the panel clear and as he'd seen on the other panels he'd discovered, the buttons all had different shaped icons imprinted on them and were designated in varying colours. Andy moved in beside him and surveyed the array of possibilities.

'D'you think it's safe to start pressing some of these?' he quipped.

'I dunno,' said Ed. 'But we're not going anywhere if we don't try.'

'What about that one?' Andy asked, just meaning to point to a blue one on his side of the panel, but because of the thickness of his glove he brushed it.

A thump behind had them spinning around and bringing their weapons up. The stairway was activating.

'How the fuck did you know it was that one?' Ed asked, giving Andy a look of astonishment.

'I didn't,' he replied. 'It was just the picture of what looked like a spring on it. I thought it was the only one to have any kind of a spiral shape.'

'You jammy bastard.'

They both took up positions either side of the entrance and waited for the rock sections to complete their transition from wall to staircase. Bits of squashed bug dropped down into the room adding to the already unpleasant stink from the previous dead one.

As he had predicted, no live ones presented themselves and one foot at a time, Ed began the short climb up to the vast chamber they explored earlier. A dozen or so more flattened bugs were stuck to the treads and walls. Ed could hear Andrew gagging behind him and he turned to put his finger against his visor to quieten him down. Once at the top he poked his head up and did a quick three-sixty to ensure the coast was clear. He couldn't see very far in the gloomy light coming up from below so he risked lighting his weapon lamp and swung that around.

Nothing came out of the darkness and as he listened, there was no rattle of feet on the stone floor either. He nodded at Andy nervously peering up from below and they both ventured out and began to make their way quickly towards the exit. They trotted in complete silence, the dust on the floor helping to deaden their footfall.

It took them about five minutes to reach the exit leading to the staircase up to the arch on the surface.

'I'll talk to Linda as soon as I have a connection and get her to create a diversion a couple of kilometres away before bringing the shuttle in,' Ed whispered to Andy, getting a nod in reply.

They both hit the stairs as quickly and quietly as they could, checking around each turn before committing themselves. They found it much easier going up as the cascade of bugs descending and ascending had cleaned most of the grit and dust off the steps. Once they'd negotiated the eight flights again, they both extinguished their lights and while Ed called the *Gabriel*, Andy peered out across the regolith. He could see movement on the horizon, like waves of an ocean, but he knew it was anything but.

'Guys, can you hear me?' Ed called.

'Oh, thank heavens,' replied Linda. 'We were really worried they'd caught you over near the *Cartella* wreck. Phil is nearby in one of the shuttles, I'll get him over to you.'

'Before he commits, can you initiate a diversion in the other direction? They're like moths to a flame. Use one of the bigger drones, they'll think it's another rescue attempt.'

'Pol's on it as we speak,' said Linda. 'I'll let Phil know the plan.'

'It's okay,' said Phil, breaking into the conversation. 'I'm close and I'll watch for the distraction and move straight in.'

Ed and Andy sank back into the shadows and waited. Four minutes later the skyline lit up, followed a couple of seconds later by a faint crack as the weak sound waves in the thin atmosphere passed over them.

Andy pulled up his rifle and squinted through its telescopic sight.

'It's working,' he said. 'They've taken the bait.'

'Phil, go,' called Ed.

He must have been just above them, as even in this thin atmosphere the scream of the antigravs was loud as Phil dropped the shuttle like a stone and flared almost on top of the arch. The open airlock beckoned, as the small ship stopped its plunge only inches from the surface. They both jumped up and sprinted for the shuttle, its shield only dropping for the time it took for them to pass through it.

They threw themselves into the airlock, and Phil had the shuttle up and away before the outer door was fully closed. They remained sprawled on the floor for a few moments, breathing hard to catch their breath.

The small ship ripped upwards, heading for the *Gabriel*, the alma drive quickly taking over from the antigravs.

Ed's suit alarm sounded again, closely followed by Andy's. They both looked at each other and shook their heads. Nothing was said, but they both knew it had been a dangerously close call.

10

The starship Gabriel's *bridge, non-system space*

THE *GABRIEL* HAD QUICKLY JUMPED OUTSIDE of the system as soon as the shuttle entered the port hangar. Ed and Andy gave Phil their thanks and a hug, then made their way towards the tube lift, glancing at the spot where the *Cartella* would normally be parked.

'I'm going to miss that ship,' said Andy.

'You and me both,' agreed Ed. 'You don't realise how much of an emotional attachment you have to something until you lose it.'

Andy went suddenly quiet as Ed realised he'd probably said the wrong thing.

'Come on,' he encouraged. 'Let's go and suffer the wrath of Linda.'

. . .

'So, that went well then?' she growled, the second they disembarked the tube lift. She was sitting bolt upright, glaring at them with her arms folded across her chest.

'Actually, it might not be as bad as you think,' said Ed, waving a finger in the air.

'Is that a fact?' she snapped. 'Forgive me for not getting the whole picture then. I was under the impression you'd lost the *Cartella* and very nearly your own lives. Perhaps you'd like to enlighten us as to why that operation wouldn't be considered a complete gang fuck?'

'We have an important guest,' said Andy, cheerfully.

Ed grimaced, as he knew being cheerful when Linda was in castigation mode wouldn't end well.

'Don't tell me—you have a bug that wants to defect,' she said, sarcastically.

Ed produced the data nodes and held them up.

'No, but there's someone here you'll want to meet and can explain a lot of what's going on.'

Linda sat back on her couch and waved her hand as if to say "you have the stage".

Ed looked up.

'Cleo, can you provide me with an interface for these, please.'

She appeared next to him and took the two nodes and inspected them closely.

'Ah,' she said. 'I believe we've seen this design before.'

'Indeed we have,' he said. 'Just make sure you have full authority over the contents.'

'You want me to firewall myself and the ship from what's on here?' she asked.

'For now, yes,' he said. 'All will become obvious in a few moments, but allow access to the holo emitters in here.'

She nodded and waved her hand. A small console appeared next to them. She inserted the two nodes, which began to glow and emit a low hum.

Ed heard Pol and Callon gasp as Pyriaeus materialised in the centre of the bridge. He glanced down at himself and then around the room, stopping at Ed and smiling.

'You escaped the bugs,' he said. 'The end of the tunnel was clear?'

'Ladies and gentlemen, may I introduce Pyriaeus the Fourteen,' Ed announced.

'You're one of the Ancients,' exclaimed Linda, all the earlier angry body language dissipating away.

'Yes, I understand from your friends that is what the twelve of us are collectively known as in this time period,' he said, turning in a circle so he could address them all.

'In answer to your question,' said Ed, 'the tunnel did indeed come out amongst the remains of a large building.'

He nodded, his gaze settling on Andy.

'Did you discover how long I'd been in stasis?' he asked.

Andy held up one finger and produced the bone.

'What the hell is that?' Pol asked, pulling a slightly disgusted expression.

'It used to be him,' said Andy, pointing at their guest.

They all turned back to stare quizzically at Pyriaeus.

'Hmm,' he grunted. 'A bit weird, I know.'

Andy approached Cleo and held out the bone.

'Are you able to date this?' he asked.

She took the proffered tibia and inspected it closely, her hand emitting a blue glow where it was in contact with the bone. She nodded and handed the bone back to Andy, before turning to face Pyriaeus.

'I'm afraid you died approximately three hundred thousand years ago, although, you'll most likely know that as chronia,' she said.

He looked down at himself again.

'Wow, I don't think I look that old, do I?' he said, with a smirk.

Everybody chuckled.

'A god with a sense of humour,' said Andy. 'Earth could certainly do with one of those.'

'Is that your home planet?' Pyriaeus asked.

Andy nodded.

'Well, let's hope these bugs as you call them don't find it,' he said.

'I'm afraid it's too late for that,' said Ed. 'They already have.'

'They're on your world already?'

'They came to steal things,' Phil said, joining the conversation.

The Ancient's expression became more studious.

'What did they take?' he asked, staring at Phil and then over at Ed.

'Frozen human bodies and embryos,' said Ed.

'And Phil's computer containing a lot of his races technology,' said Linda.

Pyriaeus rubbed his chin in thought.

'Tell me, was there anything on that computer

pertaining to memory reprogramming or such like?' he asked.

They all glanced at Phil, who nodded.

'Why would you ask that?'.

'We discovered some sort of a laboratory on a raid once,' said Pyriaeus. 'They seemed to be attempting to rewrite a human brain with one of their own.'

'Did they succeed?' Ed asked.

'We didn't think so.'

'Bloody hell,' said Phil. 'They most likely will with the Theo tech they have now.'

It went quiet on the bridge for a few seconds before Pol piped up.

'I don't get what all this means,' she said.

'It means, they're attempting to infiltrate GDA space with humans with bug brains,' said Ed. 'Can you imagine the sabotage they could undertake before an invasion?'

'Oh, shit,' said Pol, glancing around at everyone. 'What do we do?'

'You need to destroy that capability before they perfect it,' said Pyriaeus.

He stepped to one side and glanced up at the holomap.

'Is that Tessamaine?' he asked, his intonation remaining sombre.

'I'm afraid so,' said Ed.

It remained quiet on the bridge for a few moments while they let Pyriaeus circle around the dead world that had once been his home.

'Can I see Tessamaine City?' he asked and after receiving a few quizzical looks, he added. 'It's the one you found me in.'

The footprint of the ruined city grew as Pol panned in. A shadow of deep sadness washed over the Ancient's face as the completely barren landscape swept into close-up.

'You were right,' he said, dejectedly. 'There's nothing for me here anymore.'

Turning his back to the projection, he sighed and glanced at Ed.

'You mentioned you were part of a group of human worlds,' he said. 'I will give you any help I can to try and prevent this happening to those. How many planets are there in your group?'

'Over sixteen hundred,' said Ed.

Pyriaeus's eyes widened as he took in what Ed had said.

'Really?' he said. 'Sixteen hundred worlds in just this one galaxy? My colleagues have been busy. But I suppose a lot can happen in three hundred thousand chronia. If they perfect that brain transfer technology, there'll be no stopping them. You need to move quickly or all those worlds will be turned to dust.'

11

The office of the Admiral of the Fleet, Dasos, Prasinos
system

ADMIRAL LOFTT SIGHED as another avalanche of messages appeared on his computer screen. Years ago, as a captain and then commander, he could weed out the critical ones and deal with them first, leaving the rest to answer at his leisure. These days, since the Xavier Lake attack, everything was critical and had to be dealt with yesterday. Even delegating a lot of the workload hadn't seemed to reduce the burden.

Everyone was a critic too. He wasn't even in charge when the attack happened, but both public opinion and the media pointed the finger firmly at the failure of the GDA navy to thwart the attack and ensuing catastrophic climate change on the planet. That was of course his fault.

He glanced out the window of his seventy-fourth floor

corner office window. The snow was again piling down in the seemingly never-ending winter. The scientists had assured him the effects of the engineered change had been reversed by utilising their own terraforming technology. Watching the snow storm outside, he wasn't so sure, but they had said it would most likely be a decade before the climate was back to previous temperatures. Maybe a little warmer, which wouldn't be a bad thing. Shame they couldn't do anything about the heavier gravity on Dasos. After decades of living aboard starships that on the whole had lower gravity to appease the crew members from lower gravity worlds, he had got used to being a lighter weight. Edward Virr had once said "On this planet you literally do have the weight of the world on your shoulders." He smiled at the thought, before rolling his eyes as yet another message arrived at the top of the list with the annoyingly cheery pinging noise.

Although, his mood was momentarily buoyed as he noticed it was notification of a jump drone-delivered video message from his aforementioned friend. The moment of animation was short-lived however, as he played the message and Ed explained the situation out in the halo.

Oh, joy of joys, he thought. *An alien invasion now, while I've only got half a fleet spaceworthy, that's just perfect.*

He called recently promoted Commander Mye and now personal adjutant to the admiral into the office.

'Come in Zaphir, there's something I want you to see,' he said, as she entered and closed the door.

She watched Edward Virr's message play out on a wall screen and rolled her eyes as it ended.

'Pardon my Earth language but, oh, shit,' she said. 'That's all we bloody need.'

'Have we got any spare ships?' Bache asked, already knowing the answer as he saw Zaphir return his gaze with a "you've gotta be kidding" expression. 'I know, I know,' he said. 'But if what Ed says is true, this could be a massive problem if those insects get loose in our region. Especially if they can potentially disguise themselves as humans.'

Zaphir sighed and pulled out her tablet.

'I might be able to spare *K52*,' she said. 'It's just completing its space trials this week, but I'll want it back as soon as the situation has been managed. I did have it earmarked for simpler operations that would break the crew in a little more moderately.'

Bache adopted a more pensive expression.

'That's Captain Grogun Whipper isn't it?' he said. 'Her first command.'

Zaphir nodded and gave her boss a knowing look.

'She still carries a torch for you, you know,' she said.

'She's a good kid,' Bache replied, a faraway look in his eyes. 'She's got a sensible head on her shoulders, just like her father who'd probably come for me with a laser cannon if I made moves towards his daughter.'

'Oh, I don't know about that, Gastion has a lot of respect for you. I think he'd be thrilled.'

Bache puffed out his cheeks and gazed out at the snow again.

'Yeah, well, I haven't put any thought into dating again since my divorce. I've just been too busy. It might've been a different story if I'd remained retired like I was supposed to be.'

'You're a martyr to the cause, Bache,' she said, smiling. 'You always have been. You could never abandon the love of your life.'

'And who might that be?'

'The navy, you idiot.'

Bache shook his head and tutted.

'Disrespecting a senior officer, I could have you court-martialled.'

'Oh, please do,' she said, the grin getting wider. 'I could retire and live on a tropical island on some distant planet and live happily ever after.'

'Not going to happen,' said Bache, turning back to the ever-growing list of messages. 'Now, as Andrew Faux would say, "bugger off" and make sure you send Grogun and the *52* to help Edward with this infestation of insects thing.'

Zaphir turned, tucked a lock of hair behind an ear and made for the door.

'I'll send a jump drone to the *52* straight away,' she said, hovering in the open doorway. 'But knowing Ed as I do, I think this could be a bigger threat than you might realise.'

As the door closed, Bache scratched his chin in thought and stared at a large snowflake as it fell and settled on the outside window ledge.

'You might be right, Zaffie girl,' he said, to an empty room.

12

The bridge, Katadromiko 52, *Tenerai system*

CAPTAIN GROGUN WHIPPER grinned from ear to ear as she read the classified message from the office of the Admiral of the Fleet. She hadn't expected her ship and crew to be entrusted with such a critical mission quite so soon after completing an already shortened shakedown flight. It was a long way from home too, with no backup readily available. But she knew that since the Dasos attack, the fleet was considerably depleted. Ninety-one percent of the vessels in the vicinity of Dasos at the time of the disaster were either destroyed or so severely damaged, they had to be scrapped. The reconstruction, although well under way, was far from completed and the navy was desperately short of serviceable vessels. She, her father and the admiral went back a long way, so she was adamant the level of trust shown here wasn't to be underestimated or indeed given grounds for regret.

Transmitting ship-wide, she informed the crew of the upcoming operation and they had orders for a resupply stopover en route at Earth in the Sol system. She could hear the buzz of excitement around the bridge once she'd finished and hoped this enthusiasm extended throughout the forty-seven thousand crew on the huge fourteen-kilometre vessel.

The ship's eight-foot tall first officer, Quill De'Maars, sidled over to the captain's dais, a perplexed expression on his dark narrow-featured face. He was the same height as the captain, even though she was standing on her raised dais. De'Maars was a Xallionite from the planet Xall on the outer edge of the Milky Way. Xall is an extreme low-gravity world which has produced a race of very tall spindly humans, some as tall as nine feet. They need to wear a specially designed servo assisted leg and back brace in standard and high gravity areas and worlds. They're dark skinned and their thin gaunt faces make them appear almost malnourished.

'Eeerth?' he queried, in his slow Xallionite drawl. 'Wiey theerre?'

'Because the insects went there and stole some human embryos and Theo technology,' said Grogun, staring at Quill. Grogun was only five foot three and tended to find Xallionites made her feel a little uncomfortable when they stood too close. The high-pitched whirring of their brace servos didn't help either and sounded eerily android-like. 'The report also states,' Grogun continued, 'that they seem to have developed a personal jump capability.'

'Yoo meeening aan inndividduaal caan juump?' De'Maars asked, raising a thin eyebrow.

'So it says,' answered Grogun. 'While we take on supplies, I want to scan for any residual signatures.'

'Theey maay bee tooo faaint, beeing thaat smaall aand soome tiime aago.'

'Even so, we will need to be able to detect their movements and the sooner we can do that, the better.'

Grogun stepped down from her dais and approached the lead navigator.

'Time to the Sol system, Lieutenant?' she asked.

'Twenty-one hours, Captain,' he said, after a moment, his hands flashing over the floating icons.

'And then on to the rendezvous in the halo?'

Again he concentrated on the calculation.

'Nine days, ma'am,' he stated, as the route flashed up on the holomap.

'A bit convoluted isn't it?' said Grogun, eyeing the circuitous red line. 'Is there some reason why we're not able to take a more direct line?'

The navigator stroked a few more icons, looked up and pointed at the holomap as it panned in to an area about two thirds of the way to the rendezvous. An enormous black circle swelled into focus.

'Black hole, ma'am,' he said. 'One of the biggest in the galaxy, it's almost six hundred billion kilometres in diameter. We have to give it a very wide birth.'

Grogun nodded and waved an arm at the projection.

'Okay, get us to Earth as quickly as you can. Mr De'Maars you have the bridge, call me when we arrive,' she ordered and strolled off the bridge in the direction of her cabin.

The call came just over nineteen hours later and as Grogun entered the bridge, she could hear the constant chatter between her crew, Earth and several freighters lined up in high orbit, awaiting to discharge their various loads onto the mammoth cruiser.

She strolled directly to the semicircle of array officers and surveyed their various screens. Selecting the operator of the ship's largest and most powerful array, she pointed at the officer's screen and made a request.

'Can you project the track of the strange comet they witnessed at the time of the infiltration?' she asked.

A thin green line traced slowly across the projection of the Sol system. It had appeared from behind the Sun and didn't reappear after disappearing behind Jupiter.

'That's it, ma'am,' she said. 'I'll throw everything we have at that trajectory and see if we can isolate any signatures we can work with.'

'Excellent,' said Grogun. 'We really need to be able to detect them if they try to jump aboard our vessel.'

Walking back to her dais, she nodded at De'Maars.

'Give the order for everyone to be issued with a side arm,' she said. 'Also, when we arrive in the halo, I want all the marine armoured suits permanently manned and distributed around the ship. I don't know if these bugs can jump through our shields, but I don't want to find out when they suddenly appear all over the bloody place and we're not in the least bit prepared.'

De'Maars nodded and began having a conversation with the ship's chief security officer.

Grogun turned and pointed at the communications officers to her right.

'Get those freighters in and unloaded straight away,' she ordered. 'I want to be under way in less than four hours.'

13

─────

The starship Gabriel*'s bridge, non-system space*

'ARE we at the agreed rendezvous yet?' Ed asked Phil, as he stepped off the tube lift.

Phil opened his eyes and scratched his chin.

'Not long now,' he said. 'One jump away. 'I'm kinda leaving it to the last minute, just checking we're not being tailed.

Ed slid into his couch and indicated the other empty seats.

'Have you been on your own all day?' he asked.

'Ah, no, Callon was here keeping me company until I said she ought to get some sleep.'

'No, I suppose we don't all have to be here just to meet another friendly ship. Do we know who's coming?'

'*Katadromiko 52*, so I'm informed,' said Phil, shrugging.

'I didn't know there was fifty-two of those monsters.'

'It's brand new apparently, only finished its trials a few days ago.'

'Well, let's hope one's enough to sort this crap out. Do we know who the captain is?'

'Grogun Whipper.'

Ed cocked his head to one side in thought.

'I know that name, but I can't picture him.'

'It's a her,' said Phil. 'You're thinking of her father Gastion, a good friend of Bache's.'

'Yes, Gastion,' blurted Ed, pointing at Phil. 'I remember…came to Andy's wedding with Bache.'

'That's the one.'

'So…he has a successful daughter too?'

'So it seems,' said Phil, raising his eyebrows suggestively.

'Hey, don't go there…I already have Pol. You on the other hand?'

Phil rolled his eyes and adopted a downcast expression.

'Human and Theo relationships don't have a good rap,' he admitted.

Ed looked across and was about to question that, but Phil spoke before him and swiftly changed the subject.

'How's Andy getting on now?' he asked.

'Good days and bad days,' Ed replied. 'But overall, he's doing the only thing he can and keeping busy.'

'Yeah, I saw the two old motorbikes he's doing up down in the hangar. He has Cleo fabricating new parts for them.'

'Good,' said Ed. 'It's the best therapy for him.'

'What is?' said Andy, the tube lift depositing him in the room.

'You, fixing bikes with Cleo,' said Phil.

'Not as straightforward as it might seem,' Andy replied, his hands on his hips. 'She's the galactic expert on particle physics, but trying to teach her the intricacies of a seventies Kawasaki triple is a different matter.'

'I don't have to help you, you know,' said Cleo, her voice booming around the bridge.

'You love it really,' chortled Andy, giving Ed a wink.

'Oh, yes,' she replied. 'Having to vent the hangar every time you start up that eighty-year old smelly and overly loud two stroke.'

'Sounds like a choir of angels,' Andy replied.

'A tin of ball bearings in a tumble drier, more like,' Ed interjected, shaking his head.

'You have no appreciation of classic engineering,' Andy muttered under his breath, while adopting a phoney anguished expression.

'Anyway, moving swiftly on,' said Ed, glancing forlornly at Phil. 'Do we have any evidence of a pursuit?'

'No, boss, all clear.'

'Okay, take us to the rendezvous point and uncloak so that monster doesn't jump onto us by mistake.'

The three of them glanced up as the holomap reset post-jump. Ed had chosen the empty non-system location deliberately as there were no hiding places for the bugs and it was a single hundred light year jump back to the dead planet of Tessamaine and bug central.

'Uncloaked,' said Phil, leaning back and sliding his hands behind his head. 'Now we wait.'

'Keep an emergency jump icon primed,' said Ed. 'If anything other than the *Katadromiko 52* jumps in nearby, hit it.'

They didn't have too long to wait. Twenty-two minutes later a whole slab of stars vanished fifty kilometres away on their starboard side. The monstrous fourteen-kilometre cruiser had arrived. It remained uncloaked and after righting itself to be on the same plane as the *Gabriel*, approached slowly and stopped ten kilometres away.

'Greetings, Captain Virr,' said Grogun, her image appearing in mid-air above the three crew on the *Gabriel*'s bridge.

'Captain Whipper, we're very glad to see you and congratulations on your first command,' said Ed, smiling. 'I imagine your father's very proud.'

'Hmm,' she grunted. 'More overly paranoid and protective is nearer the mark. Probably why it's taken me three times as long to achieve this than most and most likely now only because half the navy's captains are dead, making them desperately short of senior officers.'

Ed noticed Andy give him a harried look that spoke volumes, to the fact he'd seemingly and unwittingly opened a large can of worms. He decided it would be prudent to quickly change the subject and talk about the operation. He was about to speak again when he saw Grogun's head snap to her right. When she looked forward again, it was with a questioning expression.

'Have you just initiated a localised jump?' she asked.

Ed saw both Andy and Phil look at each other, then back at him and shake their heads in puzzlement.

'Negative,' said Ed. 'Has your ship just detected something out of the ordinary?'

'A faint jump signature, similar in structure to the reading we detected in the Sol system on the track that fake comet took.'

'You've been to Earth?' Ed asked, noticing Grogun was issuing commands and not really paying attention to what he was saying.

'Have you any evidence the bugs have any cloaking technology?' she asked, glancing back at Ed.

'Err, well, no,' said Ed, getting shrugs and head shakes from Andy and Phil.

'Hmm,' Grogun grunted again. The expression on her face was not one of contentment. 'I don't like enigmas,' she said. 'I've ordered a complete ship-wide search, which as you can imagine on a vessel this size is no small task. Perhaps you should do the same.'

Ed glanced up.

'Cleo, can you scan for any anomalous signatures in and around the ship during the last few minutes?'

'Already done,' she said. 'Nothing out of the ordinary detected.'

'I'm transmitting the odd echo we found to you,' said Grogun. 'Try scanning for that. It's faint and almost impossible to pinpoint, but we feel there's too much there to ignore.'

There was momentary quietness on the bridge as Cleo inputted the data and analysed the ship using the new information. She appeared suddenly wearing her black ninja outfit, her arms crossed and a stern expression.

'I concur, this is worrying,' she said, her usual jovial

attitude absent. 'I'm afraid they're correct…something I can't quite get my holographic head around did occur on the *Gabriel*. It's hardly there, but at the same time it is, or was. I think we might very likely have or have had a stowaway.'

'Is there any way to improve on that?' asked Ed. 'Like —what, where and when?'

She shook her head and frowned.

'It's as frustrating as hell,' she griped. 'But that really is all I can confirm.'

Ed slumped in his seat and glanced at Andy and Phil opposite him.

'There's just not enough of us to search every corner of this ship,' he grumbled, shrugging. 'There must be a better way, Cleo?'

'I've adjusted our internal detectors to warn of any fresh echos,' she said, not sounding overly convinced. 'But then again, if anything occurs now, I'm most likely going to know about it.'

'Saying "most likely" isn't very reassuring, Cleo,' said Phil. 'Especially for you?'

'This tech, whatever it is, is new and clever. I need more than a faint unreadable echo to be able to assess and design a reliable detector and/or defence against it.'

Grogun, who'd been watching and listening to the conversation with interest, suddenly snapped her head to the right again.

'What the Ancients was that?' she demanded, before her image disappeared.

'Bloody hell,' said Andy, staring at his seat display and then up at the holomap.

'What?' asked Ed, following Andy's gaze up to the map.

'The *K2* just shut down.'

'Shut down what?'

'Everything,' said Cleo. 'Propulsion, shields, environmental, lighting, artificial gravity…everything…it's suddenly become a dead floating hulk.'

'Oh, shit,' said Andy, as the holomap lit up with thousands of rocks suddenly jumping in close by and converging on the *Gabriel* and the helpless *Katadromiko* at a frightening velocity.

'Weapons and shields up,' shouted Ed.

The holomap image changed suddenly. The *Katadromiko* and the thousands of rocks descending on them disappeared in an instant.

14

The bridge, Katadromiko 52, *non-system space*

No sooner had Grogun asked what the shudder she felt through her seat was, the lights went out and she was forced to grab the arms of her seat as gravity disappeared, causing her to go on the float. The orange emergency lighting began to glow, producing eerie shadows around the large room. She jumped as the hidden emergency float handles flicked out from the walls, ceiling and floor with a loud snap. They were some of the few systems independent from the main power supply, along with lifeboats and a basic environmental system that had a limited battery life, this being only designed to allow the crew time to get to a lifeboat and not for prolonged periods.

'Systems report?' called Grogun, squinting around in the gloom at her new bridge crew busy belting themselves into their seats.

'Main and secondary drives down, Captain.'

'Navigation down, ma'am.'

'Shields down.'

'Environmental down.'

'Weapons down.'

Grogun, like her father, was a ship's engineer and knew full well what was happening was an impossible scenario. The vessel was state of the art and had more backups and redundancy built in than you could throw a stick at.

'This is fucking madness,' she shouted. 'Do we have control over anything?'

Rows of shaking heads with scared eyes stared back.

'Is this another drill, ma'am?' quizzed a nervous voice from communications.

'No, it is not,' she snapped back. 'Does anyone have contact with the engineering decks?'

Before anyone had a chance to reply, the vessel shuddered again twice and then after a short pause a third time.

'Does anyone have any clue as to what's causing that?' she asked, fruitlessly tapping at the dead controls in her seat arms and secretly praying for her personal holographic control display to somehow reappear.

'Peerhaaps yoou shouuld maake foor thee ROR, ma'am,' said De'Maars, meaning the hidden remote operations room, used in extreme emergency situations. They were sensibly another of the independently powered systems.

She nodded and pointed at the chief engineering officer, who had been on the bridge at the time.

'Mr Qatts, accompany me,' she said, releasing her

belts. 'Mr De'Maars, you have the bridge, I'll do the best I can to get the power back on.'

Kicking against her seat, she launched herself towards a smaller door at the side of the room. It led to a long corridor leading through several bulkhead doors to the captain's private shuttle hangar. She floated from handle to handle until roughly halfway along, she grabbed a handle and this time didn't let go. Chief Engineer Qatts did the same behind her. She entered a code into a hidden touch keypad that illuminated as she ran her hand over it, causing a small section of the wall to sink in and slide to one side. Dropping down, they both pulled themselves inside a small four-metre by four-metre room. A series of lit screens lined one wall with glowing icon touch panels below. Two bunk beds were opposite with floor to ceiling cupboards and a door to a small bathroom on the third wall.

'Who turned all this on?' Grogun asked.

Qatts shrugged and stared up at the screens in horror.

Grogun pulled herself into one of the two seats and looked up at the random scenes from around the ship.

'Oh, shit,' she muttered under her breath. 'We're being boarded.'

The outside cameras showed countless lumps of rock of various sizes had punctured the unshielded hull. The inside cameras revealed hordes of bugs flooding into the ship attacking anything or anyone that got in their way.

'How the hell do we counter this without any power?' Grogun hissed. 'The lack of gravity doesn't slow them at all.'

'Nor does the cold of space,' said Qatts, pointing to a

bunch of bugs appearing on the outside of the hull and proceeding to open an airlock with consummate ease and just pile on in.

They watched helpless as the bug army surged through various areas of the ship. The only time they appeared to suffer casualties was when they encountered the marines in the armoured suits. But the bugs were soon able to overwhelm them by sheer weight of numbers.

'There's no blood,' said Qatts. 'They're using some sort of stun shots on us, and look, they're carrying away the bodies.'

'What, theirs?'

'No, ours, ma'am.'

'What in the name of the Ancients are they up to?' said Grogun, experiencing a deep sense of foreboding as she watched her new command suddenly going to pieces.

'They're doing what they're told,' said a voice to their right.

They both almost levitated out of their seats. Only the float restraints prevented them from doing so. A female figure stood in the bathroom doorway. She was young and attractive and wore the uniform of a senior engineer. Once the shock had worn off, Grogun realised she didn't recognise the officer. Engineering was her faculty and she knew them all well, she'd selected them personally.

'Who the fuck are you? And what are you doing in here?' she demanded, sliding her hand down to where her side arm hung.

'I wouldn't do that if I were you,' said the newcomer, swinging up a hand weapon that Grogun didn't recognise as one of theirs.

She also noticed the girl's voice was a little odd too. The intonation was off, very monotone like an early android with a basic speech programme.

'I asked you some questions,' she said, a little more forcibly this time.

The girl clunked a step forward. Grogun realised she was wearing engineering gravboots, designed for use when repairing the outer hull which were enabling her to walk around in the weightless environment. The strange weapon swung across at Qatts and discharged a red bolt of energy. He grunted, slumped and went silent, his arms floating up into a horizontal position above the control panel.

'There are consequences if you question a queen's wardress,' she snapped, the weapon returning to point at Grogun. 'You will order your crew to stand down and await subsumption.'

'And if I refuse?'

'You will get the same as him and be subsumed anyway,' she said, nodding at Qatts.

'And what is that exactly?'

'Immersed into the hive mind.'

'I take it that's what happened to you?'

'The amelioration of the hive is primary.'

'To the detriment of other life forms it seems.'

While the conversation was taking place, Grogun had turned in her seat and with her left hand now out of sight, had pressed her belt release button on the chair arm. Instead of shrugging the belts off and letting them retract into their housings, she held them in place, braced her left foot against the chair base in anticipation of a lapse of concentration from her uninvited roommate.

'The amelioration of the hive is primary,' the girl repeated, waving the weapon in Grogun's face. 'You must make the announcement now.'

Grogun found the girl's monotone voice irritating. She was also beginning to run out of procrastinating conversation while she waited for her opportunity.

She was on the verge of giving up and just as she'd decided to attack the girl anyway and hang the consequences, a nearby explosion rocked the ship and gave her what she was waiting for. The girl's eyes flicked upwards and off Grogun for a brief second.

She didn't hesitate, and the belts flew off Grogun's shoulders as she launched across the three metres separating them. She heard the weapon discharge as she slapped it to the left. Appreciating the fact that she was still conscious and the red bolt of energy must have missed her, Grogun utlised her continued momentum to smash her right palm under the girl's chin. The girl's head whipped back and crunched into the door frame, rendering her immediately unconscious.

15

The starship Gabriel's *bridge, non-system space*

'DID WE JUST JUMP?' said Ed, his eyes darting from the holomap to Phil and back.

'We did,' said Cleo. 'Sorry to overrule, but the sheer weight of rock heading at us would've overwhelmed our shields in seconds.'

'What about the *K2*?' asked Andy. 'They had no power, they would've got mullered.'

'What is mullered?' asked Phil, giving Andy a questioning glance.

'English slang for smashed,' said Ed, trying to think what to do. 'How far away are we?'

'The jump was ten light years,' said Cleo.

'Can we jump back outside the danger zone and see what's happened?' Ed asked. 'Just make sure we're cloaked this time and well away from all those bloody rocks.'

Phil plotted and executed a jump close and behind a distant planet in the nearest system, cloaked the ship and powered out towards their previous rendezvous point.

'Cleo, you'd better wake the others. I don't know what we're going to be able to do when we arrive, but we'd better be fully manned up here.'

The three of them gazed up with various degrees of trepidation at the holomap as the array updated the feed. It wasn't pleasant viewing. Even at this distance, they could see the *K52* was still dead and unmoving. It was completely surrounded by an immense swarm of rocks, some of them buried deep into the hull. The closer they got and as the definition improved, it became more and more evident the huge GDA cruiser was in significant dire straits.

'Oh, shit,' mumbled Ed.

Phil went white and said nothing.

Andy just sat with his mouth open.

'How the fuck were they able to do that?' he said, eventually.

'Override codes,' said Cleo. 'It's the only way. Those ships have a bundle of backup and redundancy systems to make just this scenario impossible.'

'Do you think the traitor was the stowaway we had?' Phil asked.

'It's not out of the realms of possibility,' said Ed.

'Bloody hell, I hope not,' said Andy. 'Bache'll never forgive us.'

'Forgive what?' Linda asked, stepping off the tube lift with Pol.

No one answered, so she stopped and gazed up at what the other three were staring at.

'No way,' she gasped. 'Is that who we were supposed to meet?'

The others nodded.

'How did they find them so fast and most importantly, how the hell did they penetrate the shields of one of those bloody things?' Linda asked.

Phil gave Ed a worried look, which didn't go unnoticed.

'What are you not telling us?' said Pol, giving Phil an accusatory glare.

'We might have had a stowaway,' said Cleo, appearing in person and looking contrite. 'Who may have jumped onto the Katadromiko and been in possession of the over-ride codes. Don't blame the boys, it was all my responsibility. I should've detected it.'

'Hiding where?' Linda asked, a tone of alarm in her voice.

'One of the hangars most likely,' said Cleo. 'It's really difficult to pinpoint.'

'Which one is it?' Pol asked, sliding into her seat and nodding at the holomap.

'The *K52*,' said Andy.

'Fifty-two?' exclaimed Linda. 'I didn't know they'd got that many.'

'It was new,' said Ed. 'First operation, it had only just completed its trials.'

'Oh, crap, a rookie crew too, I should imagine. We need to help them.'

'I'd love to,' said Ed. 'But if these bugs can just jump through our shields almost undetected, we can't risk getting even remotely close. Which reminds me, Phil, can you hold up here? We don't know if they can see us through our cloak. So bearing in mind they seem to be a lot smarter than we first presumed, I don't want to get too near.'

The pitch of the sub-light engines changed as Phil slowed their momentum, eventually holding station at around eight hundred and sixty million kilometres from the *K52*.

Callon joined them. Her initial chipper demeanour soured somewhat as she was filled in on the situation and sitting down she stared up at the holomap, her shoulders sagging.

'Okay,' said Ed. 'Now everyone's here, I'm open to suggestions.'

'Couldn't Cleo synthesise some sort of bug spray to wipe them out?' Andy asked.

Ed arched an eyebrow and puffed out his cheeks.

'Firstly, that would be committing genocide of a sentient species and I'm not sure the GDA's strict regulations would look favourably on that. Secondly, Cleo, as you know, has no kill programming. She wouldn't be permitted to design a weapon to wipe out an entire species, no matter how cruel or dangerous they are.'

'Why don't you wake Pyriaeus and ask him?' said Pol. 'After all, he's got more experience of the bugs than anyone else.'

'He was defeated though,' said Phil. 'And they seem to be more technically advanced than in his time anyway.'

'All true,' said Ed, turning to nod at Cleo. 'But I don't think it could do any harm to have his input.'

Cleo waved a hand. Pyriaeus appeared in his familiar gold-trimmed garments, his expression brightening as he gazed around at everyone.

'Greetings,' he said, speaking in Ellinika, the principal language of the GDA. 'I take it, as I'm here, there have been developments?' He turned and gazed up at the holomap. 'What in the universe is that thing?'

'A dead starship,' carped Andy. 'The one sent here to supposedly sort out our bug problem.'

'How big is that thing?'

'Fourteen kilometres,' Pol answered.

He turned his head slowly and stared straight at Ed.

'You let the bugs overrun it?' he blurted. 'Don't you have some kind of shielding on something that big?'

'Of course,' Ed replied, dejectedly. 'They must've somehow got hold of the master codes and shut its systems down before boarding it.'

'Would the codes have been on that computer you said was stolen?'

'No,' said Phil. 'Definitely not. However they did that, it didn't come from there. It must've been the stowaway.'

Pyriaeus turned suddenly and stared at Phil.

'Stowaway?'

Ed explained what they knew. Pyriaeus's face dropped as the information sank in.

'They must've succeeded with the mind transfer technology,' he said flatly. 'They've had plenty of time to do it, I suppose.'

'So, you think the stowaway could've been in human form?' Linda asked.

'It would've been easier for it to move around on that ship and set up the shutdown from within,' he said, pointing at the *K52*.

'Is there any way we can help to power it up again?' asked Pol. 'The crew will be at a huge disadvantage with no gravity.'

'Not without boarding the thing,' said Ed.

'That isn't going to happen under any circumstances,' grumbled Linda. 'You were plain lucky last time. It'd be a suicide mission.'

'She's right,' said Pol. 'There's forty-seven thousand crew over there. If they can't sort it out, what chance have we got?'

'I could,' said Cleo, with a wry smile. 'I could play them at their own game.'

The forward ROR, Katadromiko 52, *non-system space*

GROGUN DIDN'T WASTE any time. Code locking and shutting down the systems in the ROR, she quickly exited after checking the corridor was clear. Doing a similar code change to the door to ensure the girl couldn't escape, she pulled her way as swiftly as possible to the captain's hangar.

Peering through the inner airlock porthole, she could see her personal shuttle was still there on its magnetic struts – although, it had been dragged nearer the hangar exit by the rapid decompression of the room as the power had failed and shut down the atmosphere shield. Any loose equipment had gone, the hangar was very bare and she could make out deep gouges in the main door frame where some of the equipment had smashed into it on its way out. She hoped there hadn't been any of her crew working in any of the other many hangars big and small on the vessel. She felt sick in her stomach the more she thought about it; there was always maintenance taking place day and night to keep the hundreds of smaller vessels spaceworthy.

Taking a few deep breaths to calm herself, she turned and albeit a little awkwardly, she managed to open a storage locker to the left of the airlock and removed one of the grey Hostile Environment Suits or HESs from within. Checking it was fully prepped and charged she activated its magnetic boots and donned the slightly bulky piece of kit before running its start-up diagnostics.

Once she had a row of green lights shining on the inside of her visor, she re-entered the airlock, closed the outer door and vented the chamber. She could feel the cold through the suits many membranes as soon as the inner door slid away and allowed her access to the hangar.

Ignoring her shuttle, she clunked straight to the gaping outer door and sticking her head out, she peered rearwards. The hull wasn't crawling with bugs as she'd feared and seemed reasonably clear. Suddenly thinking of something, she clunked her way back to the shuttle, opened its small airlock and disappeared inside. Reappearing a moment later cradling an assault laser rifle, she returned to the door and carefully stepped around the frame until she was standing on the outside of the hull.

Checking the suit's status one last time, she took a deep breath and began walking towards the stern. Walking thirteen kilometres in normal gravity is a long walk, but doing it in a HES, on the outside of a ship's hull in mag boots was going to test her stamina to its fullest degree. She certainly wasn't a stranger to the ship's many fitness rooms, but even so, the trek was going to be long and arduous.

After an hour or so, she was beginning to wish she'd taken the captaincy of a destroyer. The boots were becoming heavier to disengage from the hull and the stern seemed just as far away. She stopped in the lee of one of the larger laser gun turrets and rested for a few minutes. Staring upwards into the complete blackness, she could make out the occasional vague shadows of something or somethings moving around. It was only the sweeping disappearance and reappearance of distant stars across the void that gave their existence away.

She shivered, gathered her thoughts and continued.

Reaching the middle of the vessel, she dropped down to one of the many larger gaping hangar openings and peered down inside, illuminating her suit lights. It was full of assault landing ships of various sizes, their magnetic struts the only thing keeping them attached to the deck in their neat regimental columns.

Movement in her peripheral vision caused her to shrink back and extinguish the lights. Turning her head slowly, she gagged as the frozen body of a crew member floated slowly up towards her. Its empty eye sockets seemed to stare accusingly as it bumped into the door surround and began to float back down into the darkness. Swallowing the bile in her throat, she took a few deep breaths and continued quickly on her way. A mixture of renewed anger and dogged determination gave her legs an extra boost of endurance. She marched the rest of the way to her destination without a break, only slowing once as she gave a wide birth to one of the huge jagged rocks buried in the hull. She noticed some sort of shiny sticky residue had been injected around the edges of the penetration.

Her destination was an airlock on one of the upper recreation decks and on arrival, she clunked her visor against the small outer door inspection window and checked the interior. Confirming the airlock was empty, she keyed in her security override code and waited while the door sank inwards and slid aside into the hull. She waited a few moments, watching for any movement in the inner door window before carefully entering and closing the outer door.

She knew there was a narrow corridor inside with access to the chief engineer's ROR not too far away. She'd changed the design and position of the ROR right at the last minute. It hadn't gone down well with the shipyard or the project manager, but she'd argued that engineering was genuinely one of the first targets for any attack. It was pointless having an emergency ROR right where any initial strike might render it unoperational. The attackers had somehow known where the captain's ROR had been located and even knew the access codes. She was relying on this eleventh-hour change of position being unknown to the enemy.

Holding her breath and her rifle with the safety off, she equalised the pressure and stood by the inner door. The small window only showed what was within a couple of metres of the door, so she couldn't be sure what might be further up the corridor to greet her. Igniting her suit and rifle lights she entered the code to open the airlock. As it turned out, no armed six-legged bugs were anywhere in sight in either direction, so after closing the door, she clunked her way quickly deeper into the ship.

In a stairway, she came across the floating corpses of dead bugs, hundreds of them. It was the first time she'd seen her enemy and she slowed to get a closer look as she pushed them to one side. Noticing they all had some form of body armour and carried a similar weapon to the girl in the ROR, she stepped by them carefully. She found it was impossible to avoid all of the floating bubbles of ugly grey goo seeping from the corpses and it stuck to her suit and made the stairs extremely treacherous, especially under-foot where some had settled.

'FREEZE,' said a sudden loud electronic voice from above on the next landing.

She did as directed, as an armoured marine suit clunked into view, its weapon pointed straight at her face.

'IDENTIFY YOURSELF,' the unnerving voice continued.

'Whipper, Grogun, Captain,' she said as confidently as she could with an activated heavy laser pointed at her head.

'CODE?'

'WHIP11442233,' she repeated from memory, at that moment really glad she'd been issued a number that was easy to remember in stressful situations.

'Thank you, Captain,' said the voice, a little less demanding in tone this time. 'Do you have any idea what the Ancients is going on? I've had no contact with my section commander for a while.'

'I'm as much in the dark as you, marine,' she said. 'But

I believe these bloody insects are attempting to commandeer the ship.'

'That cannot be permitted to happen,' he said, standing back to allow Grogun to pass.

She stopped and thought for a second.

'Were you on your way up or down?' she asked.

'Down, Captain,' he said. 'Then I bumped into that lot coming up towards me.'

'I have to go up another seven decks,' she said. 'Is it clear that far?'

'It was a few minutes ago, but I can't vouch for the deck level itself, as I came from one of the marine hangars higher up.'

'In that case come with me,' she said. 'You can provide my forward defence and a diversion if I need it.'

This slowed Grogun's progress somewhat, as she had to wait for the armoured suit to clunk its way up the stairs in front of her. Eventually, they reached level 209 and Grogun peeked through the small circular window and out into the corridor beyond.

'Shit,' she muttered under her breath, as she ducked back out of sight. 'The passageway's busy with bugs.'

'Just wait a few moments,' the marine said. 'I've noticed they travel around in groups, so they might have moved on in a bit.'

Sure enough, when she checked the window a couple of minutes later, the corridor seemed deserted again.

'Which way are we headed?' the marine asked.

'To the right,' Grogun replied. 'Then left at the first junction.'

'That's away from engineering,' he said, sounding surprised. 'Aren't you going to the engineering ROR?'

'How d'you know about those?' she asked, as he opened the door.

'I was escorting a senior engineer on his way there when he was taken. Unfortunately I was unable to save him.'

Grogun nodded and pointed in the direction they had to go.

'First on the left up there,' she said. 'It's a dead end, so you guard the junction and I'll fire up the control room.'

It was only about a hundred and fifty metres to the turning and they both arrived without incident.

'Wait there,' she said, indicating the wall opposite the turning. 'Don't make it obvious you're guarding this passageway. I don't want them getting too suspicious about what might be down here.'

'Understood,' said the marine, taking up station with his back against the wall she'd pointed at.

Grogun counted her paces as she walked almost halfway down the corridor, before stretching up and waving at the left-hand wall high above her head. The hidden keypad she was looking for illuminated and she quickly keyed in the code. As a lower panel of the wall sank inwards and then slid upwards, she became aware of another noise behind her. She turned to find the marine in the armoured suit directly behind her. His laser cannon pointing at her head again. The big mistake she'd made struck her immediately. He'd checked her identification, but she hadn't returned the favour. She'd just presumed he'd killed all the bugs on the stairs and was on her side.

'Fuck,' she mouthed silently, knowing what was coming.

'Thank you for showing us where this was,' he said, the whirring of the suit servos and the whine of the fully charged cannon loud in the quiet corridor. 'The queen will be very pleased.'

Grogun frowned in puzzlement as a small black canister rolled past the armoured suit. It popped open almost immediately, ejecting a handful of black objects around the corridor that stuck to the walls, ceiling and floor.

'What is this?' asked the marine, turning to see where it had come from.

Grogun's eyes nearly popped out of her head, as a young girl dressed in a skintight matt black jump suit and a large backpack appeared directly behind the marine. She winked at Grogun and reached out, her hand passing straight through the suit's personal shield and touched it on the shoulder.

Grogun shielded her eyes as a shower of sparks turned the dark corridor into daylight and the noise of the suit went silent. Puffs of smoke effused from the suit's joints and the smell of burnt electrics and plastic filled the passageway.

The girl relieved the marine of his cannon, slung it up on her shoulder and pointed at the open doorway.

'You'd better get in there and start taking your ship back,' she said, with a wry grin.

'Who the Ancients are you?' Grogun asked, still rooted to the spot, her eyes wide with astonishment.

'My name's Cleo, I'm here all week and programmes are available in the foyer.'

17

The engineering ROR, Katadromiko 52, *non-system space*

CLEO, after explaining who she was and where she came from, had disposed of the armoured suit in a utility room, back down the main corridor. After adhering some more holo emitters around the walls of the ROR, she'd joined Grogun inside and they'd sealed up the door.

'I'm hoping he hadn't informed the hive of our where-abouts,' said Grogun, activating the controls and screens.

'It was a her,' said Cleo.

'What, in the suit?'

Cleo nodded

Grogun grunted. 'The girl in the forward ROR called herself one of the queen's wardresses. Perhaps she was another of those, whatever they are.'

'Bugs in human form,' said Cleo. 'It seems they've perfected it.'

'Not entirely,' said Grogun. 'Their speech is a bit robotic still, well, the one I met was. It's certainly something to watch out for.'

The screens had started to come to life and they both went silent for a moment as they scanned them for more up-to-date information.

'Are you able to reactivate the ship's systems from here?' Cleo asked.

'It seems they were shut down from one of the other RORs, so I would think so,' she replied, sliding into one of the seats.

'Perhaps lighting, shields and environmental first,' said Cleo. 'Just to give anyone on the float, time to get back to the deck or grab something solid before you initiate the gravitational plating.'

The screens became a lot brighter once power was restored to the vessel's lighting systems.

'Ah, notice how the bugs are bumping into things as the lighting was restored,' said Cleo. 'That's something to remember. Their eyesight takes a while to adjust.'

'You say the *Gabriel* is nearby?' Grogun asked.

'It is.'

'I noticed on my walk outside, there are some dark shapes flying around out there.'

'Bug rocks,' said Cleo.

'Does your ship have the capability to get rid of them?'

'There are hundreds,' Cleo replied. 'We could destroy quite a lot of them, but would eventually get overwhelmed and be in the same situation as you. Every simulation I've run reaches the same conclusion.'

'How many ships would you need for the odds to run in our favour?'

'I see where you're going with this,' said Cleo. 'It depends on the ship in question, but if you could crew twenty to thirty gunships, then we might have a fighting chance. The downside of this is the bugs have thought of that.'

Cleo pointed at a couple of the screens.

'You see, they've stationed a load of bugs inside all the major hangars where the gunships and fighters are. They've been planning this for a while. They were expecting you to turn up, they had the master codes and an intimate knowledge of the layout of the vessel. The only thing they weren't expecting was your last-minute design change.'

'This room being here instead of engineering. Yes, I was counting on that and now I come to think of it, I haven't asked you, how did you know where I was?'

'Scanned for humanoid movement. I knew it must be someone important when you were traversing the hull, but I couldn't meet you out there as there's nowhere to suspend my emitters.'

They both paused to scan the screens again. It was obvious the reducing bug movement had suddenly increased again when the lights came back on.

'Have you shut out the other RORs?' Cleo asked.

'Yeah.'

'Perhaps the shields next. It'll stop any more getting aboard.'

Grogun's hands flashed across the illuminated icons and on the screen showing the vessel's pictographic real-time status, a thin blue line formed around it. Next, the two vents in the ceiling began wheezing quietly as Grogun reinitiated the environmental system.

'Okay,' she said, sitting back in her seat. 'I hope everyone's ready.'

'Gravity next?' Cleo asked.

'Yep.'

Grogun reached forward and tapped one last icon. She immediately felt the weight of her suit for the first time and there was a clatter as a couple of loose items in the room dropped to the floor. They watched on the screens with mild amusement as a few bugs caught high up in the central atrium crashed to the deck, most remaining there unmoving.

The ship shuddered slightly. Grogun switched some of the monitors over to exterior views to find rock debris flowing around the newly reinstated shields.

'They were trying to send in reinforcements,' said Cleo. 'Communication around the hive mind can't be all that immediate. The shields had been up for twenty-three seconds.'

'Let's have a bit of payback,' said Grogun, activating the main array and bringing the weapons online. 'The *Gabriel*'s not in the vicinity is it?' she asked, glancing over her shoulder at Cleo.

'No,' she replied. 'You're free to target anything that moves.'

Grogun smirked and programmed the heavy cannons to automatically target anything that moved.

'Have some of this,' she growled, touching the initiate icon.

Immediately all the cannon turrets began tracking and firing. They had hundreds of targets and within a few seconds the area of space around the cruiser was a blizzard of laser bolts criss-crossing in all directions and all finding their targets. A hailstorm of rock debris began rebounding off the *52*'s shields.

'Edward would call this a turkey shoot,' said Cleo, watching the carnage on the exterior view screens.

'What's a turkey?' asked Grogun.

'A flightless bird they eat at times of celebration on his home planet.'

'They eat birds?'

'You wouldn't believe what they eat on that world.'

'Shame they don't eat bugs,' Grogun replied, rolling her eyes.

'Actually they…'

A series of bangs and crashes close by stopped Cleo mid-sentence. Grogun flicked through a bunch of corridor scenes until she found the view outside the ROR. The passageway was full of bugs feverishly ripping off wall panels and encroaching on their position quickly.

'Shit, they know where we are,' she said, grabbing her tablet and rifle.

Cleo put her hand on Grogun's shoulder and whispered in her ear as she tried to stand, then promptly vanished.

18

The starship Gabriel's *bridge, non-system space*

'SOME OF THE 52's systems are coming back online,' said Callon.

'Lights are on and shields are back up,' said Pol.

Both of them looked over at Ed as he peered up at the holomap to witness several bug rocks impacting the reinstated shields.

'That's a good sign,' he said. 'They weren't expecting that.'

'Which means, someone on board that ship is fighting back,' said Linda.

'It's Grogun,' interrupted Cleo. 'She's in one of the vessel's remote operations rooms.'

'How did it get shut down in the first place?' Andy asked.

'Grogun says one of the crew had somehow been brain

washed by the bugs. She was in the forward ROR with all the codes.'

Pyriaeus appeared suddenly rubbing his chin in thought.

'That is not an encouraging piece of information,' he said. 'That's what they did to us. Although the human converts weren't difficult to spot, as they walked awkwardly and spoke strangely without emotion or intonation.'

'Cleo, how many bugs are there on the *52*?' Ed asked.

'The number is inconclusive,' she answered. 'The majority of them are constantly on the move, but it is in the thousands.'

'Shit,' mumbled Andy. 'How do we combat that many?'

'We need a bug spray,' said Linda.

'That's what I was thinking,' said Ed.

'We tried that,' said Pyriaeus. 'They have the ability to develop an immunity to them within hours.'

'Weapons have just come online,' announced Pol.

All eyes raised up to the holomap to witness a blizzard of heavy laser fire rip into the circling bevy of powered rocks and asteroids.

'Go, Grogun,' whooped Andy, turning to Ed. 'Can we go in and kick some bug arse too?'

Ed watched the carnage unfold as the massive cruiser unleashed its arsenal of heavy weaponry on an unsuspecting bug fleet.

'No, I think she's doing just fine all on her own. We really wouldn't want to get mistakenly targeted by anything that ship's dishing out.'

'They seem to have developed a large range of technology, but not cloaking or shielding it seems,' said Callon, as they watched dozens of bug rock ships disintegrate. The shrapnel bloomed out in all directions, causing mayhem amongst the swarm.

'They were never concerned about losses,' said Pyriaeus, waving a hand at the holomap. 'Their philosophy was to overwhelm with numbers. It seems nothing has changed.'

The sudden appearance of a massive planetoid completely overshadowed the holomap view and made the *52* appear minuscule. It was hundreds of kilometres in diameter, its surface scarred and cratered. Wide ravines, kilometres wide and deep, meandered randomly across its dark crust. Worst of all though, were the millions of smaller powered rocks, ranging from a few metres in size to over a kilometre, swarming in and out of its craggy outer layers.

'Oh, fuck me,' called Andy. 'As if things couldn't get any worse.'

Ed glanced at Pyriaeus questioningly as the holomap image panned back to incorporate the huge newcomer. Pyriaeus, noticing Ed's unvoiced query, shook his head and rolled his eyes.

'They didn't have anything that big in my day,' he said. 'They've been busy.'

'This is a whole new level of bad,' declared Linda.

'I've never seen a Katadromiko made to look so small and insignificant,' said Andy. 'What the hell do we do now?'

'We need to talk to Bache,' said Ed. 'If that thing gets

into GDA space, we would have an infestation that could wipe out every human world in a matter of months.'

The conversation on the bridge stalled at that point, as everyone let that fact sink in. Ed continued staring at the planetoid as it rotated in front of him. He had his head tilted to one side and as he tapped his chin with a forefinger, his expression changed.

'I think I've seen that moon before,' he blurted, turning to the others. 'Forgive me if I'm wrong, but doesn't that thing remind you of something we've met before?'

They all stared at Ed and then back at the holomap.

'It's not the *Arena* is it?' Pol asked.

'I was thinking that,' said Andy. 'It can't be, surely?'

'Oh, crap,' said Linda. 'I sincerely hope it isn't.'

'It's the same size,' Ed said, almost in a whisper.

'What was the guy's name we dealt with on the *Arena*?' Andy asked, turning back to Ed.

'Conor.'

'That's the man.'

'Is there any way of confirming that, Cleo?' Ed asked.

'Difficult,' she replied. 'That rock is too dense to penetrate with my scans.'

'As was the *Arena*,' said Pol.

'I will confirm, however, it is the same diameter and of a similar rock stratum as the *Arena*,' Cleo admitted.

Ed felt a sudden sense of unease develop, as he considered the thousands of people that lived in the *Arena*. It didn't bode well for them if the bugs had indeed overrun their world.

'Come on, people,' said Linda, sitting upright in her seat. 'There must be a way we can find out. If it is the

Arena, there may be people still alive and needing help on that thing.'

'Absolutely,' said Andy, turning to Ed. 'They saved one of our planets not so long ago. If it is them, we need to return the favour. Quite how we do that is another question.'

Ed spread his arms wide and gazed around the room.

'I'm open to suggestions,' he said.

Everyone turned to stare at Phil as he slowly and slightly nervously put his hand up.

'A nano-swarm?' he said, questioningly.

'Bloody hell,' blurted Andy, sitting back in his seat and throwing his arms up in frustration. 'It's so fucking obvious. Why didn't I think of that?'

'Cleo should've,' mumbled Linda. She glanced up from her screen when the room went silent, to find everyone staring at her. 'Did I say that out loud?' she asked, turning to find Cleo leaning against a bulkhead stanchion behind her, with a wry grin.

'Actually, she's right,' said Cleo. 'But in my defence, I was expending the majority of my computing power on my hologram in the *52*.'

'Well, okay,' said Ed. 'But can it be done?'

'Yeah,' she said. 'For delivery, I suggest one of the smaller cloaked drones. More chance of it squeezing through that rush hour of bug traffic. Would you like me to prepare everything?'

'Do it,' said Ed. 'If that really is the *Arena* and there's still survivors aboard, I want to know as soon as possible.'

19

———

Engineering passageway, Katadromiko 52, *non-system space*

WHEN CLEO MATERIALISED in the corridor outside the ROR, she was confronted by around thirty bugs, the nearest being about twenty metres away and all busy ripping panels off the walls. They stopped what they were doing and stared at her, seemingly frozen to the spot, but Cleo knew they were likely awaiting instructions from the collective mind.

She had appeared in Grogun's image, wearing the captain's uniform and didn't have to wait long for the reaction she knew was coming.

They launched themselves in her direction, a snarling, snapping wall of incensed metre-tall insects surged toward her. Had it been the real Grogun, it would've been terrifying and she wouldn't have stood a chance, but the holographic version stood her ground with hands on hips and a big grin on her face.

Just as the leading bugs were a fraction of a second from hitting her, she vanished. The seething cascade of hate all piled into each other and as they began picking themselves up, confused as to where their prey had gone, the holographic Grogun reappeared behind them at the corridor T-junction.

'Oi, dumb arse dipshits,' she hollered back up the passageway.

They all turned and, mad with anger, swarmed back the way they'd come, the leading bugs fighting over each other to be the first to get to her.

Grogun immediately took off to the right and flew down the passageway, head down like a hundred-metre sprinter.

'Be ready with your finger hovering,' she transmitted to the real Grogun, checking over her shoulder to see how fast they were gaining.

Gaining they were, alarmingly quickly. She thought about cheating and moving faster than a human actually could, but that might alert them to the deception. Upping her pace as much as she dared, she flashed past a right-hand junction just as another large group of bugs reached it. They stared at her as she zipped past, before realising she was the target they'd been tasked with eradicating. Without looking they piled out of the turning, straight in front of the original steam train of bugs.

The noise of them coming together had Cleo glancing over her shoulder again to witness a car crash of epic proportions. So much so, as to momentarily block the corridor. She smiled as the few seconds it took the maelstrom of bodies to sort themselves out, gave her the extra time she needed to reach the nearest hangar.

'Airlocks now,' she shouted.

Grogun, back in the ROR, having already removed the safeties, remotely opened both airlock doors into the hangar at the same time, enabling Cleo to sprint through and out of sight of her pursuers.

She promptly disappeared, reappearing as herself in the ROR with Grogun.

'Wait till they're all inside,' she said, watching the video feed from inside the hangar.

The bugs began swarming into the large hangar. Their numbers had increased considerably from the original thirty, as the collective decision must have been to throw every nearby available asset at eliminating the captain.

'Fuck me,' mumbled Grogun. 'Look how many there are. It must be more than a thousand now.'

'Have you secured the ships in there?' Cleo asked.

'The mag floor should hold them,' Grogun answered. 'How long do I wait?' she asked, as bugs continued to flow in through the airlock.

Cleo shrugged.

'Until they stop coming. They won't get in the ships will they?'

'No, I secured them all,' said Grogun, watching the sea of insects flowing around the hangar fruitlessly searching for her.

The number of bugs entering the hangar receded suddenly, as if someone had turned off a tap.

'Ready?' Cleo asked.

'I thought you being a Theo and all that, meant you couldn't take a life?' said Grogun.

'I'm not…you are.'

'But you were part of the operation.'

'I just ran down a corridor,' Cleo replied, nodding at the flashing icon under Grogun's finger. 'About time you hit that.'

The flow of bugs had ceased. They were all in the hangar circulating and searching frantically around the rows of parked freighters for the ship's captain who, unbeknown to them, was no longer there. Grogun touched the icon and both airlock doors closed again, trapping the surging mass of insects inside.

She ignored the warning siren that sounded as she removed the fail-safes on the atmosphere shield generator and turned it off.

The explosive decompression whipped the hangar clean of insects in a few seconds. A few of the smaller ships near the hangar exit shifted out of their neat lines, more to do with being struck by hundreds of bugs than their lesser weight causing them to move on the magnetic floor.

Even though the bugs could actually survive in the cold vacuum of space, Grogun had programmed the auto mini cannons on that side of the ship, designed to target enemy fighters that managed to get close in, to engage anything that moved.

Grogun adopted a contemptuous grin as the side of the cruiser lit up with hundreds of red laser bolts vaporising dozens of bugs a second.

'What was it you said they called this? A turkey shoot was it?' quizzed Grogun.

'Yeah.'

'On Kalameed II, we call it naive egotistical disassembly, although good fucking riddance sounds much better to me. Bastard things.'

'Ah, crap,' exclaimed Cleo, suddenly looking up to stare at one of the monitors displaying the exterior view behind the ship.

'What the hell is that?' asked Grogun, following her gaze. 'That better not be more of the little shits.'

'I'm afraid it is,' admitted Cleo, pulling an apologetic expression. 'This time on a planetary scale. Can't you jump the ship away?'

'I need to lock them out of propulsion first,' she said. 'I hadn't got around to that yet.'

'Did you close all the bulkhead doors in this section?'

Grogun nodded as she tapped away on the control panel.

'Means you should be left alone for a while. Would you like me to go to main engineering and mess with their heads a bit?' asked Cleo.

'Couldn't do any harm,' Grogun mumbled as she concentrated.

Cleo was just about to disappear when Grogun turned and waved a finger at her.

'Don't break anything,' she said, sternly. 'I'm going to need everything working in there.' Before returning her attention back to her task.

'I'll be very subtle,' Cleo whispered, as she vanished once more.

20
____

Main engineering, Katadromiko 52, *non-system space*

CLEO HAD to materialise blind in engineering, as the cameras had been turned off and locked out before Grogun had had a chance to gain control over them. She chose a small tool store room and thanked the ship's design engineers for their meticulous overengineering of almost everything. Fitting a couple of holo emitters into a machine workshop tool store wasn't wholly necessary, but it did enable the maintenance holobots to retrieve tools for the human engineers.

It was pitch black, and the booming thump and rumble of nearby powerful equipment echoing around the metal walled room made it feel like being on the inside of a bass drum. She knew from the detailed plans of the ship, the noise was coming from one of the four Ried-Hardsick generators that initiated the vessel's gravity plating.

Having been turned off for a while, it was working hard to recharge the system back up to optimal levels. The noise played into her hands as it enabled Cleo to crack the heavy door a few centimetres and peek out onto the main engineering deck.

She heard a groan of disappointment from Grogun, listening and watching from the ROR. The huge engineering control room was awash with bugs and in the distance she could see a human in an engineering uniform standing at one of the main consoles. He was surrounded by a ring of insects, all strangely facing outwards, seemingly guarding rather than enforcing.

'Can you pan in on the crew member?' asked Grogun.

Cleo did as requested and heard a sharp intake of breath as the captain recognised who it was.

'Who is it? Cleo asked.

'That's the chief engineer,' she replied. 'How the hell did he get here? I left him unconscious in the bridge ROR and code sealed it.'

'You left him with the brainwashed girl though.'

'I didn't have any choice, I couldn't carry him all the way here and I didn't have anything in there to restrain her.

'We need to see if he's working under duress or if he's been brainwashed too,' said Cleo.

'They can't possibly have brainwashed him that fast, surely?'

'Well, they're carrying the crew away somewhere when they stun them. Perhaps when you've jumped the ship away somewhere safer, we can investigate that.'

'Yeah you're right,' said Grogun. 'The priority is

getting the ship away from that swarm and planetoid thing outside.' She went quiet for a moment.

'I need to see that screen that Qatts is working on,' she said. 'He's got propulsion code locked to that panel only. The code should be displayed in the top right corner of the screen.'

'I need to get closer,' said Cleo. 'The screen's at an angle and even if it wasn't, my optics wouldn't be able to read it from this distance.'

'All the guarding bugs have their backs to him,' said Grogun. 'Can't you silently appear behind Qatts and peer over his shoulder? I'll do an immediate screen freeze and you can disappear again.'

'D'you know,' said Cleo, 'occasionally, humans surprise me. I've the brain the size of a planet and I hadn't considered that scenario.'

'Yeah, but you're running a starship as well as being here,' said Grogun. 'I couldn't do that in a million chronia.'

'You have an analytical mind just like your father.'

'Hmm, I don't think Mr Critical would agree with that,' she replied, sceptically. 'But anyway, I'll accept the compliment and I'm ready when you are.'

'Before we do that, I have another idea I want to throw at you,' said Cleo.

'Okay.'

'The design schematics show you have a toxika vent in this area of engineering.'

'We do and I see where you're going with that, but what about Qatts? He'd get vented into space too.'

'Can you turn the gravity plating off in just this area?'

'Yeah, I can.'

'What's Qatts trained to do if that happened?'

'Sit on a seat that will automatically swing out and strap himself in,' said Grogun. 'Ah, now, yes, that would do it and seriously thin the area of creepy crawlies wouldn't it? Are we sure there's no more of my crew in the vicinity?'

'Qatts is the only human within the catchment area.'

'You're absolutely sure? Because I couldn't live with myself if that fact proved wrong.'

'I'm sure. I take it all the emergency doors will seal automatically, so we don't vent half the ship?'

'As soon as a drop in pressure is detected the airtight doors will close and seal,' affirmed Grogun. 'It's automated and each door is individually powered.'

'Good.'

'Okay, shall we extinguish the gravity first and as soon as he sits down, you go in and get a look at the screen and then I vent the chamber.'

'I'm ready when you are,' said Cleo, preparing for her reappearance behind Qatts.

She heard the huge generator behind the wall change pitch as Grogun shut off the gravity in the engineering section. Watching closely, she saw Qatts grab hold of the console and pull himself down into the automatic emergency seat and strap himself in as the gravity faded away. Pandemonium reigned as the huge contingent of bugs suddenly found themselves unexpectantly on the float. A few were able to grab hold of things, but the majority began flailing around, their six limbs thrashing about trying desperately to paddle their way unsuccessfully back down to the deck.

'Go now,' said Grogun.

Cleo didn't need to be told twice. No one saw her disappear from the gloom of the tool store, but a couple of the floating armed bugs saw her reappear looming over Qatts's shoulder. They instinctively and without thinking it through, fired at her.

Laser rifles don't have an awful lot of recoil and especially not when they're set on stun. But when you're on the float just the smallest force will have you spinning uncontrollably, which is exactly what happened. The two bugs fired almost instantaneously, sending them spiralling away and clattering into their colleagues. The shots they fired missed by a mile and hit hapless floating bugs nearby.

'Got it,' Grogun called. 'Right, let's flush the room of these parasites.'

There was a loud clunk from the far port side wall as the vent safety clamps disengaged and red warning lights began strobing around the vast space. The vent itself was low down and almost flush with the deck. It was two metres in diameter and stretched over a kilometre long, finally venting into space between two of the larger attitude thrusters on the stern of the ship. The agitation amongst the bugs nearest the vent went into overdrive as the heavy circular door snapped away into its housing with a deafening clang.

'You might want to be somewhere else when I open the outer door,' said Grogun.

'I'm a hologram,' said Cleo. 'You go right ahead. I'm

sick of these bloody arthropods wiggling their legs and glowering at me already.'

Qatts had turned in his seat and was giving Cleo a determined glare. He snatched out with one hand, only for it to hit and then pass straight through Cleo's midriff.

'How rude,' she said, taking a step back. 'D'you mind keeping your hands to yourself?'

No sooner had she said it, Qatts was suddenly pulled sideways, his arms and legs flailing towards the vent. Cleo turned and watched as the swarm of floating bugs surged towards it too. The ones that had managed to hang onto something when the gravity failed, found their grip wasn't strong enough to fight against the vacuum of space and were quickly dislodged.

Cleo couldn't see the vent from where she was, but she could certainly hear the roaring as the atmosphere thundered into the narrow pipe. There was also a sound like a wet machine gun, as hundreds of bugs clattered the edge of the vent as they flashed away, only to be flung out into the cold void of space a few seconds later.

As before, Grogun had programmed the multiple laser cannon turrets on the stern this time to engage anything that moved and they had an inordinate quantity of targets. The whole area around the vessel's stern lit up with a blizzard of laser fire as a couple of thousand insects spewed out from the open toxika vent. Some of the bugs were already dead, but dead or not, few survived the thirty-six multi-barrelled auto-targeting laser emplacements.

Cleo watched as the last few bugs disappeared. She could hear Grogun whooping with joy in the ROR as her beloved engineering was scoured clean of insects. She also noticed Qatts was fighting for breath and looking round she found and retrieved the nearest emergency breather. He snatched it out of her hands, rammed it over his face and began gulping down the flow of oxygen.

'The queen…will be…most…displeased,' he said, in a monotone voice between gritted teeth and laboured breaths. He glared at Cleo with a contemptuous scowl.

'Well, that answers my next question,' said Grogun. 'Give me a few minutes to plot, embed and execute a jump to somewhere safe. Then you can help me with retaking my ship.'

Cleo put her hand on Qatts's shoulder. He stiffened and slumped, his eyes closing as he lost consciousness. She strapped the oxygen mask to his face and took herself back to the ROR.

21

The starship Gabriel*'s bridge, non-system space*

'THERE'S MORE OF 'EM,' said Andy. 'Flying out a hole in the stern.'

Everybody on the bridge glanced up as Andy panned in on the rear of the *52*. Hundreds of bugs were spewing out only to be immediately turned into vapour by the laser emplacements.

'How is she doing that?' Callon asked.

'That must be from engineering,' said Andy. 'All GDA ships' main engineering decks have a vent in case of a radioactive or toxic material leak.'

'Clever girl,' said Linda.

'Clever girls,' corrected Cleo, staring at Linda with a furrowed brow. 'I did have a part to play in that too.'

Linda pulled a sour expression at Cleo and held her hands up in a placatory manner.

'Nice one, Cleo,' said Andy. 'D'you know what she plans on doing next?'

'She now has control of propulsion again. So she's going to jump the ship to safety. If I'm going to be able to continue to help her, we obviously need to go too.'

'Oh, shit,' said Pol. 'What about the nanos? They've only just been deployed.'

'They won't go anywhere,' said Cleo. 'It'll give them time to fully infiltrate the moon and anyway, don't you think our priority must be to retake the *52*?'

'I do,' said Ed. 'I take it she's going to embed the jump?'

'She is.'

'Then we need to do the same and follow along.'

'Already prepped. I just need her emergence co-ordinates.'

Ed looked over at Andy and smiled.

'Ready for a bit of bug exterminating, Andrew?' he asked.

Before he could answer, Linda's brow creased and she pointed a finger at Ed.

'You're not planning on doing what I think you are, are you?' she grouched.

Ed shrugged.

'Well, we can't do much to help sitting on our arses in here, can we? and there's a lot less of 'em on that ship now.'

'You're mad…and what d'you expect us to do? Wait here for the news of your demise?'

'We'll have Cleo with us,' said Andy, hopefully.

'And our personal shields,' said Ed.

'This isn't like on the bloody movies you know,' she grumbled. 'You can't just beam out when the going gets tough.'

'I can,' said Cleo, putting her hand up and adopting a petulant grin.

'Shut up, you,' Linda snapped. 'This is not the time for humour.'

'No, but I do have eyes all over the ship now Grogun has gained control. I know where they are and in what numbers. It seems they're a bit disorganised now. It might mean their connection to the collective off the ship was cut when the shields went back up. It'll definitely be cut after the jump and from the queen too.'

Phil's ears pricked up.

'There's a queen?' he asked. 'Where?'

'Unknown,' said Cleo. 'But both the brainwashed humans have mentioned the queen won't be very happy with the current turn of events.'

'My heart bleeds,' said Andy, sarcastically. 'She can go to hell.'

'Hopefully, that's only a matter of time,' said Ed.

'I have the jump co-ordinates,' said Cleo, suddenly standing straight and staring straight ahead. 'Jumping in sync with the *52* in five seconds.'

After the usual slight dimming of the lights when the jump took place, everyone on the bridge watched the holomap as it reprogrammed itself with the new location.

'We're in a system,' said Callon. 'A hundred and seventy-seven light years travelled, supposedly uninhabited, B-type main sequence star, seventeen planets, no traffic detected except for the *52* a hundred and fifty kilometres distant.'

'Awesome,' said Phil, giving Callon a beaming smile.

Andy gave Ed a knowing glance and got raised eyebrows in response.

'Okay, full shields and uncloak,' said Ed. 'Let's move in closer now we don't have the swarm of bug rocks to contend with.'

Grogun's image appeared to one side of the holomap. Ed thought she looked tired but confident.

'Hello, *Gabriel*,' she said. 'Sorry I haven't been in touch recently, it's just I've been a little distracted with a slight infestation.'

'Understatement of the year,' said Andy. 'Did you really walk the length of your ship on the outside?'

'I never want to wear another pair of mag boots ever again,' Grogun replied, rolling her eyes. 'My legs feel like they're full of carboncrete.'

'You'll be able to crack walnuts with your thighs though!' chuckled Andy.

Grogun looked puzzled, as everyone else on the *Gabriel*'s bridge turned to glower at Andy.

He glanced around at a circle of unsmiling faces, his grin slowly morphing into a grimace.

'Err…inappropriate?' he asked, awkwardly.

'Yep,' said Ed, nodding his head.

'What's a walnut?' Grogun asked.

'Don't worry,' said Linda. 'Just Andrew being a dick.'

Ed and Andy made their way down to the port hangar, much to Linda and Pol's palpable disapproval. Cleo provided them with some GDA marine-style body armour, just as a backup in case their personal shields failed.

'This stuff's a lot lighter than it looks,' said Andy, strapping on the grey armour and doing a few kung fu-type moves.

'It's no good you practising your karate,' said Ed. 'If we're reduced to hand to hand combat we're royally screwed, they have six limbs remember. Personally, I would've pissed off long before it comes to that.'

'No, you're right,' said Andy. 'I wouldn't want to get covered in that stinking grey goo either.'

They entered one of the two shuttles parked against the side wall.

'Would've preferred the *Cartella*,' said Ed, as he passed Andy a laser rifle. 'At least it had some armaments.'

Andy gazed out the front screen to the opposite side of the hangar.

'Why don't we take one of the new ones?' he asked, pointing at two sleek black shuttles parked against the far wall.

Ed turned and followed Andy's gaze. The ships in question had been purchased on their last adventure. They were unique, gloss black, fast and had hidden laser cannons.

'That's not a bad idea,' said Ed, grabbing a rifle for himself and a couple of come-in-handy backpacks, before turning for the airlock. 'At least we'll have something to defend ourselves with if the flying rocks appear.'

'We really ought to have a name for these ships too,' said Andy, as they walked towards the nearest one. 'We've had them a while now and we can't keep referring to them as the black ones.'

'I'll give it some thought,' said Ed.

'I already have,' Andy replied.

'Go on.'

'*Scorpion*.'

Ed stopped, looked between the ship and Andy and smiled.

'They're small, black, fast with a sting in the tail, that's perfect,' he said. '*Scorpion* it is.'

Andy beamed as they boarded the small ship and prepped it for the short flight over to the *52*.

22

―――――

Cockpit of a Scorpion *shuttle, un-named system*

GROGUN HAD CLEARED the *Scorpion* through the *52*'s shields and was bringing Ed and Andy into one of the engineering hangars near to her ROR, the same one she'd re-entered the ship through earlier.

Ed, who was piloting, was glad they'd brought the smaller shuttle. The hangar was crowded with engineering paraphernalia. Strange-looking machines, crates of assorted sizes and large cable drums lay haphazardly around the deck. He managed to squeeze the *Scorpion* down on the right-hand side close to what looked like a small portable office unit.

'Bit untidy in 'ere isn't it?' said Andy.

'I'll have a word with housekeeping,' replied Ed, shutting down the drives.

They disembarked, taking with them their rifles,

ensuring the personal shield generators clipped to the weapon were both activated and the two backpacks. Cleo met them as they descended the steps.

'Welcome to the mad house,' she said. 'Come this way quickly. The way through the ship is clear at the moment, but that can change fast.'

'Is Grogun still in the ROR?' asked Andy.

'She is, that's where we're going first,' she replied, leading them through all the gear littering the deck.

'I thought the location had been compromised,' said Ed.

'It had, but since no bugs have turned up since the venting, we're kinda led to believe the location didn't get passed down the line in time. Grogun has also closed all the airtight doors leading from the front of the ship.'

'Is the rear of the ship clear since you vented engineering?' Ed asked.

'I haven't come across any yet,' Cleo replied. 'But it doesn't mean there aren't a few stragglers lurking. We must remain wary.'

Twenty minutes later, after an uneventful journey through to the ROR, Grogun let them in and resealed the door.

Ed could see the relief on her face to have human company once more, but there was also a deep-seated lethargy about her that worried him.

'When was the last time you ate?' he asked, swinging his backpack around.

'Yesterday…probably,' said Grogun, shrugging.

'Here,' said Ed, passing her a couple of protein bars. 'Get those down you.'

Andy went through the cupboards lining the far wall and found some marine issue ration packs and bottles of energy water. He gave her one each of those too.

'We need you to watch our backs as we move forward,' said Ed. 'Can't have you dropping with exhaustion at a critical moment can we?'

Grogun took a deep breath as she tucked into one of the bars.

'Never knew captaincy could be so draining,' she said, between mouthfuls.

'Look at it this way,' said Andy. 'After this is over, nothing will seem hard ever again.'

'That's if they ever give me another command,' she said. 'This is my first and it's a disaster.'

'I think you're underestimating yourself,' said Andy. 'No one could've predicted this and you haven't lost yet.'

She nodded and sighed.

'Yeah,' she said. 'I just can't help but think I've let my crew down. There's forty-seven thousand of them. Where are they?'

'That's our next job,' said Ed. 'They're taking the crew somewhere and using some form of mind-altering technology.'

'They took my chief engineer and had him brainwashed and working for them at the opposite end of the ship in just three or four hours.'

'Hmm,' grunted Ed, looking thoughtful. 'There's two big rocks buried in the hull amidships and because of the density, we couldn't scan what's inside. They spent considerable time sealing around the edges, presumably because they wanted to contain an atmosphere around and in them.'

'You think that's where they're taking them?' asked Grogun.

'It's a pretty good place to start,' said Ed, glancing up at the rows of screens. 'Can you see what they're doing there on the cameras.'

'No, all the cameras in that location have been obscured or smashed,' Cleo replied.

'What about the holo emitters?'

'I haven't tested them, because me appearing there might stir things up before we're ready.'

'Can't you appear as a bug?' said Andy.

Cleo smiled and glanced at Ed.

'There's no flies on him,' she said. 'I'll give it a go.'

'Transmit what you see onto there,' said Grogun, pointing to one of the larger monitors.

A view of Grogun and Ed in the ROR from Cleo's perspective appeared on one of the lower screens, before moving from screen to screen until she found the correct one.

'Okay,' she said. 'How does this look?'

Grogun nearly fell out of her seat as Cleo vanished and an armed bug materialised in her place.

'Fuck's sake,' exclaimed Grogun when she realised it was Cleo's interpretation of a bug. 'I nearly soiled myself. A bit more warning next time perhaps.'

'Well I can't tell the difference,' said Ed. 'But then again the ones I've seen up close have generally been in bits, or a puddle of grey goo.'

'Don't remind me about that smell,' said Andy, cringing. 'They fucking reek.'

'Well, be ready for it, probably before the day is out,' said Ed, raising his eyebrows.

Andy took a step back and wrinkled his nose.

'Don't, just don't,' he mumbled, pulling a disgusted face.

'Wish me luck,' said the bug in a weird squeaky voice that Ed thought was a bit creepy.

The large screen view changed immediately. Ed tilted his head to one side trying to make out what Cleo was seeing.

'What the hell is that?' Andy asked, squinting at the weird image.

'Looks like dirty sand-coloured wallpaper,' said Ed.

The image swept right as Cleo turned and all three of them realised what it was.

'It's a tube,' said Grogun.

'Like in a termite nest,' said Andy.

Just as he said it, a train of bugs came the other way and Cleo moved on so as to not look suspicious.

'Why does her hologram still work in there?' Andy asked.

'We're still inside the *52* and the membrane must be very thin,' said Ed. 'You can see it moving as they pass through.'

She rounded a corner and the tube ended in a recognisable human corridor. Two bugs came the other way dragging an unconscious man in a crew uniform.

'Medical orderly,' said Grogun, with a sigh, recognising the distinctive epaulettes.

'We're going the wrong way then, Cleo,' said Andy. 'Turn around, we want to see where they're taking him.'

She did as requested and followed the trio back along the thin wobbly tube. Several corners later they came to a junction and turned sharp left. The tube ended in a much gloomier space, although this was definitely not part of the 52. The walls, floor and ceiling were made of a dark rock, but polished to a high sheen.

Ed, watching on the screen back in the ROR, thought it looked similar to the polished concrete floors they had in the laboratories back at Canterbury University. The main difference was these were perfectly rounded, not a flat surface anywhere, even the floor was a series of gentle curves.

'We must be inside one of those rocks now,' said Andy.

'Cleo,' called Ed. 'Is your holo image still holding up?' he asked.

'It is,' she replied, turning slowly to give everyone a good look around the inside of the thirty-metre sphere.

'Your hologram's still working, even in here,' said Ed.

'There are emitters in here,' said Cleo. 'And they must have hot-wired into the 52's systems too, the crossover was seamless.'

The room was quite spartan except for fifteen grey couches, twelve of which contained seemingly unconscious members of the ship's crew. They watched as the two bugs dragged the medical orderly to one of the vacant couches and dumped him quite unceremoniously onto it, then retreated from the room back past Cleo without a second look. There were five other bugs in the room, four of whom were crouched over some kind of low control panels. One of them gave the fifth bug a small vial, which he placed inside a small claw-held machine. He walked up to the medical orderly and offered the machine up to the unconscious man's neck. It projected a needle and injected something into him.

'It could be nano technology,' said Cleo. 'Similar in design to our krypti stuff.'

'That would definitely have been on Phil's laptop when it was stolen,' said Ed.

One of the other humans suddenly opened her eyes and sat up.

'Ah, no,' groaned Grogun. 'She was a bridge navigation officer, a good one too.'

The girl turned and stared at one of the bugs who returned the look, before she nodded, slipped off the couch and on slightly wobbly legs, stooped down and disappeared up the low circular tunnel.

'She must've been receiving instructions,' said Andy. 'Which shows the collective mind is still working on the ship amongst the remaining bugs.'

'We need to shut this and any other similar ones down,' said Grogun. 'Can Cleo do that?'

'No,' said Ed.

'But we can,' said Andy, tapping his rifle. 'Have you got a peg for my nose?'

'You've got to get there first,' said Grogun. 'It's kilometres away.'

'Do you have control over the tube trains?' Ed asked.

'I can have,' she replied. 'Hadn't really thought about those. They don't seem to use them.'

'Find us a carriage that can take us all the way there non-stop.'

'And wait there,' said Andy. 'We might need it to get back here in a hurry.'

'I'll see what I can do,' said Grogun, turning back to her console.

'All aboard for London Victoria,' said Andy, grinning at Ed.

Ed just shook his head and wondered if bringing Andy had been wise.

23

Tube train, Katadromiko 52, *un-named system*

ED SAT CRADLING his rifle and stared out of the carriage's front window as they zipped along deeper into the ship. He half expected a sea of bugs to come surging down the tube towards them. He glanced over at Andy who was sitting sideways on and staring at the floor humming an unidentifiable tune, his head bobbing from side to side in time with the beat.

'You're remarkably chipper considering the situation,' Ed commented.

Andy shrugged.

'How far is it from the tube stop to that bug rock room thing?' he asked.

'About three hundred and forty metres,' said Cleo, materialising on one of the other seats.

'Bloody hell,' said Ed, jumping back in surprise. 'Don't do that when I've got my finger on the trigger.'

'Your weapon's not activated,' she said.

'It might've been though,' he said, looking around the ceiling. 'How can you be in here, there aren't any emitters?'

'Integrated,' she said. 'All the GDA ship trains have them built in for the holographic maintenance and cleaning bots. Anyway, I'm here because you're getting close to your destination and I wanted to recce the corridors first.'

'Good plan,' said Andy. 'The fewer we meet face to face the better, I forgot to bring a nose peg.'

The carriage had been flashing through stops every few seconds, but now it began to slow, the stops, previously just a passing blur, became an open window for a second. Ed stared at each one as they passed and was pleased to see empty corridor after empty corridor.

The low hum of the carriage suddenly changed pitch as it braked hard and Ed had to grab a hand hold to avoid falling.

'Bloody hell,' he whinged, hanging on for dear life. 'They don't normally do this.'

'Grogun's bringing the train in quick,' said Cleo. 'She's changed the operating protocols so it comes into the station fast just in case there are bugs about and you want to take them by surprise.'

As she spoke, the carriage flashed into the station they wanted, stopping so quickly, Andy slid along three seats, cursing as he went.

The concave door hissed up into the ceiling. Cleo,

being the nearest, stuck her head out and peered left and right.

'Clear both ways,' she said, as Ed and Andy stepped up behind her. 'I'll go on ahead,' she added, before promptly disappearing.

Ed staggered forward, almost falling out the door and into the corridor.

'Shit,' he mumbled, steadying himself against the door frame.

'Have you been raiding my tequila supply?' Andy asked, watching from behind with an accusing smirk.

'No,' he griped. 'She buggered off just as I was about to lean out and check too.'

'Excuses, excuses,' chuckled Andy, as he pushed past and turned left.

Ed hurried to catch up and checked his personal shield and weapon were activated and on the right setting. Once satisfied everything was in the green, he turned his attention to the route they were taking. The passageway, he noticed, wasn't as brightly lit here as it was near engineering. It was more of a yellowish glow, than the usual bright white light the GDA would normally maintain in the public areas.

'Why's it so gloomy?' Andy asked, peering over his shoulder.

'They don't like bright lights,' said Ed.

'Hmm,' grunted Andy. 'That's right, in that case I might have an idea.'

'Like what?'

'Strobe lights,' he said. 'Really bright and slow repeating. Cleo told me that when Grogun turned the lights back up, the bugs seemed temporarily disorientated and kept bumping into things. A slow strobe might bugger them up for longer periods.'

'Did you hear that, Grogun?' Ed asked, as they trotted side by side and weapons up down the wide corridor.

'I did,' she replied. 'That facility isn't available in the itinerary, but I might be able to write some code though. I'll work on it.'

Ed was about to add something when a door to their right cracked open, a face briefly peered out at them before the eyes widened in surprise and the door quickly clicked shut again. Ed and Andy stopped, looked at each other and then back at the door.

'Hello,' called Andy, moving over and tapping on the door as he was the nearest. 'We're here to help. Are you alright in there?'

After a few seconds the door clicked open a couple of inches again.

'Are you really human?' a female voice enquired.

'Absolutely,' said Andy. 'We're trying to rid the ship of these smelly bugs. Are you on your own?'

The gap between the frame and door widened, and a girl's face appeared. She was gaunt and pale. Her hair was unkempt and her eyes darted both ways up and down the passageway, before settling back on Andy. She jumped back slightly when Ed came into view from behind him.

'It's okay,' he pleaded, holding his hands up in a placatory manner. 'There's two of us.'

She glanced down, her eyes widening as she noticed the rifles slung around their necks.

'Are you marines or something?' she asked, her brow

furrowing as she looked them up and down. 'Because they're not the usual uniforms I've seen them wearing.'

'No, we're from another ship,' said Andy.

'A civilian one,' added Ed. 'We're helping your captain retake the ship.'

The girl stared at them for a moment before speaking again.

'At least you're talking normally,' she said. 'The last person we saw was speaking very strangely.'

'What, like monotone, as if they were reading it from a script?' Andy asked.

'Yes,' she replied. 'A crew member came and took my husband away, told us to remain in the cabin until we were called for. I asked them where my husband was going and they just ignored me and marched him off. They walked as if they were a bit drunk too.'

'They? there was more than one of them?' Ed asked.

'Five,' she said. 'All armed, all with strange glaring eyes and a bit unsteady on their feet.'

'What did your husband do?' Andy asked.

'He went with them.'

'No, I meant for a job.'

'Oh, right. He's a water supply engineer. They seemed excited when they found that out.'

Ed and Andy glanced at each other.

'Are you thinking what I'm thinking?' said Andy.

'Hmm,' grunted Ed. 'We need to ask Cleo if the nano tech could be introduced via the water supply?'

'It could,' Cleo said, appearing behind them.

They both jumped, the girl screamed and slammed the door in their faces.

'CLEO,' Ed snapped, turning to give her a glare.

'Sorry, too abrupt perhaps?' she said, looking contrite.

Ed exhaled and shook his head.

'Maybe walking back up the corridor might've been better.'

'Understood.'

The door cracked open again.

'I thought you said there was only two of you,' the girl said, suspicion obvious in her tone.

'There are,' said Ed. 'She's a hologram.'

'What, like a maintenance bot?' she asked, staring at Cleo suspiciously.

'Little bit more sophisticated than that,' said Andy, smirking.

Ed turned to Cleo.

'Can you let Grogun know that they might be trying to put their nano tech into the water supply,' he said.

'I already have and she's shutting the water supply down. Her reply was, she'd rather they went thirsty for a while, than have their brains scrambled.'

'You think that's what they wanted my husband for— to poison everyone?' the girl asked, her fear evident in her tone.

'Possibly,' said Ed. 'We're just being careful.'

'To stand any chance of retaking the ship we have to stop them from brainwashing the crew first,' said Andy.

A clattering sound from around the next junction caught their attention.

'Bugs,' said Cleo. 'Quick, get inside.'

She pushed Andy who clattered into Ed and they both hit the door, sending the girl flying backwards as they fell into the cabin. Ed saw Cleo morph into Grogun just as she pulled the door shut.

The girl saw it too.

'She turned into the captain,' she exclaimed, picking herself up off the floor and pointing an up-to-now concealed weapon at them.

24

——————

Crew cabin, Katadromiko 52, *un-named system*

'IT'S OKAY,' said Ed, raising his hands and ensuring they didn't stray anywhere near his rifle.

Andy did the same.

'It gives the bugs something to chase rather than coming in here,' Andy said.

She lowered the weapon, but her expression of distrust remained.

'What if they catch her?' she said.

'She's a hologram,' said Ed. 'She can just disappear.'

'Hopefully in the vicinity of an airlock that the real captain can open at an opportune moment, then it's goodnight Vienna,' said Andy.

Ed turned and grimaced at Andy.

'She's hardly going to understand what that means, is she?'

Andy shrugged.

'They get sucked out into space,' he said, giving the girl an apologetic glance.

She returned a patronising smile.

'The captain hasn't been captured then?' she asked, turning her attention back to Ed.

'No, she's in hiding and doing her best to thwart them commandeering the ship.'

'Oh, good,' she said. 'I was…'

They all turned as a door behind her cracked open an inch, revealing an eye blinking back at them. Then a nose and a second eye slightly lower down.

'I told you two to stay hidden and quiet,' she barked.

The door snapped shut again.

'Sorry,' she said.

'You have children?' Andy asked, giving Ed a forlorn look.

'Two girls.'

Ed nodded back at Andy.

'We need to get going,' he said. 'The longer we dick about here, the more crew get brainwashed.'

The mother watched them nervously as they both stood up from where they'd fallen. She made no attempt to stand however and remained where she was, staring at their rifles.

'Don't open the door to any noises again,' said Ed.

'Or drink the water,' said Andy. 'At least until we know it's safe.'

She dipped her head in a resigned nod.

'Can you save my husband?' she said, pleadingly.

'Where would they have taken him?' Andy asked.

'Where's the main water supply control centre?' Ed added.

'Deck 311,' she said. 'Room 9020.'

'We need to go there as soon as possible,' Ed said, giving Andy a determined stare as he put his ear to the door. Hearing nothing he opened it an inch and peeked through.

The corridor was empty in the direction they had to go. Cracking it a little more he leaned out and checked the other way.

'Clear?' Andy asked.

'Yep.'

'We will return—look after those two,' Ed said, indicating the door behind her.

She nodded slowly again as they exited.

'Stay safe,' they heard her call just before the door clicked shut.

'We never asked her name,' said Andy, as they trotted away from room 2397.

'Or her husband's,' added Ed.

Cleo materialised thirty metres ahead and signalled them to follow.

'How far is it?' Andy asked her as they approached.

'The bug tunnel begins just after the next junction and then it's about a hundred metres to the first rock room.'

'As a matter of interest, where did you take all those bugs?' Ed asked.

'Midships supply hangar,' said Cleo. 'Unfortunately Grogun lost all the racks of dried foodstuffs in there too, as they went out the door along with the bugs.'

'Small price to pay,' said Andy, shrugging. 'Good bloody riddance.'

Turning right at the junction, they immediately had to stoop to enter the strange circular membrane tunnel.

Andy snorted and wrinkled his nose.

'I can smell them already,' he whinged.

Ed noticed the tunnel material flexing and squirming under his feet. He thought it felt like walking on a silk sheet laid on ice.

'This is weird,' said Andy. 'Feels like I'm about to fall over any second and then the material tightens and you regain your balance.'

'Shush,' hissed Cleo, holding her finger to her lips and then pointing. 'We're getting close now.'

They both stopped and checked their rifles.

'Full power?' Andy quizzed.

'Yeah,' Ed whispered. 'We don't want any of the bugs calling for help. Head shots if you can and don't hit any of the ship's crew on the couches.'

'What if they get up and attack us?'

'Good point,' admitted Ed, thinking quickly. 'Let's have our hand guns set on stun and use those.'

Cleo morphed into a bug again and disappeared around the corner, returning a few moments later.

'There's five of them in there, two on the left, three on the right and four crew on the couches,' she said. 'I'll watch your backs.'

They exchanged a quick glance, Ed counted to three and with rifles raised into the shoulder they stepped purposely around the corner and into the rock room.

The first two bugs went down within seconds, one on

the left next to the couches and one on the right in front of the control panel. Both head shots so they were out of the game. The other three moved quickly, one scuttled behind the couches and the other two at the control panel ducked down and launched at them.

Andy had moved forward on the left searching out the one behind the couches, leaving Ed facing the two charging at him. He fired at the one on the right, scything off two of its left limbs. It crashed down on its side, right legs thrashing to keep it upright but only succeeding in sending itself into a spin.

The other bug crashed into Ed's personal shield, its front pincers snapping only inches from his face. The hit pushed him back, he tripped and sat down hard on his backside. His shield flicked off and his weapon discharged as his finger was still on the trigger. The laser bolt glanced the bug's abdomen, enraging it even more and as it came at him a second time, he managed to scramble back a few inches as its pincers snapped close, this time not restricted by the shield. He felt blood drip from his forehead as he tried to bring the rifle to bear, but the insect was extremely close now. He tried pushing it off him with the butt of the weapon, but it was too strong and as it reared up to make a final fatal attack, its head vaporised.

Ed gagged as grey goo splashed over him and the bug's body landed heavily in his lap.

'Shit, that stinks,' he complained, as he threw the body off him.

'No hugs for you, smelly boy,' said Andy, as he despatched the last bug still thrashing around in a circle.

Ed stood up again, rebooted his personal shield and

they both tiptoed across the bodies and puddles of goo and began firing laser bolts into the control panels, only stopping when the equipment was quite obviously unrepairable.

Turning, they gazed over the four unconscious crew lying on the couches. None were moving.

'What do we do about them?' Andy asked, as Cleo poked her head into the room.

Ed walked along the line of couches and felt for a pulse at each one.

'Well at least they're still alive,' he said. 'We'll just have to leave them here.'

'They might die though.'

'Do we have a staffed medical facility nearby?' Ed asked.

Andy shook his head, glancing sorrowfully at the crew lying helpless on the couches.

'Come on then, we need to shut down the second of these rooms,' Ed continued, making for the door and where Cleo was waiting.

'Do we have any idea how many bugs are left on the *52* now?' Andy asked Cleo. 'Their numbers must be becoming drastically reduced by now.'

'Grogun reckons the rear section of the ship is relatively clear now,' said Cleo. 'It's difficult to tell the further towards the bow you go as the cameras have been taken out. Quite whether this is by them or factions of the crew fighting back she's not sure.'

'There's a lot of crew on one of these and they're not going to give up easily,' said Andy.

He'd barely finished speaking when a rustling noise caught their attention and the circular tube began vibrating.

'Shit,' both Ed and Andy mouthed in unison, as they quickly jumped back into the rock room and took up defensive positions behind the couches.

Cleo morphed back into the captain and stood just outside the doorway, hoping to lead them away as they rounded the last bend. What she saw when the throng did appear, surprised her.

25

Bug tube, Katadromiko 52, *un-named system*

A LARGE GROUP of heavily armed humans thundered around the bend three abreast, completely filling the space. Cleo noticed the look of surprise on their faces matched her own.

The front rank stopped abruptly, causing those behind to clatter into them and each other.

'Captain?' a voice from somewhere within the group blurted, both questioningly and suspiciously.

'Don't worry, I haven't been converted,' she said, keeping her hands clearly visible, demonstrating she was unarmed.

One of the group from the front row spoke, eyeing her sceptically.

'How in Ancient's name have you survived unarmed?' he asked, jutting out his chin.

'I was with these two and they are,' she said, pointing into the rock room.

All eyes and weapons swivelled to cover the doorway. Cleo beckoned to Ed and Andy.

'Come on out, guys,' she said. 'These appear to be genuine crew and on our side.'

'Weapons down,' the spokesman shouted to them. 'If I see as much as a hand facing forward, you will be dropped.'

Three of the crew beside the spokesman dropped to their knees, bringing their rifles into the shoulder allowing the row behind to shoulder theirs. There were now seven rifles covering the doorway.

Ed came first, slowly, his rifle slung over his back, his palms held up and towards the newcomers, followed closely by Andy in a similar pose.

'Tell us your names, ranks, numbers and planet of birth,' he ordered.

'Edward Virr, captain, no number as not a serving GDA officer and Earth,' he said.

The spokesman's brow furrowed, but before he could speak Andy did.

'Andrew Faux, chief engineer, also no number for the same reason and Earth.'

The spokesman's gaze flicked between them until a spark of recognition registered in his eyes.

'Are you the civilian crew from that Theo ship we were sent to aid?' he asked.

Before Ed had a chance to reply a patronising voice echoed out from the group.

'That's Edward Virr from the *Gabriel*, you moron, don't you recognise him?'

The comment received a few sniggers from the rest of the group. The spokesman turned and glowered over his shoulder.

'Thank you, Corporal Fees,' he sneered. 'That's quite enough from you.'

The corporal stepped out from the throng, rounded the spokesman and approached Ed, his fist held out in front.

'It's good to see you, Captain,' he said.

Ed knew from Admiral Loftt, the proffered fist was a marine greeting. He also knew it wasn't like the Earth greeting where you bumped fists head-on. You tapped your fist on top of his and then he on top of yours.

Corporal Fees grinned when he did so.

'You're a friend of the admiral I understand,' he said.

Ed noticed the spokesman's eyebrows suddenly rise at that piece of information.

'I apologise for my colleague here,' he continued, jabbing a thumb over his shoulder. 'He's a catering manager and thinks he can order career marines around.'

'I was the senior rank,' the spokesman blurted. 'It was only right I…'

'If I'm not very much mistaken, your captain is the most senior rank and she is still in command,' said Andy.

Causing the group's attention to turn to Cleo.

'Although, that's not her,' said Ed, pointing at Cleo, who took the cue to morph back into herself.

This garnered a collective gasp from the group and a few weapons to rise up again. Ed held his hands up and shook his head.

'It's okay,' he said. 'This is Cleo my sentient ship's computer. Captain Whipper is still commanding the vessel from a hidden ROR. Cleo here poses as her to lure groups of bugs into hangars where they can be flushed out the door.'

'What a great idea,' said Fees. 'All we've been able to do is blow a load of them away with these.' He tapped his rifle and grinned again. 'I must agree, that would prove a much less pungent way to dispose of them.'

'Don't go in there then,' mumbled Andy, gurning a revolted face and nodding back through the door.

'Ah. Have you secured that room?' Fees asked, stretching his neck to peer around the corner.

'We have,' said Ed.

'Any crew in there?'

'Four, all unconscious but alive.'

'Have they been altered?'

'Unknown,' said Ed. 'Is there a medical room that's functional?'

'Not that we know of,' said Fees.

'Did you decommission the other rock room?' asked Andy, pointing back down the tube.

'Oh yeah,' said Fees, patting his rifle. 'With extreme prejudice.'

'You're my kinda guy,' said Andy, patting his.

Ed rolled his eyes.

'Can we move on before you two get engaged or something,' he said. 'We need to get to the water supply control room on deck 311, room 9020.'

'Well remembered,' said Andy. 'Come this way, ladies and gentlemen, we have a private train awaiting to depart.'

There were seventeen of them, eleven men and six women. Some were still dressed in their relative uniforms and the remainder in various styles of civilian dress. All were armed though, most with laser rifles and a handful with smaller hand weapons, a few with both.

As they reached the tube stop and piled aboard, Ed noticed the original spokesman had a face like a wet weekend. He pulled him to one side.

'When we've retaken the ship, we're going to need you to organise feeding the survivors,' he whispered in his ear. 'It'll be one of the most important jobs on the ship and everyone will be relying on you.'

He gave Ed a stern sideways glance.

'Who gave you the authority to give the orders?' he growled. 'You're not even a member of the crew.'

'I did,' boomed the captain, her sudden loud utterance over the carriage's intercom making everyone jump. 'The only reason we're in a position to retake our ship is because of them. So, Mr Hertmayor, catering supervisor from the canteen on deck 190, you do as you're fucking told.'

Ed heard Andy chuckle behind them, as Hertmayor blenched at the mention of his name and actual rank. He gritted his teeth and stared at the floor as everyone on the carriage turned to look at him.

'Ship's senior catering manager, eh?' said Fees, patronisingly. 'Well, well!'

'Doesn't matter who or what he is,' said Ed, 'we're going to need him along with the rest of you to get this ship up and running again. Is everyone cool with that?'

A round of concurring nods and verbal affirmations

echoed around the carriage. Even Hertmayor nodded his consent before sitting down and avoiding eye contact with anyone.

'Why are we going to the water supply deck?' Fees asked.

'We believe the bugs might be attempting to poison the supply,' said Andy.

'What, to kill us all? Like what happened on the *38* a few years ago?' one of the girls asked.

'It was the *Katadromiko 37*,' Fees corrected her, a faraway look crossing his face.

Ed noticed his change in demeanour.

'Did you know someone on that ship?' he asked.

'My father,' he answered, softly. 'He was a marine officer on board.'

Andy reached over and squeezed his shoulder. Fees cleared his throat and adopted a more determined expression.

'Sorry,' he said. 'Dark times.'

'Well, let's all work together and make sure this isn't another one,' said Ed, turning to face the girl who'd spoked first. 'In answer to your original question, no, it isn't,' he said. 'We believe they're attempting to add the nano technology that they're using to brainwash your crew. If they manage that then they'll convert almost everyone in one fell swoop.'

Those still standing staggered slightly as the carriage pulled away. Ed glanced up at one of the cameras.

'As near to room 9020 on deck 311 as you can please, Captain,' he said.

'Already programmed in,' came the reply from Grogun. 'The cameras are down on that deck, so I can't give you a recce on the location.'

'I can,' said Cleo, garnering a collective gasp from the group as she morphed into a bug and promptly vanished.

26

Tube carriage, Katadromiko 52, *un-named system*

CLEO WINKED BACK into the carriage only a few seconds after she left and gave Ed a worried expression.

'I take it it's not all clear?' he asked, noticing her reticence.

'To say the least,' she said. 'There's dozens of them.'

'Okay,' he said, thinking hard. 'Grogun, are there stations out of sight to the north and to the south of that location?'

'Indeed there are and I know where you're going with this. I'm reprogramming the first stop now.'

'Right,' said Ed. 'We need to split into two groups and attack the location in a pincer movement.'

Andy groaned.

'Ah, sorry,' he said. 'Pun not intended.'

Everyone else just stared at him, not understanding the Earth play on words.

Andy cleared his throat theatrically.

'Moving swiftly on,' he said, nudging Ed.

'Yes, okay,' said Ed. 'Our two groups attacking from opposite directions. It should create some confusion within their ranks for a short window. Make the most of it, make every shot count and remember, your colleagues are coming in the opposite direction, so no blue on blue mistakes.'

'Blue on what?' Fees asked.

'Shooting each other by mistake,' interjected Andy.

'Oh, right,' he said, furtively glancing at Hertmayor, who thankfully hadn't noticed.

'Do you want to take one group and me the other?' Ed asked Andy.

'What, split up?'

'Does that worry you?'

Ed noticed a slight hesitation before getting an answer.

'No,' Andy replied, unconvincingly.

Ed raised his eyebrows questioningly.

'No, really,' Andy continued. 'I'm cool with that.'

Ed nodded and turned back to the group.

'Okay, everyone on the left side of the carriage comes with me at the first stop and everyone on the right with Andy at the second. Is everyone happy with that?'

A murmur of assent echoed around the train together with a flurry of nodding heads.

'How long to the first station, Captain?' Ed asked, glancing up at one of the cameras.

'Four minutes,' came Grogun's reply. 'I've a second

carriage en route, so you'll both have an avenue of retreat if things don't go well.'

'Right, listen in my group,' called Ed. 'We're most likely to encounter targets as soon as we alight, so make every shot count and keep pressing forward. Remember there will be these guys coming the other way,' he waved his arm at Andy's group. 'So no spraying fire around willy-nilly.'

'That means randomly,' said Andy, rolling his eyes before turning to glower at Ed.

'Indeed,' Ed replied, shrugging. 'Check your weapons and my group line up in pairs. We'll disembark two at a time, weapons in the shoulder.'

The carriage slowed abruptly as it neared the station. The darkness outside in the tunnel became brighter all of a sudden as Grogun brought the carriage in hot. They all braced themselves against seats or clung onto hoops dangling from the ceiling as the tube train braked viciously. Ed noticed how quiet it had become, the murmur of conversation had ceased, leaving just the low hiss of air sucking past outside and the high-pitched whine of the train.

They all jerked a step forward as the carriage whipped into the station and shuddered to a sudden halt. Ed could see a scattering of bugs milling around out on the walkway. Some of them turned as the door shot away into its housing. Ed and Fees were the first out, guns up and firing as soon as they had targets. As the others behind disembarked, they spread themselves across the width of the wide walkway. There was no wall on the right-hand side, just a high railing with glass panels beneath that looked out over the ship's central atrium. It dropped vertically away to the bottom level dozens of floors below.

The firing was constant as they made their way forward at a fast trot. The bug casualties piled up as they left hundreds of bodies in their wake. It seemed the enemy hadn't been remotely prepared for this. Some of them tried to escape over the railing, but made themselves easier targets and ended up with lumps or limbs missing from their anatomy and falling hundreds of feet to splat on the atrium floor far below.

Very few had weapons, the ones that did also became instant targets and were quickly dismantled in a blizzard of laser fire.

'Andy, are you out and active yet?' Ed called.

'Arriving now,' came the immediate reply. 'Shit, there's a lot of 'em.'

'Pick every target, especially the few that are armed. They weren't expecting this and are luckily totally unprepared.'

Ed glanced at the door number they were passing, it had 'Store 9018' stencilled on it.

'Two more doors,' he shouted above the din.

There was a shriek from behind him. Turning, he saw one of the girls collapse and a collection of armed bugs coming at them from quite a distance behind.

'You guys,' he said, pointing out the rearmost three. 'Look after her, take them out and stay here to cover our backs.'

They immediately turned and engaged the bugs approaching from behind while protecting their unconscious colleague.

Ed could see the door he wanted now and pointed it out to the others. It closed as they approached. Designating another three to remain in the walkway, secure the other direction and wait for Andy's group to break through, he and Fees regarded the closed door to room 9020.

'You stay behind me and my personal shield,' he said to Fees, trying the handle and finding it locked.

'You have a personal shield?' Fees demanded. 'Why don't we get issued with one of those?'

'It's Theo,' said Ed. 'Designed by my ship's computer a while ago. Saved me on more than one occasion. I'll get you one when this is over.'

'Damn right,' Fees muttered, nodding.

Ed checked his shield was at its optimum strength, levelled his rifle at where he considered the locking mechanism would be and fired. It took three shots before the lock gave in and the smouldering door swung open.

'Knock, knock,' he said, as a flurry of laser fire turned his shield into a lightning show. They were only stun shots, but they still pushed him back a couple of feet. He bumped into Fees standing right behind him, who leaped back as some of the dissipating energy caught him.

'Ow, fuck, shit,' he bitched. 'You didn't warn me about that.'

'Never happened before,' said Ed, as he moved into the doorway and despatched a bug that jumped at him from the right. Another one launched itself at him from behind a cabinet on the left. It hit his shield hard and slumped to the floor momentarily stunned. Fees disposed of that one as Ed pushed on into the room.

It was some sort of reception office around four metres

square, with a desk on one side and the aforementioned cabinet on the other. A pair of closed opaque glass doors lay dead ahead, with an engraved glass panel on the right-hand side. It was marked 'Central Water Supply, Authorised Personnel Only'.

'We're in the right place then,' said Fees, stepping around Ed and trying to see through the glass. 'How big is this room then?'

'Captain, how large is this room?' Ed asked.

'I'm looking on the schematics now,' came the reply. 'I know I've been in there before, I just can't remember though. Er, it opens out through the doors into a much larger space than you'd expect. It's a hundred and twelve metres to the far wall and sixty metres wide, mostly to the right as you go in. It's tall too, about thirty metres.'

'There could be a thousand of 'em inside,' said Fees, looking down to check his weapon.

Ed noticed the sound of firing from outside had ceased and sensing someone else had entered the room, he turned.

'That was fucking awesome,' said Andy, a huge grin on his face. 'Like a first-person shooter game.'

'Only you don't have extra lives,' said Ed.

'Well, there is that,' he replied, stepping past Ed and surveying the doors. 'Are we going in then?'

'Are you going to tell him?' said Fees.

'Tell me what?'

'It's a bit of a Tardis in there,' said Ed, jabbing a thumb at the glass doors.

'Big huh?'

'Yep.'

'What's a Tardis?' asked Fees.

This time he was ignored as Andy continued.

'Big enough for how many, roughly?'

'More than we could handle on our own,' Ed said.

'What's the solution?' Fees asked.

Andy sniggered, running his finger along the room name etched into the glass door.

Ed rolled his eyes.

'Something I said?' Fees demanded.

'Sorry,' said Andy, smirking. 'I don't think Earth puns are understood when speaking Ellinika.'

The corporal stared at them blankly.

'May I be of assistance?' said Grogun, strolling into the room along with a posse of armed men in engineering uniforms.

'Ah,' said Ed. 'You got here fast, have you been recruiting friends while we were away?'

'They were holed up in an unused cabin at the rear of main engineering,' she said. 'I used to hide in a similar one as a kid when my dad was a chief engineer.'

'The more the merrier—welcome,' said Andy, nodding at the newcomers.

Grogun stepped over to the desk and began tapping away at its recessed touch panel.

'They may have taken out the cameras, but the fire detecting heat sensors are still operational,' she said, pointing up at a screen above that flickered into life.

'What's that?' Ed asked.

'That room,' the captain replied. 'Those two faint red dots here are most likely bugs and the two brighter ones are humans.'

'So, there's only four in there?' Andy quizzed.

'It would seem so,' said Grogun, sitting back and folding her arms.

'What are we waiting for,' said Andy, striding for the doors.

'Wait,' said Ed, holding up one hand. 'When we enter you go left and I'll go right. There's a lot of gear in there to negotiate around. We'll take half these guys each and meet in the middle where those heat signatures are.'

'Right, okay,' said Andy.

'And it's not a computer game,' added Ed.

'No, you're right, it's not,' Andy added, looking around sheepishly at the others in the room, who all regarded him with curiosity. Then, as he was nearest, pulled the right-hand door open.

27

Deck 311, Katadromiko 52, *un-named system*

ED PUSHED in through the door beside Andy, keeping their personal shields side by side to protect the others behind. Fortunately, they weren't needed as the heat sensors had been correct. No bugs, no laser fire and nothing sinister met them as they filed in and spread out.

'I'll go straight towards the target,' whispered Ed, pointing down the centre of the huge room. 'You could circle around the left side and flank them from there.'

Andy nodded, veered off and disappeared behind a row of large unrecognisable machinery closely followed by half the armed engineers.

Ed, Grogun, and their half of the posse headed forward, directly towards the heat signatures. They trod silently, veering in and out of various lumps of equipment, some only a couple of metres tall, others stretching up to the ceiling thirty metres above.

Sixty metres in, it opened out to a central space about twenty metres across. A raised area with a couple of steps up to it and around half a metre above the floor contained all the control consoles. They were spread in a horseshoe shape and facing outwards towards them.

Two bugs at the top of the steps regarded Ed and the group as they emerged. They chittered to each other, but otherwise remained stationary, weapons pointed at the floor and their emotionless eyes staring eerily.

A man looked up from one of the consoles, a frightened look on his face and watched them nervously. He turned his head slowly to the left and looked up at a human girl who had her back to the approaching group. Ed switched his weapon to a heavy stun and raised it towards her.

'I wouldn't do that if I was you,' the girl said in a monotone drawl, turning to regard Ed with a cool nonchalance.

Ed's eyes bugged. His mouth hung open and, unable to speak, he just stood and stared in disbelief.

'That's the girl I met in the forward ROR,' said Grogun. 'She's an assistant to the queen or something.'

The girl raised an arm and dozens of armed bugs appeared from the rear of the room, all shrugging off heat reflective cloaks.

A sudden shout from Ed's left broke the temporary silence as Andy sprinted in.

'RAYL,' he bellowed, as he vaulted up onto the platform and headed straight towards her.

Rayl raised her weapon and fired without a second's hesitation. Her rifle wasn't set to stun however and hit his shield dead centre. Although not penetrating the shield, the immense power of the bolt smashed him straight back as if he'd been hit by a truck, the energy crackling and dispersing around him. He slid back across the floor, ending up at the feet of his small group still emerging from the flank. He lay there panting, struggling to stand and staring with a look of complete disbelief.

'You're a difficult bloody life form aren't you?' she said, shaking her head. 'Do you know how many workers I've had to squander just to trick you all here to be neutralised? The queen will not be happy.'

'I'm heartbroken,' said Ed, finally recovering from the shock of it being Rayl.

'How can YOU be here and what are you doing?' Andy shrieked, at the same time as he was struggling to get to his feet again.

'Ah yes, that's right,' droned Rayl's characterless monotone, at the same time giving Andy a withering disdainful stare. 'This previously human vessel was a member of your crew wasn't it?'

'She's not an *it*,' Andy spat back. 'She was my wife.'

'Yes, that's right—your disgusting species trait of affection and coupling. It has and will continue to lead to your demise.'

'Wanna bet?' said Ed.

Her head turned slowly back towards Ed, who received the same contemptuous glower.

'We've been overcoming much more powerful civilisations than this small GDA thing for many millennia.'

'You're not doing so well this time, are you?' said Grogun, stepping out from behind Ed.

'Hello again, Captain Whipper,' she said, baring her teeth in something almost resembling a smile. 'You have been busy and even walking the entire length of the ship on the outer hull. We certainly didn't envision you doing that, and then the enticing of large numbers of workers into hangars and on to their doom. Again, unexpected. You are a very astute and surprisingly fast mover for a human.'

'Oh, that wasn't me,' Grogun replied, with a genuine smile.

Rayl's half grin vanished again.

'Well, whoever it was, it hasn't worked out for you in the end, has it? You're outnumbered here by more than twenty to one,' she swept her arm around behind her, 'and these workers don't have their weapons set to stun anymore as you've all proved to be too much trouble and expendable. To be honest, when this man here has finished introducing our little additive to the water supply, we'll have tens of thousands of human workers to infiltrate every level of the GDA and open the door to over sixteen hundred worlds.'

The man at the console glanced up at her momentarily.

'Get on with it,' Rayl commanded.

As he looked back down, his pleading eyes met Ed's for a fleeting second.

'I don't think that's going to happen,' said Grogun.

'I don't envision there's any way for you to stop us,' said Rayl, the wry smirk returning as she surveyed the room behind them. 'I don't see any hidden army coming to change the course of events.'

Ed leant into Grogun. 'Cleo's ready,' he whispered into her ear. She nodded once.

'Ah, but I'm here,' she said, before Rayl could ask what he'd said.

'I'm here too,' called a voice from high up on the machinery behind Ed.

Rayl looked up to find another Grogun grinning down at her.

'As am I,' said another Grogun, off to the right.

'Me too,' said another behind Rayl, causing her to spin around. She snarled and raised her weapon, but before she could aim and fire, that particular Grogun vanished.

'That's enough,' she shouted, turning back and pointing the rifle at the real Grogun and as Ed stepped in front of her, there was an audible click from Rayl's weapon. She turned it over in her hands and stared at it in confusion. Aiming it again and pulling the trigger only produced another click. 'What the?' she mouthed. 'Useless fucking human weapons.' She turned again to face the dozens of bugs behind her. 'Kill them, kill them all,' she spat.

Dozens of clicks sounded as every single bug weapon failed to fire. Rayl spun back around and glared.

'What have you done?' she hissed.

'I'm very astute and surprisingly fast, don't forget,' said the real Grogun as she raised her weapon and shot Rayl through the centre of her chest.

Two things happened very quickly: one, the other members of the posse opened fire and set about the bugs who, on discovering their weapons were inoperative and witnessing their leader going down, came at them in a wave, pincers snapping. Two, Andy screamed and launched himself at the dais, completely ignoring the blizzard of fire flashing around him. His shield took a couple of glancing blows causing him to stumble, but he made it to Rayl and slid down on his knees beside her.

Ed was busy dispatching bugs, but he still heard Andy's wail above the racket going on all around him. The fight that he was irretrievably involved in, didn't last long. The bugs were no match unarmed against a determined group of crew, now on the front foot, realising this was a critical moment in the retaking of their ship and armed with laser rifles set on full power.

As soon as he could, Ed moved across and squatted down next to Andy. Saying nothing, he put his hand on his friend's shoulder and gave it a squeeze.

'She fucking killed her,' Andy spat, stabbing a finger at Grogun through a tear-streaked face.

'She was one of them,' Grogun shouted back, pointing at the nearest dead bug. 'My ship and crew come first.'

'She was my fucking wife and you murdered her.'

Ed held his hand up at Grogun before she could say anything else.

'Go on now and take the rest of your ship,' he said to her. 'I'll take care of this.'

Grogun nodded once, and began issuing orders to the crew.

Ed turned back to Andy and sighed.

'You didn't have to say that to her.'

'Look what she fucking did to my beautiful girl,' grizzled Andy, hugging Rayl's head against his chest. He waved his hand at the gaping wound in her chest.

'She had no choice, Andrew. If it wasn't for your shield, Rayl would've killed you. Look, her krypti's intact. Let's get her back to the *Gabriel* and see what Cleo can do.'

28

The Gabriel, *orbiting a gas giant, un-named system*

BOTH SHIPS HAD JUMPED AGAIN into a distant system containing a particularly large gas giant and hidden in a low orbit. Grogun had initiated a ship-wide clean up on the *K52*. All the bugs remaining on the ship, dead or alive, were quickly and ruthlessly purged. The brainwashed members of the crew were rounded up and put into protective custody until a medical solution could be found. Without the collective mind to guide and instruct them, they were lost souls, confused and lacking purpose, but at the same time quite harmless.

Rayl's body had been taken back to the *Gabriel* and placed in an autonurse for assessment. Everyone was in the medical suite as Phil and Cleo stood hunched over its console.

Ed figured the prognosis wasn't going to be good, judging by the grim expressions on their faces.

'Well?' asked Andy, shifting his weight from one foot to another and almost exploding with impatience.

Phil turned slowly, his countenance dour and keeping his eyes down, he spoke softly.

'Her krypti is intact and a Theo rebirth procedure is undoubtedly quite possible.'

'Yes,' blurted Andy, punching the air. 'Back of the net.' He held a hand up to high five Ed, which wasn't reciprocated. Instead he pointed back at Phil.

'I don't think he's finished,' he said.

Phil held up a placatory hand, to quieten Andy's premature enthusiasm.

'But we have a dilemma,' he said, finally glancing up and locking eyes with Andy.

'What d'you mean?' Andy asked. 'I haven't got a dilemma. How can there be any reason not to rebirth her? She might even wake up and decide she loves me again.'

Phil took a deep breath and continued.

'The krypti is intact but compromised,' he said. 'The bug nano tech has reprogrammed certain parts of it and is so interwoven it's impossible to separate without creating…' Phil paused for a second or two. 'I'm trying to think of the best word to describe the problem.'

'Voids,' said Cleo, turning to face the others also.

'Yes,' said Phil. 'Voids would be the word to use in this case. If we did erase the alien stuff, it would also remove some sections of the Theo organic software too, creating voids.'

'And what might that do?' Ed asked.

'We have no idea,' admitted Cleo. 'It's never been done.'

'We've neutralised as much of the alien stuff as we safely can,' said Phil. 'But not all of it.'

Andy turned to the others with a determined look in his eyes.

'You all know what my decision's going to be,' he said, forcefully. 'If there's even the slightest chance of saving Rayl, we have to take it.'

'But what if we rebirth her and she wakes with a severe mental disability?' said Pol.

'Or doesn't wake up at all,' said Linda.

'What about you, Callon?' Andy asked, seemingly digging for allies.

'Oh, well, I think I am with you on this one,' she said, glancing almost apologetically at Linda. 'We've got to at least give her a chance.'

'Edward?' Andy growled with his back to him, in a tone as if daring him to vote against.

'Don't worry,' Ed said. 'As far as I'm concerned, who are we to deny her that chance, no matter how the odds stack up in either direction.' He stepped forward and turned to face the group, making sure he got eye contact with everyone, especially Pol and Linda. 'Does anyone here have any major objection to Rayl being rebirthed and then we deal with the consequences whatever they may be?'

He noticed Linda glance at Pol before she spoke.

'As you said, who are we to deny her that chance?'

Ed nodded and turned back to Phil.

'Begin the procedure when you're ready,' he said, then turned to Cleo. 'Can you be at the birth in person?'

'Of course,' she said.

'I'd like to be there too,' said Andy.

'I don't think from a female perspective, that would be very appropriate,' said Linda, holding up a hand of caution.

'But why? She was my…'

'No,' snapped Pol, surprising Ed with her forcefulness. Even Andy was taken aback and stood staring at her, his mouth still open. 'If she wakes and she's the same Rayl from before and remembers everything, she's going to be naked and feel very vulnerable. Andrew, you know very well what her reaction would be if you were there.'

Andy went to say something, stopped and stared at the floor for a moment.

'She'd be really mad at me, wouldn't she?' he said, sheepishly. 'Okay, I agree, it should be Cleo, but I want to be nearby when it happens, then if she asks for me, I can be there quickly.'

'That's quite acceptable,' said Linda. 'I think we're all going to be close by when the time comes.'

Andy walked over to the autonurse, stroked Rayl's cheek with a finger and left the room.

'Should someone go with him?' asked Callon. 'I heard about the airlock episode when she originally left him.'

'He'll be fine,' said Ed. 'It's all been a bit of a shock to him.'

'But the chances of it being Rayl,' said Pol. 'It must be millions to one.'

'I think it was cleverly planned,' said Ed, 'a long time ago, and it was Rayl who was the stowaway and jumped from here to the *K2* initiating the ship's shutdown and consequential boarding.'

'D'you think she's been manipulated for quite some time then?' said Linda, pointing at the autonurse.

'Possibly,' Ed replied. 'Don't mention my theory to Andy though. It'll give him false hope that she was brainwashed to leave him.'

'Oh, shit,' said Linda, rolling her eyes. 'I'm not sure if I want that to be true or not.'

'It certainly answers a lot of the questions, doesn't it?' said Phil, looking over from the autonurse control console. 'But if she was on this ship, how in the name of the Ancients was she able to hide from Cleo?'

'Because of this,' said Cleo, holding up the strange black jacket Rayl had been wearing when she was brought aboard.

'Some sort of cloaking tech built in?' asked Ed, walking over and inspecting the lumpy and heavy garment.

'And a miniature jump drive,' said Cleo. 'It's ingenious and how the bugs are able to initiate personal jumps. Theirs are a slightly different shape, but the internals are identical.'

'Can we reverse engineer this into something safe and usable?' Ed asked.

'I don't see why not,' Cleo replied.

'Shit,' said Linda. 'This gets more *Star Trek* every day.'

'What's *Star Trek*?' asked Callon.

Linda glanced over at Ed and smirked.

'Over to you, boss,' she said. 'It was you and Andy who used to watch all that stuff.'

29

———

*The office of the Admiral of the Fleet, Dasos, Prasinos
system*

THE ADMIRAL ROLLED his eyes and sighed as his adjutant, Commander Zaphir Mye, knocked and entered his private office for what must be the fourth time in the last hour. He looked up from his screen and tilting his head to one side, gave Mye his best "this better be important" glare.

'Sorry, boss,' she said. 'Communication drone just jumped in from Captain Whipper and Captain Virr. I believe you'll need to see this straight away.'

Mye waved the file from her tablet onto the admiral's wall screen, turned and departed, closing the door behind her.

'Please tell me it's some good news for a change,' Bache whispered to himself as he keyed in his security code to access the feed.

Over the next twenty-seven minutes, Grogun and Ed explained everything that had occurred in that region of halo space. His eyes widened and his heart sank as the true scale of the problem unfolded in front of him.

'Skata, skata, skata,' he mumbled. 'Another potential disaster I'll be blamed for. For Ancients' sake give me a day off occasionally.

He summoned Zaphir and, standing, he moved across to stare out the double aspect windows. It was snowing hard again, his usual view across the buildings and rooftops of Kentro was almost completely obscured by the whiteout. The experts had promised the weather would be beginning to improve across Dasos by now, but Bache remained sceptical of that claim. The climate change scientists were as much in the dark as anyone. The modified terraforming technology they were using to reverse the winterising effects of Xavier Lake's recent attack was completely unique and untested.

He turned as a knock at the door brought him back to his current quandary. Zaphir bustled in, her face a picture of disquiet.

'Sorry, Admiral,' she sighed. 'I've got the director of planetary defence haranguing me again for the delivery date on that next pair of defence platforms.'

'Does that man never stop whinging?'

'You installed him.'

'Don't remind me. I'll have him building toilets on some distant mining colony next time.'

Zaphir sniggered.

'I take it you've seen Whipper and Virr's report?' she asked.

'Indeed.'

'What did you think?'

'If what they say is accurate, it has the potential to be the largest threat the GDA has ever faced.'

'D'you think these insects know how undefended we are?'

'Well, if they don't they've picked the perfect time to invade,' said Bache, sitting back at his desk. 'What vessels do we have available?'

'Available?' Zaphir coughed, her eyes wide. 'A mobile workshop and a couple of catering barges maybe. You know the situation as well as me. As of yesterday our operational standing was at forty-one percent and every ship allocated.'

Bache groaned and woke his screen up.

'We're just going to have to reallocate some then. Who's nearest?'

Half an hour later, they'd managed to cobble together a seven-vessel fleet. Two Katadromikos, three older D-class cruisers and two destroyers.

'That will leave us critically thin on capital planet defences,' said Zaphir.

'Needs must,' said Bache, shrugging.

'Who are you making operational commander?' she asked.

'That'll be me.'

'You?…But you're the admiral, you're needed here. You're the only one keeping everything together.'

'You're just as capable of holding this shit show together as I am, Commander. I have every faith in you. Your first job will be to inform the council and then make educated command decisions on my behalf. You've known me long enough now to work out what solutions I would find to any problem that arises. I'm the Admiral of the Fleet and I, in this case, need to be with the fleet. The time delay between here and the halo region where they are is just too great.'

'Okay, but what do you want me to tell the council?'

'The truth. Show this message to President Onqir personally. He'll understand the urgency.'

Bache glanced down, code locked his personal computer and stood.

'Signal the seven ships with their new orders and inform Captain Twynner on the *12* that I will be coming aboard and commanding the fleet from there.'

Zaphir nodded and left, before Bache made his way up from the seventy-fourth floor to the top-floor hangar and took a shuttle home to pack.

30

———

The Gabriel, *orbiting a gas giant, un-named system*

'THE COMMUNICATION DRONE JUST ARRIVED BACK,' called Phil.

'Ah, okay,' whispered Ed. 'I'll be there in two.'

Without waking Pol, Ed dressed and crept out of the cabin. He arrived on the bridge to find Phil in conversation with Callon.

'Are you still not sleeping well?' he asked her.

'I'm similar to Phil,' she said. 'I don't seem to need as much rest as some. Which is useful at the moment, as I can sit with Phil for some of the night period and learn more of the ship's systems.'

'Excellent,' said Ed, as he slid down onto his couch. 'Just don't burn yourself out though.'

The three of them watched the report from Bache in silence and it was Phil that spoke first when it concluded.

'Seven ships?' he said. 'Is that all? Doesn't he realise how serious this is?'

'To be honest, I'm surprised he managed to assemble that many in the current situation,' replied Ed. 'He's coming along to command the operation himself too, which demonstrates to me he's definitely seeing the threat as significant.'

'Hmm, let's hope so,' said Phil.

'How long will they be?' Callon asked.

Phil touched a few icons and grimaced at his screen for a few seconds.

'The drone was despatched just over six days ago, so they'll be about two days behind,' he announced, looking up again.

They all turned as Cleo appeared.

'Just letting you know it's Rayl's birthday,' she said.

'Ah,' grunted Phil, raising his eyebrows at Ed. 'We'd better wake Andy.

'Don't rush,' said Cleo. 'It'll take me a couple of hours to release her from the fluid chamber and get her cleaned up and dressed. I'll need to assess her mind state too. Make sure she's not going to harm anyone or herself.'

'Oh, dear,' sighed Phil. 'I don't know if I'm looking forward to this or not.'

'You carry on, Cleo,' said Ed. 'Don't call us until you and Rayl are good and ready.'

Cleo nodded and vanished again.

The two hours had become almost three as everyone congregated in the blister lounge on the top deck of the *Gabriel*. Ed couldn't remember Andy ever looking so terrified as he paced around the sofa area for the hundredth time.

'Cleo asking us to meet here is a good sign, Andrew,' said Ed. 'It means she's not sedated in an autonurse.'

'Hmm,' Andy grunted, wringing his hands and turning to glance at the door again. He stopped suddenly, seemingly rooted to the spot as Cleo appeared in the doorway.

There was a collective gasp from everyone in the room as Rayl followed her into the room. Her hair was very short and darker than before. She was very thin and a little gaunt in the face, but unmistakably Rayl. She wore a ship suit that was a little too big for her and blue training shoes.

'Rayl has no memory of her previous life,' said Cleo. 'I've spent the last hour explaining who she is, where she comes from and that she was a popular member of this ship's crew. Nothing more.'

'Hello again, Rayl,' said Ed. 'Welcome back.'

'Hello,' she croaked, stopping a few metres into the room. Standing a little awkwardly, she let her eyes dart from person to person, until she reached Andy, where her gaze lingered a little longer than the others.

'Come in and sit down,' said Ed, waving for everyone to do the same as he realised she must be feeling extremely self-conscious.

Pol patted the sofa next to her, Rayl obliged and perched herself there. She glanced up out of the domed glass ceiling at the huge planet below and stars beyond.

'Are we in space?' she asked.

'Indeed we are,' replied Ed. 'This ship is the *Gabriel*, you were a member of our crew and a few months ago you disappeared from the ship, only reappearing recently having been brainwashed by an alien race. They were trying to use you to commandeer one of our ships and all its technology.'

'Did they succeed?' she asked, nervously.

'No, fortunately they didn't, but unfortunately you died in the attempt and have been reborn using some amazing Theo technology and a memory chip in your neck.'

'But I have no memories,' she said. 'Did something go wrong?'

'The aliens reprogrammed and damaged it. We've managed to remove most of it, but some of their technology remains which is causing your amnesia. In time, some of your memories may return, that remains to be seen. In the meantime, remember we all love you and we're here to help you recover and become Rayl again.'

'Thank you,' she said, shyly and peered around at all the faces again.

Ed noticed her gaze linger on Andrew once again. He was sat fidgeting with his hands and knowing his friend as he did, he knew Andy was aching to say something and decided to help him out.

'Andrew here was, is, your husband and is extremely nervous too,' Ed said.

'Oh,' she said, giving Andy an embarrassed smile. 'I had a feeling I knew you somehow.'

Ed stood. 'I think it might be prudent for us to give these two some privacy and time to talk,' he said, pointing towards the door.

Rayl stood as everyone introduced themselves and gave her a hug as they left. Ed was pleased to see Cleo walk out the door instead of disappearing. As of yet, Rayl didn't know she was a hologram, that piece of information could wait for another occasion.

Ed gave Andy's shoulder a squeeze in passing, hugged Rayl, and made for the door, only to stop and pause for a second.

'Be gentle with each other,' he said. 'You've both been through a lot. Take your time, it's not a race.'

31

The Gabriel*'s bridge, orbiting a gas giant, un-named system*

'THEY'RE HERE,' squawked Pol, suddenly breaking the silence on the bridge and making Ed jump.

'Bloody hell,' he said, sitting up abruptly after spilling coffee on his shirt. 'Who's here?'

Pol pointed at the holomap. It showed seven other ships had jumped in nearby and were manoeuvring across the system to the planet they were orbiting.

'Ah, Bache's here,' he said. 'Better inform the others.'

'And put on a clean shirt,' said Pol, grinning. 'One with a collar, he is an admiral after all.'

Linda, the only other crew member on the bridge, scoffed.

Ed stuck his tongue out as he disappeared through the

floor on the tube lift, only to return a few minutes later wearing a smart collared shirt.

'That's better,' said Pol. 'No scruffy captains on this ship.'

Ed rolled his eyes at Linda, who smirked in return and then glanced down as a shrill tone from her console informed her a message was incoming.

'It's from *Katadromiko 12*,' she said. 'Admiral Loftt is hosting a captains' meeting on the *12* in one hour.'

'If I remember rightly, that was his old command when we first met,' said Ed. 'I hope he's not getting too nostalgic.'

'I feel sorry for the *12*'s captain,' said Linda. 'Having a perfectionist like Bache breathing down his neck on every decision, you know what he's like.'

***

Ed took one of the shuttles and let Cleo pilot it across to the *12* on a supplied flight plan. It took him into a hangar on the giant vessel's starboard side and set him down amongst a mixture of small ships belonging to the other captains.

'Good morning, Captain Virr,' announced a smartly dressed officer as he stepped down from the cockpit. 'Please accompany me to the meeting room.'

Ed had forgotten how heavy the gravity was on the Dasos-based ships and grimaced as he was led away towards the rear exit. He was thankful the tube stop was close by and a carriage waiting so he could sit down and acclimatise to what felt like walking around with an over-laden rucksack on your shoulders.

As it turned out, Bache was having the meeting in a café overlooking the central atrium. Ed had been on this ship before and peeked over the railing as he was led the short distance from the tube stop to the meeting. He smiled and shook his head in wonder as he looked down on the beach far below. Waves lapped on pure white sand with hundreds of palm trees gently rustling in the artificial breeze and you had to remind yourself you were in fact on a starship.

'Edward,' came a shout from the café as Grogun waved and beckoned to him, pulling out a seat next to her.

'I was bloody glad you didn't have this gravity setting on your ship,' said Ed, flinching as he sat heavily on the proffered chair.

'Good for your bones,' mumbled Bache, appearing at his shoulder after overhearing the comment. 'Good to see you safe,' he continued, giving Ed's shoulder a squeeze. 'We owe you a vote of thanks too for aiding Captain Whipper here retake her ship.'

'Ah, we kinda had to,' said Ed. 'Can you imagine what those little shits would've done with one of these and all its technology? And anyway, the Captain here did most of it,' he added, nodding at Grogun.

'Yes,' said Bache, eying Grogun warily. 'She's just as unpredictable, scary and brilliant as her father.'

Ed smiled as Grogun squirmed in her seat, seemingly unsure how to answer that.

'Right,' said Bache. 'Let's put the fear of the Ancients

up these others, so they don't underestimate what we're up against.'

Ed held up a large data module.

'Why don't you let one of them do exactly that?' said Ed.

'Is this what I think it is?' Bache asked.

'What d'you think it is?' Ed replied, tilting his head to one side.

'The recorded thoughts of an Ancient regarding these bugs, it was in your report.'

'Perhaps I didn't make it clear,' said Ed. 'These aren't recorded thoughts. That there is the digitised data core of a real sentient Ancient. They may be Ancients, but they're still around. This is the second one I've met.'

'You've been in space ten minutes and you're already on first name terms with two of the Ancients?'

'Well, I'm not on speed dial or anything, but yes, we've spoken.'

'I hope for our sake you made a good impression.'

'Don't worry, Neferuptah was quite impressed with the GDA and its ability to keep a watchful eye on the human races they'd created.'

'Let's hope this one is too,' Bache replied, waving the data module above his head as he strode on to face the group.

Over the next hour, Bache, Grogun and Ed managed to shock and awe the assembled senior officers. Any initial ebullience was quickly replaced by a mood of contemplative solemnity. All but one of the captains had brought their respective marine commanders with them and they never smile anyway. Eyes were wide as Grogun downloaded holographic video footage from the battles to retake the *52*.

Bache called Ed up to provide a bit of background and introduce their guest.

'Many tens of thousands of years ago in the time of the Ancients a mistake was made,' said Ed. 'A few rocks containing a contingent of these insects was accidentally imported into this galaxy during the testing phase of a new galactic gateway.'

'If it was that long ago, why are they only now becoming a problem?' one of the marine commanders asked.

'Good question,' Ed replied, pointing at the man. 'We believe it was only recently that they perfected a crude form of jump drive and as you know, this is a very remote area of our galaxy. The Ancient who was here at the time managed to destroy the gate before more could follow and secure the majority of his technology before his developing planet was overrun.'

'And you know all this, how?' a captain asked, sounding distinctly sceptical.

'Because he's explained it all to us,' said Ed, staring back deadpan.

'You've spoken to an Ancient?' he said, a sly grin crossing his face as he glanced around at the others. 'I've heard some fanciful briefings in my time but this has to be the most creative.'

A chorus of chuckles spread through the group.

'It seems my existence is proving a little difficult to grasp,' stated Pyriaeus, from behind them, having to raise his voice over the hubbub to be heard.

The room went silent as he strode through the seated group and stood next to Ed. He was wearing the now familiar white and gold robes with blue sandals that laced halfway up his calves. Ed noticed the gold headdress was absent, but the short black goatee remained. Pyriaeus stroked it as he flicked his eyes from person to person.

'You're trying to make us believe you're an Ancient are you?' one of the captains asked cynically.

Pyriaeus raised an eyebrow, and lifted a hand palm upwards. A pretty blue planet around half a metre in diameter materialised, spinning slowly a couple of centimetres above his fingers.

'This was my home planet in spiral 271,' he said. 'It was destroyed unexpectedly over three hundred thousand chronia ago when our star went supernova without warning.'

A flash followed by a loud crack made everyone in the room jump and the planet vaporised in a split second.

'Poof,' he said, quietly and languorously. 'Shockingly in a millisecond, your entire race with its complete fifty thousand chronia history, every scientific breakthrough, every animal and plant that evolved over billions of chronia, gone in the blink of an eye.'

'Apart from you?' the same man quizzed, folding his arms and remaining just as cynical.

'There were twelve of us on our most advanced science vessel, luckily distant enough to have time to initiate an emergency jump and avoid the all-enveloping pressure wave that engulfed the entire system.'

'Where are the other eleven then?' the man asked, not giving up.

'I wish I knew,' Pyriaeus said. 'After a few chronia and when we had the resources, we split up to seed new human races around the nearby galaxies. I was on my first civilisation when the arthropod disaster struck. It appears, owing to your existence, that my colleagues were a lot more pioneering and effective.'

The mouthy captain turned to the others shaking his head.

'I don't know about the rest of you, but I don't believe a word of it,' he said. 'You're trying to make out you're one of our gods. What a load of fucking rubbi…'

He suddenly went silent and levitated out of his chair. He grunted a couple of times and could be seen shaking and struggling against whatever force was restricting him. Everyone's eyes were wide as they backed away from him, including his own marine commander.

'Pyriaeus, this won't help,' said Ed. 'Please put him down, he's going blue.'

'It's not me,' said Pyriaeus, shrugging and backing up a step.

'Cleo, is that you?' Ed asked, glancing up at the ceiling.

'No,' said a familiar voice from behind him. 'It's me.'

He spun around to find a scowling Neferuptah sitting on a throne of gold. It was a huge chair and interlaced all over with intricate filigree designs of planetary systems. He realised at once, it wasn't the mouthy captain or Pyriaeus the others had been backing away from.

'NEFERUPTAH,' shouted Pyriaeus, stumbling towards her.

She grinned and stood to meet him in an embrace. The

ship's lighting flickered alarmingly as they enveloped each other. Everybody instinctively ducked as sparks flew from all the electrical appliances in the vicinity. The background hum changed pitch and the entire starship shook as the two leviathans of the Ancient creator civilisation came together.

'Shit, the earth really does move when these two get together,' Ed mumbled to himself as he struggled to keep his balance. He turned again, as a shout and a crash sounded behind him. The mouthy captain had dropped back down and crashed into his chair as Neferuptah became otherwise engaged.

'I'm hoping this is a good scenario?' Bache asked, giving Ed a concerned stare.

'I believe this could be very good for us,' Ed replied.

The Katadromiko 12, *orbiting a gas giant, un-named system*

'WHICH SHIP'S HE FROM?' asked Ed, as he watched the mouthy captain carried off to the medical centre with a broken ankle and suspected concussion.

Bache rolled his eyes.

'Captain Ziggermount of the old D-class cruiser *Rund-cillyt*,' Bache replied, sighing. 'If I could've left him behind I would've, but we were short of vessels. The man can never keep his mouth shut. What's that Earth expression Andrew uses?'

'Gobshite,' said Ed, with a smirk.

'That's the one. Sums him up perfectly. I demoted him to the oldest shittiest vessel we have and he still won't take the hint and retire. Been in the navy for over fifty years, been busted more times than a cheap tablet. I believe he's nearly seventy now, you'd think he would've mellowed with age wouldn't you?'

'Does anyone know where our two gods disappeared to?' Ed asked, nodding at the space where the two of them and the throne had been.

Bache shook his head.

'Ah, well,' said Ed, shrugging. 'I'm sure they'll be back. If you haven't seen your wife for over three hundred thousand years, you probably deserve a bit of privacy.'

Bache rolled his eyes and turned back to the group. They went silent as he held his hands up to indicate he was about to speak.

'Lady and gentlemen, I hope you now realise the severity of the threat we have here. These insects don't rely on huge amounts of firepower, just weight of numbers to overwhelm their targets,' he said. 'Never under any circumstances do you lower your shields. The moment you do, they will jump inside your ship in their hundreds, thousands even.'

A murmur of incredulousness spread around the gathering.

'You mean they can jump ships inside our hangars?' the lone female captain asked.

'No,' said Ed, taking over the conversation. 'They wear personal miniature jump suits and can appear anywhere inside your ship.'

'You're joking?' she said.

'No,' Ed continued, glaring at her stony-faced. 'They can also survive in space, jump onto your hull and enter through an airlock and as far as ships go, they don't have any. They have hollowed out powered rocks of varying sizes, thousands of them, and they'll ram them through your hull given half a chance. So, as the admiral said, do not lower your shields for any reason whatsoever.'

'Do we launch our fighter squadrons?' asked one of the other Katadromiko captains.

'Not unless you want to lose them all,' said Grogun, standing to face the others. 'Give your weapons officers a fire at will order, but they must target every shot. Especially the asteri beam operators. No spraying it around randomly as there'll be friendly vessels in the vicinity.'

'What are we planning to do about the *Arena*?' Ed asked, turning to Bache.

'We need to confirm it really is the *Arena* planetoid before taking any action against it,' said Bache. 'If it is, the original human population may still be alive somewhere inside and in need of help.'

'We've been inside,' said Ed. 'It's pretty immense. It's like a mini inside-out planet with the gravity reversed and an artificial star in the middle.'

'You know where the entrance is?' Bache asked.

'A long tunnel terminating in a ship-sized airlock if my memory serves me right,' he said. 'Opens into a huge hangar where there are small elevators to take you up into the central habitable zone.'

'Where's the control room?'

'Now that's something I don't know,' said Ed. 'They were very secretive and paranoid about aliens knowing virtually anything about the *Arena*. It took Callon a while to persuade the ruling council to even let us out of the hangar and even then we were under virtual house arrest within a short walk from the elevator.'

'Wasn't that where you were kidnapped from?' asked Bache.

'Hmm,' grunted Ed, shivering as the awful memory of how that episode concluded swept by.

'Sorry,' said Bache, realising his faux pax. 'Would you be able to lead a team of my marines in there to retake it?' he asked, changing the subject quickly.

'A team?' said Ed, raising his eyebrows in surprise. 'It'd take a hundred battalions if that thing's overrun with bugs and you'd probably lose most of them in the process.'

'Ah, okay,' he said. 'We need a recce first don't we? Find out what we're up against.'

'Cleo could produce a nano swarm,' Ed admitted.

'How would you get it inside?' Bache asked.

Ed shrugged and rubbed his chin.

'Andy and I could sneak in with the mini fighters perhaps.'

'That could work,' Bache admitted, before giving Ed a worried look. 'I can just see Linda's face at the suggestion though.'

'She'll be absolutely fine with it.'

33

The Gabriel*'s bridge, orbiting a gas giant, un-named
system*

'ARE you absolutely out of your fucking mind?' said
Linda, seemingly aghast at the mere suggestion. 'There
could be ten million of the bloody things in there.'

'It's just a quick in and out,' said Ed. 'We've got to get
the nano swarm inside the main airlock and into the
elevator shafts.'

'Why can't Cleo do it?'

'Because she would lose connectivity to the *Gabriel* as
soon as her ship entered the tunnel and they don't have
holo emitters on the *Arena*.'

'G'day all,' said Andy, cheerily, appearing on the tube
lift.

He looked at Linda and frowned.

'Are you pissed at something?' he asked, stopping and

raising his eyebrows. 'Your brow is furrowed. Normally means trouble afoot.'

Linda smarted and gave Ed a furtive glance, giving Andy the cue to avert his attention across to him.

'Is there something I'm not a party too?' he asked Ed.

Ed explained the happenings and decisions made at the captains' meeting.

'I should've come too, shouldn't I?' Andy admitted after digesting all the information.

'You were busy,' said Ed. 'And talking of busy, how is she?'

Andy slumped into his seat and sighed.

'Confused,' he said, pensively.

'Has any more of her memory returned?' Linda asked.

He shook his head and stared at the floor.

'She doesn't even remember her childhood, parents or anything,' Andy said, solemnly.

'After what happened to them, that could be a blessing,' said Linda.

'Hmm,' grunted Andy. 'Depends which way you look at it. I still don't know whether she genuinely left me because she wanted to, or if some manipulation was already in play.'

'Cleo, can I talk to you for a moment?' Ed asked, glancing up.

Cleo appeared sitting on the couch next to Ed. Today she was sporting a grey business suit and patent grey leather brogues.

'Very formal today,' said Ed, noticing his reflection in her shoes.

'I had a captains' meeting to go to,' she said.

'You were there too? You didn't show yourself.'

'I didn't think the captain of the *12* or the admiral would be overjoyed at my ease of penetrating their systems,' she said.

'Ah, no,' said Ed. 'Probably a wise decision. Anyway, my reason for calling you is, can you go back and scrutinise all the video footage of Rayl and search for anything strange? Absolutely everything you have from the ship, to the island, to visits to Earth, everything.'

'What exactly am I looking for?'

'Any evidence she could've been drugged or brainwashed, without her or our knowledge.'

'How far back?' she asked, turning to glance at Andy.

'A couple of years,' Andy replied. 'We were as happy as Larry till about twenty months ago.'

'Consider it done,' she said.

'Lastly, can you flight check and arm the mini-mes?' Ed asked. 'They haven't been used for a while and probably need a bit of love.'

'Sure thing.' She promptly disappeared again with a thumbs up.

At the agreed time the fleet moved off, jumping one at a time to a pre-determined co-ordinate close to the *Arena*'s last location. On arrival, it immediately became obvious they were in the wrong place. No powered rocks, no *Arena*, just an expanding debris field of rock shrapnel and dead bugs.

'There's nothing here, Ed,' said Pol, her eyes flicking up to the holomap that told the same story as her screen.

'How about jump signatures?' he asked. 'I remember from last time, the *Arena*'s not particularly quiet on that front.'

Pol bobbed her head from side to side, a habit Ed had noticed she had when concentrating hard.

'Multiple noisy signatures heading away, about forty-two hours old judging by the echo diffusion,' she said a moment later.

'Heading back to Tessamaine?' he asked.

Pol shook her head.

'Opposite direction,' she said, glancing up at him with a worried frown. 'Straight towards GDA space.'

'Shit,' he mumbled. 'Bache won't be very happy about that.'

'Communication from the *12*,' said Andy, pointing up to the holomap as a frowning image of the admiral appeared.

'As you all may have already gathered, the bug fleet, along with the *Arena*, are heading directly towards our region of the galaxy. This is obviously a complete disaster as they have an almost two-day lead. We have no choice but to pursue at flank speed. Your fleet specific jump co-ordinates will follow shortly. Admiral Loftt out.'

'I've never seen him so grumpy,' said Linda.

'Or abrupt,' said Andy.

'He hates being outwitted,' said Ed. 'This might've been a ploy of the bug queen from the start.'

'I'm sure the plan was to have taken the *52* and used its entire brainwashed crew to cause untold sabotage around the GDA navy,' said Phil. 'So she's not as strong as she wanted to be.'

'The timing for this was right though, wasn't it?' said Linda. 'She would know the GDA is at its most vulnerable at the moment and now she's got the few defensive ships that could be mustered thousands of light years away and a two-day lead.'

'They could do a lot in two days,' said Phil. 'I hope the destination's not Paradeisos. Can you imagine trying to get those bugs out of all the old underground cities?'

'Don't remind me about those,' mumbled Andy. 'I still get nightmares about riding that scooter down that hole several kilometres underground.'

'Co-ordinates are in,' said Linda, entering the waypoints into the ship's navigation and hitting execute. 'Jumping in three seconds.'

The bridge lighting dimmed slightly as they watched the starscape change on the holomap above them.

'You can all piss off now,' she said, jabbing her thumb at the tube lift. 'We've a long way to go and I've got the first shift.'

34

The Gabriel, *stationary outside the Prasinos system*

'OH SHIT,' said Andy, looking across at Ed. 'You were right. She's attempting to cut the head off the snake.'

It'd taken just over eight days for the small fleet to make it back into GDA space. The bug fleet had bypassed all the outlying human planets and had headed into the heart of the controlled region.

The *Gabriel*'s crew stared anxiously at the holomap as it refreshed to show the *Arena* in low orbit around Dasos. It was parked menacingly just fifty kilometres from Stathmos Vasi space station. Less than halfway through its reconstruction, the station was again under attack.

'This is not good,' said Ed, staring at the dozens of rocks buried in the station's superstructure and hundreds more circulating the structure like flies around a lamp. 'If they're up to the same tricks as they were on the *52*, then we've got serious problems.'

'The new planetary defence platforms didn't last long then,' said Andy.

'They only had four out of the seventeen up and running when we left anyway,' said Phil, focusing the scan in on one of them. Its weapon systems had been crushed, most likely by multiple rock strikes.

'What do we do now?' asked Callon.

'We wait for the admiral,' said Ed. 'It's his call.'

The wait was not a long one as the admiral's hologram appeared above them moments later, his expression grave.

'Fleet will immediately jump in and adopt attack formation beta six. Attack anything moving that isn't a GDA vessel. Watch your shields closely, they will throw everything at you. If they get anywhere near critical, jump away and return when restored. Do not under any circumstance let them fail. *Gabriel*, I need eyes inside that planetoid, operate as previously discussed. Admiral Loftt out.'

'Cleo, are the fighters ready to go?' Ed asked, standing.

'All good and nano'd up,' she said. 'I transferred the prepared swarm from the drone. You both have a swarm big enough to do the job, but if you can release both, then more is wizard.'

'Wizard?' repeated Linda.

'Wizard,' said Andy, nodding.

'I take it wizard means good in this case?' Linda asked, sighing.

Andy just grinned.

'You both know my opinion of going ahead with this,' she continued in a fractious tone.

'We'll be back in no time,' said Ed, glancing at Andy and nodding towards the tube lift.

'Just make sure you are,' said Pol, not even looking up.

———

The tiny pentagonal personal fighters, or mini-mes as the crew affectionately knew them, sat on their mobile cradles in the corner of the starboard hangar. Ed and Andy both climbed up onto the hull and slid down into the confined cockpit in the centre of their respective ships. In reality, they didn't look like spaceships at all, just a small five-sided weapons platform with a seat in the middle.

'No letting them know we're there, Andrew,' said Ed, over the ship's comms. 'We go in, dump the swarm where it's needed and get out. No blasting bugs this time.'

'Yeah, yeah, I know,' came the reply. 'The fun bit starts later.'

'At least we won't be able to smell the bloody things all sealed up in here,' said Ed, as his canopy motored shut and the cockpit pressurised.

They powered up their fighters, lifted them off the cradles and moved across the hangar to loiter by the main door.

'In position, Phil,' called Ed.

'Roger, stand by.'

Ed watched as the bright hangar lights dimmed slightly and the view of a vast star field outside changed to a huge planetoid. It hung above a blue and white planet turning slowly below and the corner of the space station just visible around the edge of the hangar door frame.

'Let's go,' he said, cloaking the tiny vessel and powering it straight out and angling in towards the *Arena*.

With shields at maximum, they had to negotiate the busy rock traffic with the utmost concentration and after swerving through the outer more random traffic, they joined a stream heading towards the passage opening. Bache had promised them a time lapse before the fleet came in all guns blazing, so they couldn't hang around.

The entrance to the tunnel seemed to be permanently open with the non-stop weight of traffic coming and going. Ed chose to head straight down the middle as the rock traffic was keeping left and right. He remembered bringing the old *Gabriel* down the tunnel a while back, so there was plenty of room and very little danger of a collision. The giant airlock at the far end was just beginning to open, so they stayed clear of the huge doors as they arrived.

'Hold on,' said Ed. 'Let them load themselves and we'll nip in at the last moment when we can see a gap.'

'What d'you think all these bug rocks are doing?' Andy asked.

'I'm hoping they're just moving bugs around and not brainwashed Arenians,' Ed replied.

'I imagine the bugs are taking a lot of casualties.'

'Yeah, especially on the planet's surface. Bugs don't work very well in the cold and it's permanent winter down there.'

'I thought they could survive in space?'

'They can for short periods, but after a while they go dormant. Grogun told me they had some supposedly dead bugs in an area of the 52 that had got exposed to space.

They suddenly came back to life when the deck was sealed and repressurised.'

'Hmm,' grunted Andy. 'I need to think about that with my engineer's hat on.'

'Look, the doors are closing and there's room for us in the middle, let's go.'

When the airlock had cycled, they had to wait till last before moving across and exiting. What Ed witnessed as they scooted out made all the hairs on the back of his neck stand up.

'Holy moly,' he muttered.

Andy said nothing.

The huge cavern was as he remembered it. Three kilometres across, with an expansive gravity-enabled landing platform over on the right. The difference was that now, the whole place was full top to bottom with suspended egg sacks connected by flexible mesh tunnels. Row upon row upon row, up, down and stretching away as far as the eye could see. Millions of them, all made out of what looked like the same material as the strange flexible tunnels they found on the *52*.

'Oh fuck,' whispered Andy.

They moved quickly up to the ceiling and watched the thousands of worker bugs moving eggs up and around the maze of tunnels. It was mesmerising and although at first glance it seemed every bug was moving around randomly, when you watched closely, it was apparent every single one knew what it was doing and where it had to go.

'We are so in the shit,' Andy continued. 'Can you even see the elevators?'

'Not from here,' Ed admitted. 'We should be able to.

They've been busy though, haven't they? I mean, how long have they been in here to construct all this?'

'Can we even get down there?' Andy asked.

'Not without being detected,' Ed admitted. 'If we are, they could shut down the airlock and trap us in here.'

'Do we release the nanos up here and hope for the best?'

'Only thing we can do. Let's hope they're not noticed.'

They both ejected the nano sacks downwards and roughly towards where they remembered the elevators to be. Cleo had constructed the sacks out of an ultra-thin membrane, almost like a small condom so they wouldn't clatter around and gain attention like the usual metallic ones would. They'd just burst on impact with something solid, disperse the cloud, then shrink and be almost invisible.

The sacks quickly disappeared from sight and they waited, watching their screens with bated breath.

35

The mini-mes, inside the Arena, *Prasinos system*

THEIR SCREENS REMAINED blank for what seemed like an exorbitantly long period of time.

'I don't think they've work…oh, hang on,' said Andy as their screens flashed a light mauve, then went a reddish brown, before fading into a slightly out of focus web effect. 'What the hell is that?' he asked.

'It's a close-up of some of this bug tunnel material,' said Ed. 'I think we need them to disperse more before we'll get a better picture.'

Even as he spoke the image panned back and up to reveal a line of bugs traipsing along a curving tunnel.

'That's good,' said Ed.

'What is?'

'They seem to be oblivious to the swarm expanding around them. If they don't detect it when it's this dense, once it's thinned out around the planetoid it's much less likely.'

Ed started panning around the swarm as it expanded, trying to orientate himself. Finally after a few minutes the swarm exited a tunnel onto what seemed to be the landing platform. He swung the view around until he found an elevator door and headed straight for it.

'Got 'em. Have you found them yet?' he asked Andy.

'No, I seem to be in an endless tunnel and eggs keep zipping by,' Andy replied.

'What, on their own?' Ed asked.

'Yeah, it's weird.'

'If it was a weightless area they'd continually hit the sides of the tube and gradually come to a standstill,' he said, thinking hard. 'Ah, now I think I know where you are.'

'You do?'

'You're heading straight up. I'm hoping you might be in one of the elevator shafts. The eggs aren't being laid in here, so that must be happening in the main cavern.'

'How did I get in a shaft without knowing it?'

'No idea, but keep going with your nanos.'

Ed's view reached the elevator door in his view. He panned left and right, immediately spotting why Andy didn't know he was in the shaft. The doors next to his had been removed and lay on the ground nearby. One of the bug tunnels was stuck out of the aperture about three feet off the ground and continued for about five metres before turning back up and disappearing in amongst all the egg racking. A hole underneath dispensed an egg every few seconds. It was collected by a bug at the front of a long queue and whipped away to be stored in the racking until it hatched.

Lifting his view upwards and gazing over the top of this tunnel, he could see three more elevator shafts had been utilised in a similar fashion, leaving only two elevators out of the six in working order. He timed and counted the eggs as they emerged.

'Andy, they're producing around a hundred and twenty eggs a minute and if they're hatching at that rate too, that's…'

'Seven thousand two hundred an hour or nearly one hundred and seventy-three thousand a day,' replied Andy.

'Did you just work that out in your head?'

'Yeah.'

'Show off.'

'I have light ahead.'

'I'm going to leave my swarm on auto record down here and join yours,' said Ed.

'Roger that, I'm about to…oh fuck!'

'What is it?'

'You're going to want to see this…don't worry about changing over to my swarm, just switch over to my feed, it's easier.'

Ed's screen flickered and changed over to the same feed as Andy's. He caught his breath as he saw the result.

'Shit,' he mumbled.

'My thoughts exactly,' said Andy. 'Big isn't she?'

The queen was about fifty metres away, about eight metres tall and laying an almost continuous supply of eggs. A plethora of thin tubes jutted from her abdomen, down which liquids could be seen flowing into her body.

'That's pretty gut churning to watch too, isn't it?' he continued. 'I bet it stinks in 'ere as well.'

'Hang on,' said Ed. 'She's only producing one egg every few seconds. Go up, so we can see further out, there're eggs coming in from other directions.'

Andy steered the nano view upwards and the reason for this quickly became evident.

'Oh, bollocks,' Andy muttered. 'There's more of 'em.'

'There's twelve,' said Ed. 'All producing.'

'The atmosphere's a bit dingy, isn't it,' said Andy. 'Perhaps the filters aren't getting serviced.'

A dull flash from above caught their attention and as they peered through the murk towards the surface several kilometres up and across the internal void, they witnessed a series of smaller flashes.

'Laser weapons,' said Ed, excitedly. 'Some of the Arenians are still alive and fighting.'

'Fuck, yeah,' Andy exclaimed. 'If only we could get the mini-mes in here, we could kill all the queens and help them out up there.'

'Something tells me I think it would take more than just the two of us.'

'No, we don't even know where the control room is,' said Andy. 'All they'd have to do is shut down that airlock and we couldn't get out to re-arm.'

'You know, I've been thinking…'

'Did it hurt?'

'To have done everything they have in here,' Ed continued, ignoring Andy's jibe, 'there must have been another way into here other than the six small elevators.'

'Hmm, that's a fair call,' said Andy. 'They can't've hollowed out this entire planetoid with only hand tools.'

'It might be sealed up now, probably at both ends, but the tunnel to the surface would most likely still be there,' Ed said, rubbing his chin in thought.

'And an airlock somewhere along its length,' Andy added.

'It'll be almost impossible to detect because of the density of the rock,' said Ed.

'But there could be a slight difference in the return,' said Andy. 'So long as they didn't plug it too deep on the outer skin.'

'We need to get this footage back to Bache and our thoughts on the second tunnel back to the *Gabriel*,' said Ed. 'Our scanning arrays are as good, if not better than anything the GDA has. So, I'm not going to mention my theory to him until we know it's actually there.'

'Okay, are we shutting down the nanos before we leave?' Andy asked.

'No,' said Ed. 'They might prove useful when we return. Come on, let's get out'er here before we push our luck too far.'

36

The mini-mes, inside the Arena, *Prasinos system*

'I'VE INSTRUCTED the nanos to hide in the walls and go dormant,' said Andy. 'Less chance of them being discovered.'

'Good idea,' replied Ed, as they both crept towards the giant airlock again.

'Look at that,' Andy exclaimed. 'Down on the landing area.'

Ed panned in using his onboard camera as they moved out of cover.

'A constant supply of reinforcements,' he said, watching hundreds of bugs loading aboard rows of awaiting flying rocks.

The two cloaked ships secretly cycled themselves through the airlock again and giving the rocks a wide birth, negotiated the wide tunnel back to the entrance.

The first thing Ed missed was how quiet it was outside as he neared the tunnel mouth, and the second thing was that the flying rocks heading in the same direction had all come to a standstill. Naively, he sailed straight out into empty space.

Andy, following along around a hundred metres behind him stopped abruptly, staying just inside the tunnel as he realised something was awry.

'Hang on, Ed,' he called. 'We're not at Dasos.'

It was too late, the star field outside changed abruptly as the *Arena* jumped and Ed was gone, left behind wherever the planetoid had been at that moment.

'Ah, shit,' Andy swore. 'Silly bastard's got left behind.'

Just as he said that, the *Arena* turned, both Dasos and the enormous space station came into view. The region was a firework display of laser fire and explosions. What also appeared was debris, large lumps of ship wreckage spiralling away spouting gasses and bodies. Andy's eyes stood out on stalks as he realised what the bugs were up to.

'They've jumped the fucking *Arena* onto a battle cruiser,' he shouted to himself. 'That's just outrageous. I've had it now, I've had enough. Bunch of stinking fucking cocksucking parasites, it's payback time.'

He transmitted all the data they'd collected to the *12*, turned the mini-me around and fired it back towards the airlock, this time not worried about the speed. He arrived just as it was closing and zipped inside. While he waited for it to cycle, he checked his weapons inventory.

When the giant doors began opening, he slipped through and powered quickly up to the ceiling of the vast space, roughly where they'd been before and opened up his jump drive screen.

'Now, this is going to be an educated guess,' he mumbled, setting some blind jump co-ordinates into the navigation computer. Once everything was prepared and the jump was just the touch of an icon, he turned his attention back to the armaments and turned the ship to point downwards towards the landing pad and the elevators.

'Have some of this, arse wipes,' he snarled, unleashing two kataligo missiles straight down.

The explosions surprised even him. Everything on the landing pads was immediately enveloped in a maelstrom of fire. It spread outwards in all directions too, it seemed the bugs' tunnel membrane was anything but flame retardant. Quite the opposite. It proved almost explosive as it rippled up the passageways at alarming speed, outrunning even the fastest bugs.

Andy grinned malevolently as hundreds of the eggs began exploding in the heat. He had been prepared to fire more of the missiles, but as it became apparent he didn't need to, he activated the multi-barrelled laser cannon and began spraying that around the higher levels. Stopping and moving every few seconds, just in case they did have some sort of weaponry secreted nearby, he revelled in the fact that this had exactly the same effect as the missiles. Fire erupted everywhere a bolt impacted and spread so fast, Andy quickly realised he'd better get the hell out or be consumed himself.

Closing his eyes, he mashed the jump icon, sending the tiny ship to the pre-prepared co-ordinate. After a second or two he opened them again when it became apparent he hadn't been crushed inside solid rock.

The main cavern was spread out before him. He was about a kilometre and a half above the ground level and falling fast.

'Fuck,' he shouted, as he realised he'd forgotten a really serious factor. The inside was gravitational.

Mashing the antigrav startup and hover icons in that precise order, he prayed he had enough height for the motors to spin up in time and offset his rather swift rate of uncontrolled descent.

He felt his seat beginning to push up hard against him and peering out the side of the small canopy, he saw the ground was coming up horribly fast. He even tried firing the attitude thrusters straight down, hoping that might help a little. He braced himself as he witnessed the roofs of tall buildings pass by, there was a loud crunch as his seat hit him hard in the back and then everything went still. The antigrav was still singing its head off, so Andy tried lifting the ship up. It responded sluggishly. He thought it was probably damaged until he peeked out the port side and discovered he was also trying to lift up part of the building roof he'd crashed down onto.

Side slipping to starboard relieved the burden and the ship shot upward just as a bunch of bugs swarmed over the partly demolished house and were left snapping their mandibles at him in indignation. There was some bad news though. Three red hexagons flashed at him.

He'd lost his cloaking system, the kataligo missiles were inoperative and, worst of all, the array was damaged so he wouldn't have been able to target them anyway. His heart sank as he also realised no array meant he had no jump drive either.

'Bollocks,' he grumbled, castigating himself. 'You're supposed to be an aerospace engineer, you idiot, how could you forget something as basic as gravity?'

He was awoken from his self-flagellation by a couple of thumps against his shields, someone somewhere was firing at him, but without his array he had no idea who or where they were, except possibly behind him. Spinning the ship around, tilting it downwards and instigating a random sideslip, he scoured the ground.

Another bolt zipped past the front of the ship from almost directly below. Traversing back, Andy searched again, spotting movement near a row of buildings and his heart soured. It wasn't a bug firing at him at all. A human head and shoulders protruded from a hatch at the base of some sort of bunker holding a rifle and tracking it around trying to get a fix on him.

'Oh, you beauty,' shouted Andy inside the cockpit. 'Some of you are still here.'

37

Ed's mini-me, alone in unknown space

'SHIT…WHERE THE FUCK ARE WE?' Ed wondered.

He spun his small ship around when he got no reply from Andy.

'Oh, that's just brilliant,' he said, finding no Andy, no *Arena*, no Dasos, just a canopy full of stars. 'Where the hell did everybody go?'

Glancing down at the ship's manual control panel he switched the small scanning array from armament to navigation. This was not a starship however and its navigation array capability was short range. Yes, it had jump capability, but nothing on the scale of a larger vessel.

'Oh, bollocks,' he muttered under his breath. 'Light years of bugger all.'

There was nothing recognisable within a single jump

range of the fighter, so Ed set about orientating his location and setting off back towards Dasos.

'Ah, great, more good news,' he mumbled, after the computer fixed his position. 'That *Arena* must have a big range.'

He found that Dasos was just under four days away with the mini-me's short jump range. He checked his environmental lifespan and groaned as he discovered that was only seventy-two hours. Paxx, however, a class M planet in the Paxx'Ondor system, was closest at only thirty-one hours.

He pulled up the planetary information file on Paxx and quickly ran through its data. Young planet, almost two thirds the size of Earth, gravity point eight Earth, sixty percent ocean, twenty percent desert, four percent green around the edges of the three main continents, the rest polar ice sheets.

'Tidal chart must be a bit complicated,' he said to himself as he noticed it had fourteen moons. Although, they did range in size from a few hundred metres to Earth's moon.

It did state the survey was done from orbit and many decades ago, generally considered a little too warm and as yet unsettled. Probably more because it was well off the regular shipping jump routes.

'It'll have to do,' Ed sighed. 'There's nothing else within range.'

He set the navigation computer and began the journey.

He awoke to a low pinging noise and while rubbing the sleep from his eyes, he cancelled the navigation alarm. Scanning the Paxx'Ondor system, into which he'd just arrived, he inputted a course to Paxx into a low orbit where he could initiate a scan for a good landing site.

Thirty-six minutes later, as the tiny vessel dropped into orbit, he prepared the ship's distress beacon to remain in space and transmit on all the main GDA communication and emergency channels. He rolled his eyes as it reminded him the beacon's battery life was a maximum of four years.

'I hope I don't need to prove that,' he murmured, as he touched the launch icon.

Choosing a strip of green coastline near to one of the poles, he prepared the ship for insertion. It became quite claustrophobic as the heat shielding whined out of its housings and it went almost completely dark in the tiny cockpit. The blue glow from the backlit instrument panel was all he had for the next few minutes and he didn't waste any time hitting the execute icon.

Although he couldn't physically see where he was, the gradual increase in buffeting announced his arrival in the upper atmosphere. The whining of the antigrav spinning up was extremely loud in the confined space, but very welcome all the same.

He peered around nervously as soon as the canopy shield retracted. Wispy clouds zipped upwards as the motors' scream increased to a crescendo and he grunted as his seat pushed up hard against him. This time as he looked out, he could see desert stretching away to the horizon, but below a wide strip of green, becoming denser as it neared the coast.

Probing with his array, he found the temperature on the border between desert and trees at fifty-two degrees and on the coast forty-seven degrees.

'Right,' he said, examining the results. 'I'm going to get a tan wherever I go. At least on the coast I can cool off in the ocean.'

The mini-me was only designed for one planetary insertion in an emergency situation and acted similarly to a lifeboat. Ed decided he didn't want a computer programme to decide where he would end up and at ten thousand metres, he took manual control. Steering towards the coastline, he searched for any signs of fresh water, as he knew the emergency supply on the ship was limited. A ping from the scanning array caught his attention. Something metallic nearby on the coastline.

It was difficult to gauge the lie of the land from height, so dropping quickly to a few hundred metres, he scooted along the beach line and before long came across a small stream snaking across a rocky section of the beach and emptying into the ocean. Nearby and fifty metres inland, a line of sand dunes stretched back to the tree line. A flat metallic grid, around twenty metres square, sat amongst the dunes. He knew he couldn't land on it without struts so picking a slight depression in the sand, he brought the small ship down and as gently as he could, to avoid damaging any of the critical systems underneath the vessel, he landed.

Keeping the antigrav ticking over, he sat and surveyed his surroundings for a while, just in case something big, hairy and pissed off appeared out of the trees. Although he did chuckle to himself; considering the average temperature on this planet, monsters were most unlikely to be thickly pelted.

Satisfied he wasn't going to be eaten as soon as he climbed out, he checked the atmosphere once again, just to make sure, then cracked open the canopy with a slight hiss. He gasped as the heat hit his face with a slap.

'Holy moly…like midday in Singapore,' he muttered, releasing his belts and standing on his seat.

The breeze wafting off the ocean made it like standing in front of a giant hairdryer. He unzipped his ship suit a bit and stepped up and out, before grabbing his rifle from its clip in the cockpit and dropping down onto the ground. He reached down and ran his fingers through the sand, snatching his hand back as if he'd been stung.

'Ouch, shit, hot, hot,' he blurted, waving and huffing on his hand. 'No good for a nudist beach then.'

Crossing the dunes and clambering onto the rocks, he made his way over to what he hoped was the fresh water flowing out from the forest. Cupping a handful, he took a small sip. It seemed okay, but he had no way of checking, he just hoped it wasn't laced with arsenic or something else equally terminal. He checked out the metal grid, sunken slightly into the sand, and reckoned it to be a small landing pad. Looking around, he couldn't fathom why it was here.

Returning to the ship, he reached in and dragged out the survival pack hidden behind the pilot's seat. Opening it, he was surprised to find squeezed in on the top, two tins of corned beef and a bottle of Châteauneuf-du-Pape.

'Andrew,' he said, with a grin. 'You little shit, when did you do that?'

He grabbed the fork from the pack, sat on the edge of the ship and ate a whole tin of corned beef, knowing full well it would taste better than anything in the standard GDA survival ration packs.

Dropping down and lying back under the hull, he closed his eyes, listened to the waves slowly lapping around the nearby rocks and pondered how long he'd be marooned here. It went slightly darker and everything went into shadow. Opening one eye and expecting to see a cloud shrouding the planet's star, he nearly had heart failure to discover a dark face staring down at him.

38

Andy's mini-me, inside the Arena, *Prasinos system*

FURTHER MOVEMENT from behind the human caught Andy's attention. Only this time it wasn't human, it was bugs, lots of bugs, and seeing that the human wasn't turning around to engage them, he obviously didn't know they were there.

Andy soared over the head of the human and sprayed the oncoming swarm with cannon fire. The bugs weren't used to this, they seemed confused, the ones not cut to pieces ran in all directions. Including out into the open, where both Andy and the armed human could pick them off at will. In a matter of seconds the bug numbers had dwindled to just a handful. Andy flew down past the human and waved, before turning and heading in what he hoped was the direction of the egg layers.

A column of smoke in the distance was his target. He

surmised that the fire in the bug tunnels had ripped up the elevator shaft and was now creating problems inside the habitable zone. He thought right, egg production had ceased, but the egg layers he'd hoped to kill were noticeably absent.

'Where the hell are they hiding them?' he said to himself, searching around the area. 'They're huge.'

The bugs present were making a valiant attempt to the extinguish the fire, so he spent a few minutes disrupting their efforts and destroying everything in sight that was of obvious bug origin. Disappointed he hadn't managed to kill the egg layers, he returned to the area he'd seen the human and hovered around seeking the hatch again.

The antigrav drive on the tiny fighter certainly hadn't been designed for stealth – its high-pitched howl could probably be heard for kilometres – and it wasn't long before the hatch reopened and a head popped up. Whoever it was wasn't being caught out from behind again, as he swivelled around checking in all directions, before paying Andy any attention.

Andy swung in close and waved again, getting a wave back and a pointing finger jabbing enthusiastically off to the right, so he turned the ship in that direction.

In the distance, some five hundred metres away, he could make out a flashing white light. Sitting at about ten metres up, he moved slowly towards the beacon, arriving to find two heavily armed humans gesticulating downwards with their weapons. A section of what looked like a landing pad or vehicle park opened slowly to reveal a dark space below and while the humans kept one eye on their surroundings with their weapons at the ready, they continued gesticulating madly downwards into the gloom, seemingly wanting Andy to hurry up.

'In for a penny,' he mumbled, turning on the mini-me's lights and settling it down into what looked to be a small hangar of some kind. As he was doing so, the two humans disappeared down into another smaller hole in the ground, reappearing in a corner of the hangar, their weapons in the shoulder pointing at Andy's ship. Six more rounded a corner, again weapons up and bearing anxious expressions.

Andy winced as he clunked the mini-me down in the centre of the room. It instantly tilted to one side and settled with a rather ominous crunch and rattle. It didn't have its cradle and it had sustained damage in its earlier crash, so it was never going to be a particularly attractive landing.

The antigrav scream died quickly down to a low whine before going quiet. Andy unsealed the small canopy and slowly stood. He smiled, keeping both hands in clear sight.

His armed meet-and-greet committee weren't smiling however, and approached tentatively, keeping their weapons trained on him.

'*Calla heen adifay*,' one of them said officiously and gesticulating with his rifle for Andy to get down.

Andy remembered that the inhabitants of the *Arena* didn't speak Ellinika, so he delved around in his DOVI's language menu for the Arenian file.

'Sorry, can you say that again?' he said in Arenian, once he'd found it.

'I said, get down here,' the armed man said.

Andy clambered down and two of the armed men frisked him for weapons, removing his pistol from his belt.

'Clean,' one of them said, nodding to the man who'd spoken first and handing him the weapon.

'Who are you?' the leader demanded, his eyes flicking between Andy and the fighter behind. 'And what the hell is that thing?'

'I'm Andy, a friend of Conor's' he replied. 'I'm with Edward Virr and the *Gabriel*.'

'He was on that damaged ship that came into the hangar a couple of years ago, sir,' said one of the others. 'I recognise him. I was on guard duty that day.'

'Hmm,' he grunted, turning his attention back to the mini-me. 'How did this get in here? It wouldn't fit in the elevators.'

'I jumped it in,' Andy said, shrugging.

The man stared at him as if he'd just grown another head.

'You're trying to tell me you jumped a ship inside a moving planetoid?'

'Well, I was already inside the hangar destroying all their eggs, so that reduced the risk.'

'GDA,' said the man, shaking his head. 'You're all crazy.'

'I'm not actually GDA,' said Andy. 'More private contractor. But anyway, enough about me, let's concentrate on getting the *Arena* bug-free.'

'And why would you want to help with that?' the leader asked, shouldering his rifle and crossing his arms.

'Because at present, the *Arena* is attacking Dasos and the GDA naval fleet,' Andy replied.

The man's eyes widened. He glanced at the others before turning back to Andy.

'They don't think it's us do they?' he said, nervously.

'No,' Andy replied. 'The bugs have commandeered it as a staging post to conquer more human worlds, so my first question is, how did they get on here in the first place?'

'We were betrayed by some of our own people. They just let them in.'

'They would've been kidnapped and brainwashed,' said Andy. 'They wouldn't have had any knowledge or choice in the matter.'

'How could you possibly know that?'

'Because they did the same to my wife,' Andy replied, taking a deep breath and swallowing the wave of sadness that suddenly came over him.

'Oh, okay.' The man recognised Andy's anguish. 'We've been fighting the stinking things ever since,' he continued. 'But not with any great success.'

'They hit you with weight of numbers, don't they?'

'Every time we think we might've got them on the back foot, another thousand of them appear and we end up worse off than before.'

'How many of you have survived?'

'About a third we think, but it's hard to know exactly. There might be other groups holding out elsewhere that we don't know about.'

'The construction tunnel and airlock, is it still operational?'

The man took a step back and stared at Andy.

'How d'you know about that?' he asked, concern washing across his face.

'Educated guess,' said Andy. 'I'm an engineer and it's

what I would've utilised to get the heavy boring machines in here and the waste rock out.'

'Hmm,' he grunted again. After a pause and another glance at his colleagues, he continued. 'It's sealed at both ends. Well, that's not completely true as there is a pedestrian walkway in there from this side, but there's several hundred metres of replaced rock and carboncrete on the outside.'

'The airlock is still operational then?'

'Who knows? It wasn't decommissioned, if that's what you mean.'

'We could get a few more of these in here and wipe the bastards out,' said Andy, nodding over his shoulder at the mini-me.

'I would need to run this by Conor,' the man said, his eyes lingering on the fighter.

'Conor's still alive?' Andy asked, raising his eyebrows.

'He is, but he was wounded a few days ago when the fighting got a bit up front and personal.'

'How badly?'

'Lost a leg,' said the armed man.

'Is he well enough for a meeting?'

'I'll find out.'

39

A beach, planet Paxx, Paxx'Ondor system

He froze, quickly opening the other eye. At first, because it was upside down, he thought the dark scaly face was a Klatt. But he quickly discounted that, as the more he studied the facial features, he realised this was another dark scaly humanoid race, but new to him.

The slitted eyes were bigger and the nose and mouth protruded further, in a similar way to a monitor lizard, but not nearly as far. It had holes for ears and where the Klatt's scales were brown and small, this race had pure black scales, they were much larger and rounder than anything Ed had seen before.

None of this overly concerned Ed, but the double-headed spear with vicious-looking reversed barbs kinda did. He eyed his rifle, lying half a metre away, but discounted making a grab for it, as this was probably a first contact sort of occasion and he didn't want to make a bad first impression.

He chose to sit up slowly and swivel round to face the local humanoid. On doing so, it became apparent the newcomer wasn't standing on a high bit of dune or anything as Ed had presumed, he was genuinely over eight foot tall and the spear longer than that.

The local remained completely stationary, his large unblinking eyes and expressionless face considered Ed with an eerie coolness. He didn't seem remotely afraid, but just remained rooted to the spot.

Ed, surmised he'd seen a spear similar to that before on Earth and remembered that the design was for fishing and not for combat.

He smiled and nodded at the man – well, he presumed it was a man, but he'd been wrong before with some of the strange races that made up the GDA.

'Hello,' he said, in Ellinika and getting no response, he leaned over slowly and retrieved two protein bars from the food pack.

'If language doesn't work, next best thing…food,' he said, smiling at the newcomer, who still remained motionless and silent.

He unwrapped the two bars, placed one as far in front of him as he could reach and sat back. Taking an exaggerated bite out of the other bar, he pointed at the one he'd placed and then at the local. He smacked his lips and made a few hmm noises as he chewed. It was a kind of chocolate flavour, or the GDA's equivalent of chocolate anyway, but Ed thought it was worth a go and hoped lizard man wasn't allergic to it or something; he didn't want to unwittingly start a war.

After a few moments, Ed detected a slight relaxing in the local's demeanour and sure enough, he slowly reached forward and picked up the bar with four long clawed scaly fingers. Standing straight again, he sniffed it a couple of times and before Ed could stop him, popped the whole bar in his mouth with a clop.

Ed froze. '*If he chokes on it I'm in the shit,*' he thought. But he needn't have worried, the lizard man swallowed it and remained standing. Nothing changed in his demeanour though, he just returned to standing and staring.

'Want another one?' Ed asked, turning to find another bar. He rummaged in amongst the ration packs as he knew there were always plenty of those. Finding one, he turned back to find the man had vanished. He looked left and right up and down the beach, across at the tree line, but there was no sign of him.

'Fuck me, I've just met Usain Bolt,' he exclaimed, remembering his dad's favourite athlete from his childhood.

It reminded Ed that he ought to sleep in the sealed-up mini-me at night, '*That's if this planet has nights here,*' he thought. '*It might be like Scandinavia.*' He didn't like the thought of sleeping in a bolt upright sitting position, but reminding himself of that long spear and how quick and silent the lizard man had been made it a necessary new house rule. A second rule was to always have his rifle slung over his shoulder when walking around with his personal shield activated.

'Right,' he said, picking up the rifle and water bottle. 'Time for a siesta.'

It had quickly dawned on him that he could have a long wait for rescue and loitering around in the full glare of the star was a fast lane to heat stroke. He lay down behind and on the shaded side of the hull, checked his shield was activated, and had a doze.

40

Main chamber, the Arena, *Prasinos system*

CONOR DID NOT LOOK WELL. His expression was sallow as Andy entered the temporary medical room, but he managed a half smile. His left leg ended in a bloodstained bandage just above the knee and he tried to sit up as Andy approached.

'Don't,' said Andy, indicating for him to remain as he was.

'It's good to see you again,' said Conor. 'As you can see, things haven't gone well since we last met.'

'No, but I'm here to rectify that,' said Andy. 'We need your permission to reopen the construction tunnel and airlock.'

'What good will that do?'

'One, enable us to get some serious firepower in here

to eradicate your infestation and two, get you into one of our autonurses and sort that leg out.'

'I don't know that the council would approve that,' he said, coughing and wincing as he jarred his leg.

'And where might they be today?' Andy asked, theatrically glancing left and right, as if he might find them in the room.

Conor paused, his expression downcast.

'Err…we don't actually know where the other council members are,' he said, dejectedly. 'I'm the only one we know survived the invasion.'

'Then make the decision on their behalf.'

Conor turned to three colleagues standing on the other side of his bed.

'Do you think that airlock will still operate after all this time?'

'It's of the same design as the other bigger one in the hangar, sir,' said a young lady who seemed to be dressed a little over formally for the occasion.

'Have the insects got control over that location?' Conor asked.

'Not that I'm aware of, sir,' she said.

'The tunnel was sealed at both ends I seem to remember.'

'Not completely on this side, sir,' said the armed man from before. 'A pedestrian access does remain, although it is well hidden and locked.'

'Can you take me there?' Andy asked.

'It would mean traversing a few hundred metres in the open, but yes, probably,' he replied.

'Okay,' said Conor. 'Before we do anything drastic, I

want you to take a couple of our engineers in there and ascertain whether that airlock will operate. If it doesn't then we'll never get anything bigger than hand weapons in here and we'll have to have a rethink about putting boots on the ground and doing it the old-fashioned way.'

'Well, let's make sure it does then,' said Andy. 'And by the way, where's the control room?'

'For the airlock?' Conor asked.

'No, for the *Arena*.'

'In an impregnable bunker under the main administration building in the city.'

'Impregnable eh?' Andy said, raising his eyebrows.

'Nothing's impregnable when you're just let in,' snapped Conor, staring at the ceiling and gritting his teeth with the pain.

'My name's Quaid,' said the armed man, as he escorted Andy through a labyrinth of underground passageways.

'Andy,' said Andy, thinking about something as he walked. 'Is there some way of disabling the jump drive?' he asked. 'We need to slow them down and stop them jumping into any more battle cruisers.'

Quaid pointed upwards.

'It's built into one of the main support pillars way above us all,' he said. 'There is an elevator, but that's in insect territory and well guarded, as is the control room.'

'Couldn't I go up in my ship and accidentally damage something?'

Quaid seemed to ponder this for a few moments.

'Those pillars stretching across are critical to the planetoid's structural stability, although they are over-engineered. I really have no idea what might happen if one of them were damaged. It might do nothing, on the other hand it could cause a cascade effect and kill us all.'

'Okay, I'll rule that out then,' said Andy, shrugging.

'On the other hand, there is a large blocked-up doorway about halfway up that was used to get all the machinery inside.'

'How did you get the gear up there to get it in?'

'At one time during the excavation that door was at ground level,' he said. 'It all got installed then before that level was dug away, down to where we are now.'

'What's behind the door?'

'Everything,' he said. 'It had to be a small room, reasonably central to the planetoid and just big enough for the equipment, so as not to compromise the integrity of the pillar.'

Andy smiled and looked at Quaid.

'Is the door obvious?'

'Probably not to the eye,' he replied. 'But a scan would pick up the different density.'

'How thick is it?'

'No idea. This was all done way before my time. Unfortunately the engineer's drawings are all on the computer in the main control room.'

'No matter, I've probably got a key that'll fit,' Andy said with a wry smile.

A couple of minutes later, they reached a very substantial guarded door. The men on duty nodded at Quaid, checked a screen, presumably to make sure there were no nasties on the other side and pressed a button. The steel door rumbled back presenting some steps going up.

Quaid nodded and gave Andy his pistol.

'Might be needing that,' he said. 'But I'm hoping you won't. If it gets too hot out there, return here and these guys will assist.'

Quaid went first and trotted up two flights of stairs that ended with a hatch above. Checking a small screen on the wall, he nodded, pulled back a heavy latch slowly and quietly and cracked open the hatch a few inches.

'Okay,' he said, after listening for a moment and heaving the hatch upward.

Andy was surprised to emerge onto a grass lawn. It made sense when Quaid closed the hatch and it completely disappeared.

'Remember where it is,' he said, pointing to a slight indentation where the handle was.

Andy nodded before being led at a trot towards a group of what looked like warehouses.

'We need the third one,' he whispered as they ran. 'The one with the big red doors.'

They arrived without incident and Quaid entered a key code into a small recessed pad next to the huge doors. A loud clack sounded from within and a smaller-sized door in the middle of the bigger left-hand door swung open.

'In quick,' he said, pulling a face. 'They might've heard that.'

Quaid grabbed Andy's arm and dragged him inside a dark space and closed the door as quickly and quietly as possible.

'Shhh…complete silence,' he whispered in Andy's ear.

They both stood stock still for a few minutes, until Quaid lit a small light on his rifle, tiptoed over to a red box on the wall and silently turned a switch. Several rows of lights set into the ceiling high above flickered to life and Andy squinted as his eyes adjusted to the sudden brightness.

In the centre of the roof some forty metres up were several massive winches with cables as thick as your arm dangling down and ending in two-metre-wide hooks that sat about ten feet from the ground.

'Wow,' whispered Andy. 'You could lift a starship with those.'

'Used to bring up construction materials once we'd installed the gravity engines,' said Quaid. 'Big bastards aren't they?'

'So…the old tunnel is beneath here?' Andy asked, pointing at the ground.

'This way,' Quaid answered with a slight nod, then turned and walked off towards the centre of the room.

'Won't these bright lights be seen from outside during the night period?' Andy asked.

'They haven't given us a night period since they came,' he said. 'They don't need sleep so they keep the artificial star turned up in bright daylight mode to mess with our heads.'

Quaid began scraping here and there in the fine grey gravel covering the ground.

'It's around here somewhere,' he said, looking forward and right to gauge his position in the room.

'How d'you know?

'Lines,' he said, pointing out two small vertical white marks on the walls, one in front and one off to the right.

Andy got the picture and started scraping around too.

'Got it,' said Quaid, bending down and clearing out a hand hold.

The gravel fell away as he heaved open a metre-diameter hatch. A metal ladder on the inner wall dropped away into the blackness below.

'Any lights?' Andy asked, as Quaid clambered onto the top rungs and headed down. His head soon disappearing below ground level.

'Not till the bottom,' he replied, as Andy followed him down into the gloom.

'How deep is this?' he asked.

'Thirty metres, so don't fall,' came the echoey answer from below.

Quaid's rifle light flickered on again as Andy neared the bottom and he disappeared from view. His eyes had to adjust again as he stepped through an arched doorway onto a walkway illuminated by wall-mounted light panels. It was circular and open on the inside, with a waist-high metal railing stopping you falling into the huge central void.

'Woah,' exclaimed Andy, peering nervously over the edge. 'How far down?'

'One and a half kilometres,' said Quaid. 'And that rail is very old, so I wouldn't lean on it.'

Andy snapped his hand off the rail and stepped back as if it was electrified.

'Shit,' he said, as Quaid adopted a wry grin and chuckled. 'Airlock's at the bottom, yes?' Andy asked, ignoring Quaid's amusement at his discomfort.

'It is…and don't look so worried. It's not a ladder this time.'

'Thank fuck for that,' Andy admitted. 'A thirty-metre ladder makes my legs go wobbly,' he said, jabbing a thumb over his shoulder.

'The thirty metres is the plug at the top of the tunnel,' he said, over his shoulder as he strode away around the walkway. 'We have an elevator taking us down to the airlock control room.'

'Good,' said Andy, breathing a sigh of relief. 'Although, how old is it? And when was it last used?'

Quaid stopped at a recessed metal door that opened immediately as he pressed a palm against a black plate.

'The same age as the ones up from the hangar,' he said, stepping inside the elevator as the lights flickered on. 'An engineer goes down regularly to check the integrity of the airlock seals.'

'Hmm,' Andy grunted, tentatively following Quaid inside and staring apprehensively at the floor. 'I just don't fancy falling a kilometre and a half in a tin box.'

The door closing with a whump and his feet almost leaving the floor as the elevator dropped away didn't help with Andy's trepidation. Quaid chuckled again at his obvious discomfort and leant against the back wall with his arms folded.

'I thought Conor wanted us to bring engineers to check the airlock?' Andy said.

'I was an engineer many years ago,' said Quaid. 'I know how it operates.'

It took over four minutes to reach the bottom. Andy was mightily relieved when the door swept open again and Quaid led him out into a small rectangular room and hit the lights. Thick glass windows looked out across the bottom of the shaft at the huge inner airlock door.

'As you can see, the airlock is horizontal and has gravity,' said Quaid. 'On the other side, the tunnel continues down a gradually increasing slope all the way out to the other plug at the planetoid's surface.'

'Removing the outer plug will be relatively easy,' said Andy, then pointed upwards. 'How are we going to clear that one up there without it all dropping down here and smashing everything?'

'Shall we see if this thing still operates first, before we start worrying about that,' said Quaid, waving his hand at the windows and the huge doors beyond.

41
___

The Gabriel *'s bridge, Dasos, Prasinos system*

'EVERY BLOODY TIME,' fumed Linda, as she watched the *Arena* disappear. 'Why is it with those two, everything they attempt quickly goes to rat shit?'

'It's back,' shouted Phil. 'Oh, shit.'

There was a collective gasp from around the bridge as the planetoid jumped back into existence right on top of one of the GDA's heavy cruisers.

'That poor crew,' said Pol, the look of horror on her face mirroring everyone else's.

The *Gabriel* had been cloaked and hanging back from the fleet's activities in thinning out the bug traffic. Linda quickly moved the ship further away as they watched the GDA vessels all cease firing, then begin moving and cloaking as one.

They all winced and swore under their breath as a large

chunk of the cruiser hit Stathmos Vasi space station and ricocheted off, heading straight down into the planet's upper atmosphere.

'I hope that falls somewhere remote,' said Phil.

'Doesn't help those still alive inside it,' mumbled Linda. 'I feel so bloody helpless.'

Just as she said that, a lifeboat launched, closely followed by another.

'Hitting the station reduced some of the wreck's rotation,' said Phil. 'Allowing a few to reach a lifeboat.'

The space station's positioning jets fired, rectifying the nudge it had just received and repositioning it in its recognised orbit.

'Well, at least that's still working,' said Pol. 'The last thing we need now is that monster de-orbiting.'

'It'd be a planet killer,' said Phil. 'I always thought they'd allowed that station to get far too big.'

'Data file from Andy,' said Callon. 'It's the nano footage from inside the *Arena*.'

'Has he sent it to the admiral?' asked Linda.

'Yes.'

'Tell 'em to get back here now,' she said, giving Callon one of her more serious glares.

'Err…the signal's gone again,' Callon replied. 'They must've gone back inside.'

'What the hell are they playing at?' she raged. 'Their mission's completed.'

'Probably trying to avoid all the wreckage flying about,' said Phil.

'Oh,' said Callon, not looking up from her screen. 'I think I might know what they're doing.'

Once she had transferred the nano footage from her screen to the holomap, everyone witnessed the huge cavern stuffed full of bug eggs from ground to ceiling and the labyrinth of flexible tunnels connecting the different levels.

'Oh, crap,' said Phil, slumping in his seat. 'There must be millions of them in there.'

'The queen,' said Pol, pointing excitedly, as footage of an egg layer from the main cavern appeared.

'Hang on,' said Linda. 'There's another one…and another.'

'So that's how they're able to reproduce so rapidly,' said Phil. 'Multiple queens. We've always gone under the misapprehension there was only one.'

'Or perhaps they're different to insects we're accustomed to,' said Linda. 'They have soldiers and workers and maybe drones too, but perhaps they have special egg layers that the queen has no part in.'

'Well, whatever it is, those layers are your number one target,' said Phil. 'Get rid of those and the battle is almost won. I mean, look at the speed they're producing those eggs. No wonder they can afford to throw such numbers at us.'

'Communication from the admiral,' said Callon.

Linda pointed up at the holomap.

Bache appeared looking harassed and stoney-faced.

'*Gabriel*, have you got all your crew back aboard?' he asked.

'Negative, Admiral,' said Linda. 'Both are still inside the *Arena*.'

'ETA for their return?'

'Unknown, they were about to return when the *Arena* attacked your cruiser.'

'Inform me as soon as they're out. I don't want them as collateral damage when the marines go in. We have no choice now.'

'Admiral, we don't know how long....'

'Linda, we're detecting smoke from the *Arena* and the stream of bug traffic has ceased,' interrupted Phil. 'I think the boys witnessed the attack on the cruiser and are already doing the marines' job.'

'Admiral, did you copy that?'

'Affirmative,' he said, looking away at something on his bridge. 'We're getting the same data...*Gabriel*, stand by.'

The admiral disappeared and a close-up of the tunnel mouth appeared. Sure enough, a thin trail of smoke had become visible.

'It's not very much smoke,' said Pol.

'There's the airlock down there,' said Phil. 'It's only what had got into it from the other side before it cycled. I'm hoping they've torched all those eggs and that's why their flow of traffic has dried up.'

'None are going back in either,' said Callon. 'Let's hope the boys are okay.'

'I think they're fine,' said a voice from the tube lift.

They all turned to see Rayl step onto the bridge.

'Ahh,' grunted Linda, jumping up and welcoming her with a hug. 'How are you?' she asked, holding her at arm's length and gazing at her face. 'You've got a bit more colour in your cheeks.'

'Fine…I can hear them,' she said. 'I thought you might want to know.'

'The bugs?' asked Linda. 'You can hear the bugs?'

'Yes…the queen is flapping big time,' she said. 'The egg hatchery has been destroyed and egg production has been postponed. The workers are reporting a flying monster spitting fire in the hatchery and the main chamber too.'

'Yeah…back o' the net,' cheered Phil, punching the air.

Linda let Rayl go and turned to face him.

'You're getting very animated about large-scale slaughter,' she said. 'I thought Theos were complete pacifists?'

'They're not human though are they?' he said, shrugging. 'Just smelly insects.'

Linda pulled a thoughtful face and nodded.

'No, I suppose you're right there.'

'Hang on a minute,' said Phil. 'Did they say a flying monster's in the main chamber too?'

'Yes,' said Rayl.

'What of it?' asked Callon.

'The only way into the main chamber is by elevator and they're no way near big enough to get a mini-me inside.'

'I see where you're going,' said Linda. 'At least one of them must've jumped inside the *Arena*'s main chamber.'

'That's pretty cool,' said Callon.

'Andy's done it before,' said Rayl, startling everyone with the comment. 'Jumping into battleship hangars and firing missiles. It was in the Messier galaxy.'

'You can remember that?' Linda asked.

Rayl stared at the floor for a moment and raised one eyebrow.

'It seems I can,' she said. 'Don't know why.'

'That's a good sign,' said Phil, grinning. 'It might be returning slowly, but at least it is coming back. I imagine random bits and pieces will return here and there. Most likely brought on by things happening that jolt your brain into remembering similar events previously.'

'Thank you, Doctor Phil,' chuckled Linda. 'I must remember to book in for my psyche analysis too.'

Phil grinned back.

'What are we doing then?' asked Pol, pointing up at the holographic *Arena* floating above them.

'We keep out the way and wait,' said Linda, sliding back into her couch and adopting a more enigmatic expression. 'As per usual, the boys have gone off piste again, so all we can do is wait and watch.'

42

A beach, planet Paxx, Paxx'Ondor system

ED AWOKE WITH START. He had no idea how long he'd been asleep, but the star was setting out on the ocean's horizon. The deep crimson globe was creating multi-coloured ripples which stretched as far as the eye could see.

How incredibly beautiful is that, he thought to himself. Turning off his personal shield, he stretched and suddenly froze, as there, not ten metres in front of him, were six of the lizard men. All standing in a line bolt upright with spears in the same hand. Well, he presumed they were all men, he had to admit they did look very masculine and incredibly similar.

'Hello,' he said, staying very still and very glad he had his rifle in his hands this time.

One of them, it might well have been the one he met

earlier, stepped forward, bent down slowly and placed some sort of fish on the sand two metres in front of him. Then they all took one pace back in perfect unison, as if it was a military tattoo.

'Bloody hell,' said Ed. 'That was impressive.'

He glanced down at the fish. It was about a foot long and reminded Ed of a small cod, but with several extra fins on the sides of its body and its eyes were bright red.

'Thank you,' he said, nodding. 'Got any chips and mushy peas?'

They remained completely impassive and expression-less. He stood slowly beside the mini-me, unsealed the canopy and again rummaged in amongst the ration packs. He found he had eight of the protein bars left. Opening six, he walked carefully forward and placed them on the sand about two metres or so in front of the six men. He picked up the fish, backed away and returned to stand by the ship.

One of the lizard men broke ranks, knelt down, retrieved his protein bar and as before popped it in his mouth with a clop. The others all watched him, then turned and glanced at the bars sitting enticingly on the sand in front of them. One at a time they retrieved them, sniffed them and five clops later the bars were all gone.

Ed smiled and placed the fish on the ship's hull. He hoped he wasn't insulting them by not eating it raw. It was at this moment as he glanced out to sea, he realised the star wasn't setting at all, it was rising.

'How bloody long was I asleep?' he mumbled to himself and looked around at his honour guard to find them gone. No sign of them up or down the beach and it was a hundred metres to the tree line. Again, they'd defied the laws of physics as far as the speed of normal humans go.

'They'd clean up at Olympic track events,' Ed murmured, shrugging. *How long were they standing there waiting to give me a fish*, he thought.

He hadn't worn a watch for years as all he had to do was ask his DOVI and the time would be displayed in his peripheral vision. For whatever reason, on this planet his implant didn't seem to function.

A sudden crack from above made him jump.

How can there be a thunder storm, he thought. *There isn't a cloud in the sky.*

Then it dawned on him.

'Sonic boom,' he said, out loud and scanned the sky for an incoming vessel. 'Didn't take them long.'

He spotted it a few seconds later. A black dot moving fast towards the beach and growing larger every second. Deciding not to fly up and meet them, he sat up on the hull and watched as the ship descended. The scream of its anti-gravs reached him and he squinted up as it approached to see which member of crew was flying the shuttle.

Something registered as being slightly off. The anti-gravs sounded weird…more resonant, deeper maybe and not a tone he recognised. Sliding his rifle off his back, he activated his shield, checked the gun was set on a medium stun and slid down beside and under the ship out of sight where he'd been sleeping.

Peeking out from his hiding place, Ed saw the ship up close for the first time. It was certainly not a new model; judging by the deep pitting and scarring on its underbelly it had made countless planetary insertions in its lifespan.

'Who the hell are you?' he whispered.

The ship was definitely a shuttle of some kind, very angular in design, one Ed hadn't seen before. It might have originally been white, but years of use, or misuse even, had turned it grubby and multiple shades of grey and black. There were a few unidentified closed nacelles hanging off it in places, which Ed discerned to be most likely disguised weapon systems. He watched as it circled twice before struts motored out from their housings and it landed softly on the sand about thirty metres away. Its deep rumbling motors dropped in pitch, but remained spinning for several moments.

Seemingly, when the newcomers were satisfied nothing was going to jump out at them, the engines quietened. Again, a slight delay until the door slid up into its housing, and steps slid out from underneath, locking into place with a loud snap.

Two armed humanoids dropped down onto the sand and warily, both checking constantly all around them, approached the mini-me. As they got closer, Ed could see one was male, overweight, dressed in a grubby ship suit, sporting an unkempt beard and a baggy red rasta-style hat. The other was female, much younger, with surprisingly broad shoulders, a slim waist and wearing old worn-out military clothing that looked as if it had been through a hundred wars. Long ratty blonde hair tied back, hung limply down her back to her waist.

They both carried a hand weapon of some kind out front in a double-handed grip as if they were expecting trouble.

'It's one of the new GDA fighters all right,' the female said, speaking Ellinika. 'You were spot on.'

'We'll get a fortune for this from the Klatt,' said the male.

Ed crawled out from his hiding place and stood up. They both balked and took a step back, weapons pointed straight at him.

'Name and rank?' the male blurted, as the female moved sideways to flank him.

Ed decided to pretend he didn't speak Ellinika and just stared, turning his head nervously from side to side. He wanted them to think he hadn't understood what they'd just said to see what other information he could glean from them.

'I don't understand what you're saying,' he said in English, pointing at his ears and adding a shrug for good measure.

'He doesn't speak Ellinika,' said the female. 'That makes things easier.'

The male toggled a small unit hooked to his chest.

'Giner, have you destroyed the beacon?' he asked.

'Yes, boss,' came the reply.

'Anyone else around?'

'No, boss. Nothing within many light years.'

The two of them looked at each other, wry grins appearing on both their faces.

'Can I do it to this one too, boss?' the female asked, licking her lips in anticipation.

'You may, Kul'man,' he said, rolling his eyes. 'This time use a lower stun setting, or you'll have to wait again before you get your perverted sexual gratifications and this time clean the blood out of the airlock.'

'Yes, boss,' she said, checking the setting of her weapon. She looked up and smiled at Ed.

He grinned back.

I'm so going to fuck you up, but not the way you're hoping, he thought.

She brought up her pistol and fired. Ed's shield flared, taking the weaker stun bolt with ease. He swung his rifle around, and the smile disappeared from her face as she started to turn and run. She only managed two metres when Ed's rifle snapped back in his hands, the bolt catching her between the shoulder blades. She dropped like a sack of spuds, her pistol firing into the sand as she slammed into the ground.

The boss had frozen for a second, seemingly unsure as to what to do. He raised his hand to his communicator, but that's all he managed. Ed's second shot hit him in the neck and he dropped on the spot.

'Fucking pirates,' Ed growled, as he looked up at their ship, sat thirty metres away ticking as it cooled.

He sprinted across the sand and jumped straight into the small airlock, then peered into the cockpit as he caught his breath, his rifle in the shoulder. It was empty, there'd only been the two of them. He took a few deep breaths, attempting to slow his heart rate. He could feel it pounding in his chest. Turning and standing in the outer airlock doorway, he glanced up.

'How many more of you up there?' he pondered.

43

Construction tunnel, the Arena, *Prasinos system.*

QUAID PULLED a lever on the wall and a small control desk under the central window powered up. Its rows of knobs and buttons all became backlit and a slanted, recessed screen flickered to life.

'That's a good start,' he said, sliding onto a dusty chair, reading some text that appeared on the screen and depressing a couple more buttons.

Two more flat screens set above the window shimmered before displaying opposing views of the outer airlock doors and the tunnel leading away and downhill on the space vacuum side.

'There we go,' said Quaid. 'Now for the moment of truth. Let's see if the outer door opens and closes.'

He turned a large lever to the right and pressed a

flashing green button. A clunk sounded from somewhere deep in the surrounding rock, followed by a faint hissing.

'Airlock is venting,' Quaid announced with a small nod.

A slow creaking began, getting much louder as the huge volume of air gradually forced its way out of the mega airlock.

'Inner doors taking the strain for the first time in a while,' Quaid said. 'Nothing to worry about.'

'Hmm,' was the only reply Andy could muster. Being an engineer himself, noises like that made him nervous.

Quaid was correct though, the creaking did eventually subside and with a low boom and a shudder that Andy felt through his feet, the massive outer doors began to rumble open.

'Yeah,' said Quaid, leaning back in his chair and folding his arms across his chest. 'Never in any doubt.'

'We haven't tried the inner ones yet,' Andy reminded him.

'Ah...it was the outer ones I was more concerned about,' he said. 'After all, they're the ones that've been in the cold and vacuum of space for a long time. The inner ones, much warmer and not under any pressure.'

A clunk signalled the doors were fully open and Quaid reversed the switch and hit the flashing button again. He smiled up at Andy as they began to rumble closed again.

Once they were shut and sealed again, Quaid repressurised the lock and a few minutes later they were both very thankful to see the inner doors also operated as they should.

'Plugs,' said Andy, raising his eyebrows.

'Yeah…plugs,' repeated Quaid, looking thoughtful. 'The outer one we can just blow out with charges set behind it. The one up there,' he pointed at the ceiling, 'creates a problem.'

'There must be a way we could somehow dig it out from above,' said Andy.

'It would take days and the bugs would hear and be there in seconds,' he replied.

'Hang on,' said Andy, staring at the floor for a moment. 'My ship has an asteri beam weapon that still works.'

'What's that?'

'It's a beam weapon that vaporises stuff,' Andy said. 'It might take an hour or three, but it would do it without dropping the whole lot down here.'

'Your ship is not quiet…and again, the bugs would intervene before you've got started,' Quaid countered.

'Yeah…but maybe not if I fly it inside the warehouse and we keep the doors shut and defended. I only need to cut a hole big enough for me to get down through and to get a load more of the same fighters coming in the other way.'

'Right,' said Quaid, staring into space for a moment before shrugging and throwing his hands up in the air. 'It might just work…anything's better than doing nothing. I'll organise some explosive charges for the outer plug. It'll take a bit of time to get them in place mind.'

When they'd returned to the underground tunnels, Quaid had shot away to inform Conor of their idea and hopefully get the go-ahead. Andy had been escorted back to his ship, where he spent some time trying to fix some of the damage inflicted to its underside. The array was beyond repair with the limited resources he had at hand, but he did manage to straighten the kataligo launcher sufficiently to render it operational again. Although, he did appreciate wielding a large sledgehammer in close proximity to ten high explosive missiles wasn't something a health and safety officer would be particularly good-humoured about. But needs must.

'Conor has given us the go-ahead,' said Quaid, eyeing Andy's hammer suspiciously as he trotted in.

'I've been making a few modest adjustments,' said Andy, noticing the frown and swinging the hammer up onto his shoulder.

Quaid noticed the dented, almost straight launcher, his frown becoming more earnest.

'Is that thing going to work?' he asked, knocking it with his foot.

'Well it might if you stop kicking it.'

'Conor had an idea that we hadn't thought of,' he said, turning back to Andy. 'We're going to create a diversion half a kilometre away when you're cutting through the inner plug. Lots of bangs and smoke and stuff. Should have them scuttling about in completely the wrong place.'

'Okay, sounds good,' said Andy. 'How long till you're ready to blow the outer plug?'

'Couple of hours,' he said.

Andy grimaced.

'I know, I know,' said Quaid. 'It only takes a few minutes to set the charges, it's the time it takes to get down to the plug and back, that's the time waster. It's a long way in a space suit with no gravity.'

'Right,' said Andy, patting the hull of the mini-me. 'Let me know when you're ready with the diversion and I'll spark this little monster up.'

44

A beach, planet Paxx, Paxx'Ondor system

Ed STRUGGLED with the man's unconscious body and found dragging it over to the shuttle was the best way to get him there. The girl had been no problem and she was already aboard, bound with some strong tape he'd found in a locker and attached to one of the rear seats.

'You're no stranger to a pie shop are you?' he grunted, heaving the overweight body up the steps before securing him in a similar way on the seat next to the girl. He'd checked over the controls of their ship earlier to make sure they were familiar and was pleased to see they were of standard GDA design and that it seemed to have a tractor powerful enough to lift his small ship too.

Returning to the mini-me, he was surprised to find a single lizard man watching him. Was it the same one from the first time? He didn't know. He smiled and nodded as he approached and began to seal up his ship. Pulling out the two emergency ration containers, he laid them on the sand in front of the local.

'For you. I go now,' he said, pointing upwards and turned to walk away.

'Thunk yoo,' the lizard man said, stopping Ed in his tracks.

Ed turned and stared at the man quizzically.

'You speak Ellinika?' he asked.

'Smal bit,' he said, tilting his head to one side. 'Thay com befur,' he added, pointing to the shuttle. 'Thay steel owr roks.'

'Rocks?' said Ed. 'What rocks?'

The man dipped his hand into a small cloth bag he had over his shoulder and held out something. Ed approached and was given a jagged lump of opaque rock about the size of a tennis ball.

'Holy crap,' he mumbled, realising it was most likely an enormous uncut diamond. He pointed back at the shuttle. 'They come and steal these?'

The man nodded once.

'Thunk yoo fur kylling thum. Thuy kyll sum eldurs befur.'

'They've killed some of your elders?' he asked, his eyes wide.

Another nod.

Ed realised they hadn't come here to answer his distress call at all. He reached out to return the diamond, but the lizard man took a step back and shook his head.

'Gyft,' he said, in his strange slurry accent, picked up

the food packs and placed them in his bag, then promptly vanished.

Startled, Ed took an involuntary step back.

'What the fuck?' he uttered, before noticing he could just see the bag and spear moving swiftly back towards the tree line. In a few more seconds, they too had blurred into the background.

'A chameleon…of course,' he said, realising they were a large lizard with the ability to change their colour to match the background. Only these guys had perfected it to another level. 'Wow, that's impressive.'

He looked at the huge stone in his hand and wondered what it would be worth on the diamond markets back home. Thrusting it into his pocket, he sealed the mini-me and made his way across to the shuttle.

'You fucking GDA scum-arsed bastard,' the girl spat, as he entered the cockpit.

'Good morning,' he said, with a smile. 'Lovely warm day,' he added, wiping the sweat from his brow with his sleeve.

'You do speak Ellinika…I'm gunna cut your dick off and stick it up your fucking arse,' she continued, with as much venom as she could muster. Her head was shaking with rage.

'Does your mummy know you speak to strangers like that?' asked Ed, as if he was talking to a four-year-old.

If her face wasn't red before, it certainly was now. He could see her straining at her bonds and in a weird kinda way, because of her dark eye makeup, she reminded him of one of the evil witches from a Harry Potter movie he remembered seeing as a child.

'You patronising piece of excrement, you don't deserve to be fucking breathing, I'm gunna...'

Ed stunned her again just as the man stirred. So he re-stunned him too.

'Give me a bit of peace and quiet while I'm trying to fly this piece of junk,' he muttered, as he closed the airlock and sat in the pilot's seat.

It wasn't the flying part that concerned him, it was operating the tractor that he had to get his head around. He couldn't remember actually operating one before. It was always Linda or Phil that did that. Andy would know too. He wrinkled his nose as he donned a rather smelly pilot's POK and brought the ship's systems online. After spinning up the antigravs, lifting the ship and setting it to hover above his fighter, he activated the tractor. It took a few minutes of trial and error to grab hold of the mini-me and pull it close underneath the shuttle. But eventually he got it there and gave himself a pat on the back. He also hoped whoever was up in the mother ship wasn't watching his clumsy efforts too closely.

Arrowing the ship straight up, he headed to get back into space as soon as possible. He didn't want these two screaming at him while he was trying to sneak aboard whatever ship was waiting for him.

As he ripped up through the upper atmosphere, his DOVI came back online and he was happy to be able to discard the stinking POK. He was also able to detect the mothership now, sitting in a high orbit.

It was an old Krix'IR registered ore carrier with one or two odd bits hanging off of it that the GDA ship register didn't recognise. Ed checked out the usual crew number for one of these and was pleased to see it was four: captain, pilot, engineer and load master. Although, it didn't guarantee there were only two more on board, he just hoped it wasn't ten.

As he got closer, he saw that where the four ore hoppers would normally attach in the centre of the ship, a one-piece habitat had been constructed in the space, the back end of which slid open as he approached, presenting a small hangar.

Creeping through the atmosphere shield and carefully turning the ship, he gritted his teeth as he dropped down and released the mini-me. It crunched down on the deck and tipped over to one side. He hoped he hadn't broken his bottle of wine, then chastised himself for worrying about something so trivial.

Remembering the struts at the last minute, he took a deep breath to slow his heart rate and calm himself. He sat the ship facing the rear hangar door and sitting low in the seat, paused to see if anyone arrived. After a couple of minutes he reckoned no one was, so he shut everything down, checked his two captives were still breathing and opened the airlock doors.

He stopped and picked up and donned a grey jacket from one of the other seats and, after snatching the rasta hat off the man's head and slipping it on too, he exited the ship. He had no idea who might have eyes on him and hoped that if they did, they wouldn't look too closely. Clutching his rifle close and rechecking the shield was operational, he cycled himself through the rear airlock and followed the corridor that luckily only went in one direction.

Twenty metres along, he came to a steep staircase that went up and down. Thinking the bridge would always be high in the ship, he went up. Taking the steps two at a time he sprinted up following it around a blind right corner and ran straight into another man on his way down.

'Ah, sorry boss,' the man said, then 'Oh,' as he realised it wasn't and he was staring down the business end of a rifle.

'Where are the others, Giner?' Ed shouted, hoping he'd got the name right.

'How d'you know my name?'

Ed realised he'd got lucky and pressed the man again.

'Giner, the others, where are they?' he asked again, with equal rancour and prodded him in the chest hard with the barrel, causing the man to fall back on the stairs.

'In…in the shuttle,' he stammered. 'Where the fuck did you come from? Were you hiding in the other ship?'

Ed had got all the information he wanted and hit the man with a stun bolt from point-blank range. Picking up the unconscious body he trudged back to the hangar, placed the man on a seat with the others and trussed him up similarly. Looking at the shuttle's airlock controls, he had an idea and two minutes later and using his DOVI, he'd changed the mechanisms coding so they wouldn't be able to leave the ship even if they did struggle free. Just as he was about to leave, he realised he should lock the controls too, so they couldn't just fly off. Once he was satisfied, they had no means of escape, he turned around and went to find the bridge.

45

Underground hangar, the Arena, *Prasinos system*

ANDY LIFTED the mini-me off the deck of the underground hangar and after checking no more bits had fallen off, he signalled he was ready. The spotter up at the hatch gave a nod that everything was clear up top and the big hangar door opened slowly.

He could see the others in the hangar covering their ears as he lifted the fighter back out into the central atrium. A huge flash off to his left had him blinking for a moment. He quickly banked right as flames soared up a hundred metres off the ground as the diversion went off as promised.

Andy wasn't about to hang around and watch though, as his first job was to disable the jump drive. He didn't have use of his ship's array, so once he'd selected the correct support pillar, he scanned with his DOVI to detect the electronic equipment as he climbed ever higher.

It didn't take too long either, as Quaid had told him to put the tallest building in the main city directly behind him as he climbed the two hundred metre-diameter column. As he'd been told, it was over a kilometre up and as you wouldn't be able to see it from the ground, up here the slight discolouration of the different stone density made the old doorway quite obvious.

Andy didn't waste any time, he backed away about fifty metres and gave the area a short burst with the laser cannons. The thin outer stone layer ripped apart quickly and with a second burst from the cannons he found he had to back away even more as fire and lumps of hot metal erupted from the jagged hole. He considered sticking a missile in for good measure, but realised the Arenians would have to repair this damage at some point, so he'd best not make it too much of a shambles.

He turned and heading downwards, made directly for the warehouse with the red doors. They must've been watching as these began sliding open as he approached. He wasn't prepared for the clouds of dust and gravel the anti-gravs kicked up as he entered through and found he had to rise up to the ceiling once inside so he could see where he was supposed to be. Someone had spray painted a circle in the centre of the huge space to help him find the plug.

He tightened his belts as he had to angle the ship straight down and it meant hanging in them for the entire time he would be cutting with the asteri beam. Starting roughly in the centre, he activated the beam. It was a bit experimental to start with, as he played with the beam width. Finding around a metre wide was the optimum size, he worked in a spiral, expanding the hole out to around twice the width of his ship. It cut down about five metres on each pass and he found visibility an issue here too and had to rise up above the ash and steam every so often. It took thirty-two minutes before he finally broke through. A small amount of rock and debris that didn't get vaporised by the beam dropped into the shaft as he widened it out to the required size.

'Below,' he shouted, hoping Quaid would pick up his transmission.

'We're ready, standing by,' came the reply.

Andy checked the cockpit seals were still in the green as he dropped downwards. He switched the ship's powerful lights on too and then wished he hadn't bothered, as it became even more obvious how claustrophobic it really was down there.

'Always me that has to go down the fucking hole,' he whispered to himself, as the tiny ship plummeted down into the uninviting darkness below. 'I bet Ed's sitting in a nice comfortable chair with a chilled glass of Sancerre right about now.'

46

'I BET Andy's enjoying a nice cold beer on the *Gabriel* right about now,' Ed moaned, curling his lip, as he worked his way through the dirty, dingy and smelly corridors, looking for the freighter's bridge.

Finally, after opening about a dozen doors on three different levels, he found the bridge. It wasn't any cleaner than the rest of the ship. There were five seats, all a bit threadbare and in dire need of a scrub. Old used food and drink cartons lay everywhere, and the control screens were just about visible through years of dust and crud.

'What a bunch of grubs,' Ed moaned, as he sat at what he hoped was the pilot's seat.

Then he thought of something and went back to the door, shut and code locked it. The five seats all looked sat in, it was probably nothing but he didn't fancy two other murderous pirates sneaking up on him while he was otherwise occupied with flying the ship.

'Right, wadda we have here?' he said to himself, touching an icon on a very dirty navigation screen.

'Are you in need of navigation assistance?' a female voice boomed from behind him.

Ed nearly levitated out of his seat, as he snatched his rifle off his back and swung it around the room. The bridge wasn't big and there was nowhere for anyone to hide.

'Who is that?' he demanded, nervously.

'Preed Denamart Autonav, model fourteen ten B,' the voice stated. 'Are you in need of navigation assistance?' she repeated.

'Ahhh,' he grunted, recovering from the shock and sliding back into the seat. 'You're an old automated navigation assistant. I've heard about systems like you,' he said. 'In that case can you set a course for the nearest jump zone in this system?'

'Course set,' she said, without even the slightest pause.

'Okay, cool…take us there then,' he said, sitting back in the seat and crossing his arms.

'Do you wish me to initiate the course change?'

'Yes…please,' he said, rolling his eyes.

'Unable to comply.'

'What?…Why?'

'Only the captain can initiate course changes.'

'Why didn't you say that before?'

'It's a pre-requisite.'

Ed held his head in his hands for a moment.

'Okay…switch to manual control and I'll do it myself.'

'Unable to comply.'

'Don't tell me.'

'Don't tell you what?'

'Oh, for fuck's sake.'

'Who is fuck?'

Ed sighed and counted to ten. He closed his eyes and began searching around with his DOVI. He found the systems quite basic and quickly discovered the vessel's flight controls and the Preed Denamart software integrated into it.

'Can't be that simple, surely,' he said to himself, after finding a code lock to disengage the autonav. He'd already hacked the captain's code to lock the shuttle airlock and the bridge door.

'What are you doing?' she asked.

'System maintenance,' he said, as he changed the authorisation code and disconnected the autonav.

'This is against company regulations and has to be reported.'

'Who to?'

'The captain,' she said. 'It could lead to disciplinary action.'

Ed took control of the freighter and moved it out of orbit, accelerating it away and through its plethora of moons.

'You're moving the vessel,' she said.

'No shit, Sherlock,' Ed mumbled, as he concentrated on programming the first jump back towards Dasos.

'Your crew licence could be revoked.'

'Don't you ever bloody shut up?'

'No she doesn't,' said a voice Ed recognised from the beach.

He froze, as something cold and metallic was pressed against his neck. His personal shield was turned off and his weapon was on the floor at his feet.

'Don't even think about trying to pick that up, Mr GDA,' the captain continued, nodding at the rifle. 'Keep your hands where I can see them and move your arse out of my fucking chair, slowly.'

Ed did as he asked, slowly and carefully, at the same time decommissioning the captain's pistol still pointing menacingly at his face. It became obvious when he turned how the man had entered the cockpit undetected. A hatch in the far right corner lay open, the roar of the engines had shielded any noise of it hinging up. Then another face, grinning from ear to ear, appeared up through the hatch.

'Hello, lover boy,' she said, unable to contain her obvious excitement. 'This is going to be a glorious day, but perhaps not so much for you.'

The lights in the cockpit dimmed slightly as the ship jumped. Ed had set the autopilot to take him back to Dasos and in this ship it would require three jumps.

'Oh,' grunted the captain, stretching his neck to inspect the navigation screen. 'Going anywhere nice are we? And don't pretend you don't speak Ellinika this time.'

'Wouldn't dream of it,' said Ed, jovially, trying to appear calm when he was anything but.

The captain turned to the girl as she climbed out of the hatch clutching the roll of engineering tape Ed had used on them. She waved it in his face.

'Now it's your turn for a bit of bondage,' she said, with

a wide grin and theatrically pulling a long strip of tape off the role.

Ed decided he'd had enough and letting her truss him up was an extremely bad idea. Launching himself forward, he delivered a right-hand uppercut under her chin with every ounce of strength he could muster. Her head snapped up, she flew backwards, catching her calves on the co-pilot's seat and cartwheeling backwards over it.

Ed immediately reversed his momentum and threw himself backwards towards the captain. He didn't see the look of confusion on the man's face as his weapon failed to fire. He felt his head though as he clattered into him and the back of his head met the bridge of the captain's nose. Pushing hard with his legs, he continued backwards taking the stunned man with him. The back cockpit bulkhead soon put a stop to their uncontrolled stagger and they hit it with some force. The captain's head smashed into the covering plastic panel so hard the brittle material cracked and as he sank to the deck, leaving a thin trail of blood down the dirty greying panel.

The girl had by now recovered somewhat and righted herself. She stood on slightly unsteady legs, and a snarl crossed her face as she rubbed her bruised chin. Ed didn't see where it came from, but there was suddenly a large commando-style knife in her hand. He glanced at his rifle lying next to the pilot's seat.

'Go on…go for it, you fucking arsehole,' she snapped, stepping up on the co-pilot's seat and launching herself at him. What she didn't expect was the old dirty seat cushioning to collapse as she thrust off it and one of her legs to drop through the frame. She stumbled, which gave Ed the chance to grab her wrist, twist her arm over and slam his forearm down on her elbow. It snapped, she bellowed and dropped the knife, before collapsing down on her haunches cradling the broken arm and sobbing.

Ed sidestepped over to the pilot's seat and snatched up his rifle, but before he could initiate the shield, he was hit in the back by a powerful energy bolt. He convulsed and the last thing he remembered was the cockpit floor coming up to greet him.

'Look at the bloody state of you two,' said Giner, climbing out of the hatch, a laser pistol in his hand. 'All you had to do was shoot the fucker.'

'Get that piece of shit out the nearest airlock now,' mumbled the captain, holding the back of his head with one hand and trying to push himself up with the other.

47

Construction shaft, the Arena, *Prasinos system*

ANDY KNEW he was approaching the bottom of the shaft as Quaid had opened the inner door and illuminated the airlock. He spent a few moments with the asteri beam clearing the rubble that had fallen from the plug. Although there wasn't much of it and it had disintegrated into small lumps on impact anyway.

Quaid waved and called from the control room.

'They're blowing the outer plug in three minutes,' he said. 'I'll cycle you through when that's been done and you can go see if it's clear.'

Andy gave him a thumbs-up and scooted into the airlock, settling gently on the floor to give the hard-working antigrav a break. A couple of minutes went by and he felt a small vibration through his seat and peering over his shoulder he could see the inner door sliding closed.

He sparked up the alma drive so it was ready, listened to the atmosphere venting and watched as the outer door opened silently. The antigrav motor became redundant as soon as he left the confines of the airlock and the gravity plating's influence. He shut it down and continued on with the alma. The tunnel did indeed head gradually downwards and he met a dust cloud billowing up the passage about a minute later.

This had been expected and he reduced his speed accordingly. Just as he was beginning to wonder if the explosives had actually removed the whole of the plug and he was about to fly into a wall of rock, he saw a couple of faint stars in the distance. Two became ten and suddenly a million as he emerged into clear space.

'You beauty,' he said, craning his neck around to see where he was.

'Andy, is that you?' Linda called.

''Tis I,' he replied, excitedly.

'Did you just blow a hole in the *Arena*?'

'No, the Arenian's did that,' he said. 'It's their old construction tunnel with an airlock in the middle. We can get a load of fighters in there now and clear out the bugs. Can you inform Bache?'

'I'm on it,' she said.

'Your ship's sustained damage,' said Pol. 'Are you okay getting over here?'

'I've lost the array and jump capability, but the weapons are all still online,' he said. 'I'll be going back in to help out. Is Ed there?'

'Is he not with you?' asked Pol, a sudden edge of concern in her voice.

'No, he left the *Arena* just as it jumped a while back. I was kinda hoping he'd got back here by now.'

'Do you know the jump location?' Pol asked.

'No…I was still just inside the *Arena* and unable to use my array.'

'We need to find him quickly,' said Phil, joining the conversation. 'That planetoid can jump a long way. How much life support do you have on one of those?'

'Er…hang on,' said Andy, checking his environmental screen. 'About seventy-two hours.'

'That's no good if he's found himself more than three days away is it?'

'Shit…no…no it isn't,' said Andy, thinking about the scenario. 'How long is it since we left the *Gabriel*?'

'Fourteen hours,' said Pol.

'So, if he's been in space all that time, he has about fifty-eight hours left. You need to find him.'

'If he's anything, he's resourceful,' said Linda. 'If he's less than three days away, then he's on the way back and if it's more, he would look for a close-by habitable planet, set up a distress beacon and wait it out.'

'How's Bache doing, by the way?' Andy asked.

'A lot better now the resupply of bugs has been cut,' Pol said.

'You're welcome,' chuckled Andy.

'Was that you?' asked Phil. 'And did you jump inside the main chamber?'

'Yes and yes,' replied Andy.

'You forgot the antigrav didn't you? That's why you've got damage on the bottom of your ship.'

Andy cringed.

'You won't tell Edward will you?'

'No, but I might,' said Pol. 'Are you coming back to help us find him?'

'I've made promises here,' he said. 'There's plenty of you on the *Gabriel* to go get him.'

'Talking of promises,' said Linda, 'Bache has just ordered a couple of squadrons of mini-mes to meet you at the *Arena*.'

'Cool,' said Andy.

'What if they see them coming and jump away again?' Pol asked.

'Not going to happen,' Andy replied. 'Jump drive is disabled.'

'Was that you as well?'

'What can I say?'

'You have been a busy boy,' said Phil. 'Looks like your little army's arriving too.'

Andy watched as several tiny fighters similar to his zipped in close by, followed by a few more from another direction.

'Lieutenant Dels of 219 Wing reporting.'

'Pilot Officer Medoraine of 551 Wing reporting.'

Andy spent a few minutes filling in all twenty pilots on the details of the job.

'Follow me,' he said, once he and they were all happy with the job at hand. One at a time they followed Andy's ship into the dust-filled passageway.

48

Unnamed freighter, non-system space

A LOUD SCRAPING SOUND WAS the first thing Ed became aware of, the second was a stinging sensation between his shoulder blades. Then something clunked against the back of his head and as he gradually became aware of his surroundings. He discovered he was trussed up with tape and being dragged through the ship by his feet.

He wriggled violently and whoever was pulling him along dropped his feet.

'Ah, you're awake are you?' said Giner, leering down at him. 'It would've been better for you if you weren't. Then you wouldn't've known what's coming next.'

'They'll execute you if you murder me,' Ed mumbled, trying to work the numb muscles in his face.

'I'm wanted for murder in four systems already, so I don't think another is really an issue. Just think yourself lucky the captain didn't let Kul'man have her way with you. It gives me the shivers what she likes to do with that combat knife. She's seriously perverted.'

'Just take me down to the hangar and put me in my ship and you'll never see me again,' Ed said, a little clearer this time.

'Dream on…that ship's worth billions. It's our retirement pot,' he replied, picking Ed's legs up again and continuing to drag him.

They came to a T-junction.

'Would you like the port airlock or starboard?' he asked, then sniggered and turned left anyway not waiting for a reply.

Ed tried to implement his DOVI, but it seemed the strong pulse of the stun shot had overloaded the delicate system and all he got was white noise and gobbledygook. He grimaced again as his head bumped over a bulkhead joint in the floor, then Giner dropped his feet again as they arrived at the airlock.

'Here we are,' he said, almost cheerily. 'End of the road.'

'Less of the chit-chat and more action,' said the captain, approaching from behind.

Ed stretched his neck to look up to him.

'Just remember, when you're being sentenced to death, I gave you another choice,' Ed said, attempting to sound as unafraid as he could, when in fact it was quite the opposite.

'Oh, really?' said the captain, glancing up at Giner with a quizzical expression.

'To put him in his little ship and let him go,' said Giner, chuckling again.

The captain looked back down at Ed ruefully.

'Retire with a billion in the bank, or let the man who tried to kill me go?' He rubbed his chin comedically as if actually debating the choice. 'You know, hard decision, but I think I'd like to retire in luxury thanks all the same.'

He looked up at Giner again.

'Open the door,' he growled, nodding at the airlock. 'Get rid of this pain in the arse.'

The lock disengaged and the heavy door whirred to the right, disappearing inside the wall.

Giner rolled Ed inside, gave him a wink and stepped back.

The girl, Kul'man sprinted around the corner and waved at them.

'He sent a coded transmission to the Dasos system, Captain,' she said, panting from the exertion.

The captain glanced down and glared at Ed.

'What did you send? And to who?' he snapped.

'Full details of the three of you, this vessel and the crimes you've committed,' Ed replied.

'Shit,' said Giner, looking up at the captain. 'What do we do?'

'Sorry,' said Ed. 'Seemed like the responsible thing to do.'

'Who'd you send it to?' the captain asked again.

'Admiral of the Fleet.'

'Oh, fuck,' said Giner, putting his hand on his forehead. 'We'll have the whole GDA fleet hunting for us.'

'No system will be safe,' said Kul'man, pulling out her

knife and pointing it at Ed. 'I'm going to cut you to fucking ribbons, you bastard.'

'Stop fucking flapping,' the captain shouted. 'We'll be billionaires shortly. We can all change our identities and disappear, it's a big galaxy.'

He turned to point at Kul'man.

'Put that away, get to the cockpit and get us some embedded jumps away from here, right now,' he ordered.

Kul'man gave Ed a filthy look, sheathed her knife and sprinted away, swearing under her breath.

The captain stepped into the airlock and kicked Ed in the stomach.

'Piece a shit,' he snarled, stepped back and pointed at the airlock control. 'Shut the door.'

Ed didn't have much time to worry about what was coming. Even though he knew it wouldn't make a blind bit of difference, he held his breath and shut his eyes. He heard the inner door hiss shut again and the lock clunk as it engaged. He braced himself as he heard the outer door unlock and the whine of the door motor.

'Hello, Edward,' said a voice he recognised. Nefer-uptah floated just outside the door in all her finest regalia and her hands on her hips. Somehow she was also preventing the atmosphere from escaping. 'Having problems with some lowlifes?' she said, waving a hand at the inner door.'

The inner door snapped open a lot quicker than it was designed to.

Giner and the captain just stood rooted to the spot, their eyes wide and mouths open in shock.

'Good morning,' Neferuptah said, cheerily. 'Were you about to murder my friend?'

She wagged a finger at them, and there was a shudder from underneath the ship.

'Oh, dear,' she said. 'I think that might've been your array having a terminal malfunction. I fear Kul'man might have a problem with those embedded jumps now.'

'Who, who the Ancients are you?' the captain stammered, glancing nervously past her at open space behind her.

'Yes, I am,' she said, then noticing the direction of his gaze. 'Ah, you're wondering what's keeping you alive right now, aren't you?'

Ed felt his bonds evaporate into thin air and rubbing his stomach where the captain had kicked him, he stood up and dusted himself down. He smiled at Neferuptah and stood aside as she floated into the airlock, coming face to face the two confused pirates.

'What would you like me to do with them, Edward?' she asked.

Kul'man appeared, sprinting back around the corner.

'Something's happened to the array, boss…oh!' she grunted, seeing Neferuptah for the first time. 'Who the fuck are you? And what are you wearing?' she asked, pulling a hand weapon out of a holster.

'I wouldn't do that if I were you,' said Ed, shaking his head.

'I've had just about all I can stomach from you,' she said, pointing the pistol at Ed and pulling the trigger.

There was a little musical toot and a little red flag popped out from the barrel.

Kul'man turned the weapon in her hand and gazed at the small pennant in utter amazement.

Ed snorted.

'I think someone's been watching some old Earth comedy,' he said.

'Did you like that, Edward?' she asked, smiling.

'Oh, yeah. Andy would've loved that too. Is he okay by the way?'

'He's fine and a very busy boy.'

'Erm,' grunted Kul'man, noticing and seemingly puzzled by the fear her colleagues were showing, then suddenly becoming aware that both airlock doors were open to space. 'How the fuck aren't we all dead?' she said, peering past them.

'Because I haven't decided whether you should stay alive or not,' said Neferuptah, turning to Ed. 'You haven't answered my original question, Edward,' she said, raising her eyebrows.

'We need to secure them and hand them over to the authorities,' he said, shrugging.

'Are you sure? They were about to kill you,' she said, seemingly surprised. 'They could all pop outside.' She stepped to one side and waved her hand at the cold of space behind them.

'Too easy for them, they need to spend time regretting some of their life decisions.'

'You know…you'd make a very good junior Ancient,' she said, pursing her lips.

'Don't even go there,' he said, his eyes wide. 'I don't think I could cope with that level of responsibility. Look what it did to Lake.'

'Ah, but Lake was a liar and as corrupt as they come.'

'I'm not perfect either.'

'Nobody is,' she said. 'Least of all me.'

'Are you trying to make out you're an Ancient or something?' sneered Kul'man. 'I bet this is all a fucking holographic hoax.'

She pulled out her knife and threw it with all her might at Neferuptah. It spun through the air, slowed and the point of the blade stopped an inch from Neferuptah's nose. She inspected both sides of it as it hung there and nodded.

'Hmm,' she grunted. 'Quality blade…titanium.'

She flicked a finger and the knife flew back the way it came and buried itself in the centre of Kul'man's chest.

'NO,' shouted Ed, looking on in horror.

Kul'man dropped to her knees. With her eyes wide in shock, she opened her mouth to scream, but gurgled a cough and splattered blood in an arc around her.

'Neferuptah,' Ed cried. 'I didn't want this.'

She smiled and lifted a finger up slowly as if telling him to wait. The knife dropped out of Kul'man's chest and clattered to the floor. All the blood disappeared and as Kul'man was finally able to emit an ear-piercing scream, she stared down at her chest, the fatal wound completely gone.

'Perhaps you should remain on your knees in my presence,' said Neferuptah. 'Don't ever insult me again, mortal human.'

The captain and Giner just gawped and remained frozen to the spot.

Ed caught a glimpse of the starfield behind him change suddenly.

'Have we just moved?' he asked, turning to peer outside.

'I've brought you back to the Prasinos system,' she said. 'I believe Andrew and the rest of your crew will be very pleased to see you and you can help with the bug hunt.'

'Can't you help us with that?' Ed asked. 'After all, it was your husband who brought them into this galaxy.'

Neferuptah waved a finger again and the three pirates all disappeared suddenly. She turned to Ed, an irritated expression on her face.

'Well, it's true isn't it? Ed added. 'You could just end this with a wave of your finger.'

Neferuptah sighed.

'Indeed I could, human,' she snarled. 'But gods don't react well to being told what to do.'

'No, ma'am, sorry,' Ed said, quickly realising he seemed to have overstepped a boundary with her.

'You must realise that we're your creator but not your protector,' she said, her tone calming again. 'I am genuinely impressed with this conglomeration you call the GDA. In many ways it seems we've got at least one galaxy about right, but there comes a time when you have to face potential extinction events and overcome it yourselves with your own ingenuity. This is one of those moments and I'm sure there will be more.'

Ed nodded, as she took his arm and led him back into the corridor. The two airlock doors closing behind them.

'What the hell is that stink?' she asked, pulling a sour face.

'I don't believe these pirates know the meaning of the

word hygiene,' said Ed. 'Pretty ripe isn't it? Where are they, by the way?' he asked, staring down the empty corridor.

'In a cell on the admiral's ship,' she said, walking up the corridor with a raised hand and gradually fading out of existence. 'Go and win the war and if I were you, I'd claim salvage rights on this vessel.' Her voice boomed around him. 'And don't forget my earlier offer. It will remain open. Au revoir.'

Ed, now alone, took a deep breath and exhaled slowly. He wrinkled his nose at the smell and steadied himself against the airlock door as the realisation of how close that had been hit him and his legs turned to jelly. If it wasn't for her intervention, he'd be very dead right now. Forcing his legs to wobble him in the direction of the hangar and his ship, he said a little prayer of thanks to a god who wasn't always invisible.

'You're welcome, Edward.'

49

Construction tunnel, the Arena, *Prasinos system*

ANDY COULD SEE a huge grin on Quaid's face in the control room as he led the other twenty fighters out of the airlock in a symphony of screaming antigravs.

'Anywhere particular up there you'd like us to start?' Andy asked, above the din, as they filed past and up the vertical shaft.

'Capital city,' he answered. 'Where you saw the egg layers and around the elevators. I think they're trying to rebuild all that again. Probably doing the same in the hangar at the bottom of the elevators too.'

Andy led them up into the warehouse and through the already open doors. He could see smoke still rising from where the diversion was, but turned in the opposite direction and headed for their largest city.

A kilometre from the outskirts they spread out and

descended to about fifty feet. Andy instructed them to ignore the odd lone bugs. Conor's soldiers could pick those off as they followed along behind. He wanted to get straight in to where he hoped the layers were.

He was not disappointed. Hordes of bugs seethed around the elevator building and as they approached, Andy could see there were two lines, one line going in carrying eggs and another coming out empty-handed.

'I think they're carrying the eggs down the shaft manually this time,' he said. 'You guys get stuck in here, I'm going to follow the line of eggs. The layers aren't out in the open here this time, I'll call you when I find them.'

'Understood,' came the reply from both wing leaders.

Andy turned out of the line of fighters and followed the egg carriers meandering through the blocks of downtown buildings. He decided not to attack these as yet, so it didn't give them advance warning and they hid the layers away again.

They led him several kilometres out of mid-town and to a more industrial region where they disappeared inside what looked like a huge distribution building of some kind. He smiled and brought his cannons online.

'You're not getting away this time,' he said, firing a barrage of laser bolts at the entrance where they were streaming in and out.

His smile soon disappeared as the bolts dissipated around the building in a multi-coloured lightning display.

'Bastards have a shield…where did they get that?' he grouched, as intermittent fire came back at him from the surrounding buildings.

His shields flared wildly and he was forced to veer

away and accelerate. He didn't have his array so he couldn't lock onto any of the shooters. Turning, he dived back towards where the fire had come from and sprayed bolts manually, causing some of the surrounding industrial units to explode.

A sudden bang from underneath thrust his seat into him and his chin bounced off his chest. Momentarily dazed as the ship shuddered from the impact, he clipped an overhanging pylon arm. The fighter slewed around and cut a deep furrow in the side of a building, which caused it to spin out of control and smash into a truck parked between the industrial building and a small reservoir.

The mini-me came to a rest upside down leaning against a smaller ground car of some kind.

'Fuck…fuck,' was all Andy could muster. He was in a world of pain and when he smelt smoke he began to panic. 'Shit, anything but fire,' he shrieked. Looking up, he stretched to release the canopy. It dropped open about halfway until it met the ground. 'Bollocks,' he shouted, releasing his belts and slumping down onto his head into the part-open canopy.

He grimaced in pain as he wriggled his way around to the widest open point. The smoke was increasing and a small flicker of flame began licking around in the bottom of the cockpit. That certainly focused his attention, as he began forcing himself through the small gap as quickly as he could. He swore again as something snagged around his waist. It was his laser rifle hanging out of its cradle. Having to pull himself back up again was a struggle, but the flames now flicking around his boots gave him a big incentive to get rid of the weapon.

He slid it out of its holder and threw it outside. Now able to wriggle free of the canopy and away from the flames, he felt a surge of exhilaration. His feet were hot and he could smell the rubber of his boots melting.

Suddenly, he was being dragged away from the wreck from under his armpits and a low boom sounded from inside the ship as something flammable ignited and flames poured from underneath where the missile rack was situated. The cockpit was now a sea of fire. Waking up to the fact he was in enemy territory, he craned his neck to see who was pulling him to safety.

He breathed a sigh of relief as he found two human faces staring down at him with blank expressions.

'You are safe now,' one of them said in a monotone voice and Andy's blood ran cold. These were brainwashed Arenians and not Conor's men.

He forced a smile so as not to give away he knew and sat up. Glancing back at the fighter, he realised his rifle was engulfed in flames. His right foot and ankle were extremely painful and as he tried to stand his ankle gave way with a wave of pain.

'Ahh, shit,' he cried, sitting back on the road hard. 'Bastard ankle's bust.'

Gritting his teeth as the worst of the pain subsided slightly, he felt down his right side and found his pistol was still there. Turning his body away from them he unclipped the holster

'We carry you inside,' the monotone man said, moving around him.

He decided to continue with the pretence of not knowing they were the enemy.

'Oh, yes please,' he said. 'This road's very col…'

A huge explosion knocked him flat on his back as the missile rack detonated. The two humans were slammed into the wall of the nearby building. He rolled himself into a ball as flaming wreckage of the ship flew in all directions, some impacting the wall and dropping over and around him.

'Shit, shit, shit,' he shouted, shoving bits away from him and patting his clothes where they had ignited. He felt the hair on the back of his hands singe and standing as best and quickly as he could, he hopped across to the reservoir, slumped down and splashed water over himself.

'Fuck's sake,' he griped, as his clothing hissed. 'What a pisser of a day.' He glanced back at the other two. They lay very still and the clothes on one of them were alight.

He froze as a rattling sound he recognised reached him. Turning his head slowly, he realised his day was going to get a whole lot worse.

50

The Gabriel*'s bridge, Dasos, Prasinos system*

THE *GABRIEL* HAD JUMPED out in six directions so far, to one hundred, two hundred and fifty and five hundred light years distant, then done a full far-reaching scan.

'Right,' said Linda, the boredom beginning to grate. 'He's not back here. Phil, prepare the next direction on the grid and jump when ready.'

'Oh…that's peculiar,' said Pol, staring at both her screen and up at the holomap.

'What is?' Linda asked, half-heartedly, not bothering to look up.

Pol zoomed the holomap in and pointed at a small freighter.

'That is,' she said.

'It's just a dirty old freighter,' said Phil, staring at it closely. 'Very old too.'

'Yeah,' but it just jumped into the system right there,' she said. 'A long way from any of the designated jump zones, it's absolutely stationary and the weirdest thing about it is, its jump drive is shut down and cold.'

'What?…You're kidding,' blurted Linda, furrowing her brow and becoming interested.

'Four life signs on board but none on the bridge,' said Callon, giving Linda a weird look. 'Oh…hang on, make that one life sign now.'

'It's him,' said Cleo, appearing on the bridge.

'Who?' asked Linda.

'Edward, I've detected his DOVI,' she said, staring into space as if she was thinking. 'Hang on…it's not operating as it should though.'

'His mini-me's in the ship's hangar too,' said Pol, grinning.

'Call from the admiral,' said Callon.

Linda pointed up at the holomap.

'Good day, *Gabriel*,' he said. 'I seem to have had three very annoyed, scruffy and mildly smelly individuals appear in my brig. Anything to do with you?'

'Hello, Admiral,' said Linda. 'Erm…possibly, I think the explanation may be aboard that old freighter that's just planted itself in the middle of the system.'

'Edward, I presume?'

'It seems so.'

'Right, they won't be very happy but we'll keep them secure for the time being, I'll have their identities checked and I await an update from your captain, admiral out.'

Linda sniggered and shook her head.

'Get us over there, Phil,' she said, waving her hand at the holomap. 'What have you been up to this time, Virr?'

As Ed passed the junction in the passageway, he had a change of plan and turned towards the freighter's bridge. Once there, he activated the communications suite.

'*Gabriel*, do you copy?'

'Where the hell have you been?' Linda asked, trying to sound annoyed, but coming across more relieved than anything else.

'Having a beach holiday,' he replied, cheerfully.

'Did you build sand castles?' Phil asked.

'Don't encourage him, Phillip,' Linda growled back.

'Will this ship fit in one of our hangars?' Ed asked.

'Do we really want that dirty old thing in one of our nice clean hangars is more the question,' said Linda. 'Have you actually seen it?'

'Believe me, it's no better in here, but I have a possible use for it.'

'Are you claiming it as salvage?' Phil said.

'Yeah, the three crew are on Bache's ship. Responsible for more crime and murders than you can throw a stick at.'

'Best let him know that,' Linda said. 'He's already questioned us about them.'

'Is Andy with you?'

Linda spent several minutes filling Ed in on the last few hours and that Andy was now back inside the *Arena* with a group of fighters aiding Conor in clearing the bugs out.

'I'd better get in there and help,' he said. 'Where's this maintenance passage?'

51

———

Talken Reservoir, the Arena, *Prasinos system*

Andy slowly flattened himself down in the water. It was freezing and he shivered as his clothes and boots became sodden. Keeping just his face and the pistol above the surface, he watched around twenty bugs investigate the remains of the fighter and the two human bodies. They hadn't seen him across the road in the water and he hoped they'd soon lose interest and bugger off.

He swore under his breath as another human strolled around the corner of the building. It was female this time, she was young, slim and extremely attractive. She wore a pure white short thigh-length dress that showed off her long shapely legs.

'Bloody hell,' whispered Andy. 'Shame she's on the other bench.' Then Rayl crossed his mind and he felt ashamed.

She wandered up the road to where the fighter had exploded and peered in where it had left quite a sizeable crater. Andy noticed the bugs gave her a wide birth, the nearest ones kowtowing to her, seemingly almost frightened to go near her.

Returning to the bodies, she bent down and checked them both. Shaking her head and standing again, she gazed around, her eyes quickly finding his.

'Oh fuck,' he spluttered. He'd sunk so low, his mouth was under the water.

'Andrew,' she called, strolling quickly and confidently nearer. 'Get out of there. You'll catch the death of a cold and that ankle looks very sore.'

He really had no choice now. He struggled up with one leg, his sodden clothes pouring water and hanging off him like a wet scarecrow. He kept the weapon by his side because she seemed to be the only reason the bugs weren't tearing him apart.

'You did well to survive that,' she said, nodding at the crater. She stopped at the water's edge and beckoned him with a finger. 'Come on…come and get dry and we can have a nice little chat.'

He sighed and hopped his way out of the reservoir with a grimace as his ankle gave him its disapproval. He gave her a wide birth and stopped a few feet away. One thing that did puzzle him, was the fact she was human like the other brainwashed people, but she spoke normally, no monotone for her.

'Who are you?' he said, shivering uncontrollably. 'You're human and with the bugs, but speaking normally.'

'Yes,' she said, ruefully. 'That is unfortunate. Something we haven't perfected yet, but it's only a matter of time before you won't be able to tell the difference.'

'You didn't answer my question,' he said.

'Ah, yes,' she said. 'Depends on whose perspective you're talking about. To these beautiful little creatures, I'm their queen.'

'YOU'RE THE QUEEN?' Andy blurted, unable to keep the astonishment from his voice.

'You were expecting a four-metre tall insect with pincers that could decapitate a man in one snip, weren't you?' she said, tilting her head to one side.

Andy just stared at her for a moment.

'Well, kinda,' he said, finally. 'What's your real name then?'

'My human name is Menka the Nine. I believe you know me as an Ancient.'

'Bollocks,' he said, without thinking. 'No way are you a fucking Ancient.'

Menka laughed before glaring at him menacingly.

'Such disrespect…you should watch your manners, mortal.'

'A mortal with a gun,' he said, pointing it at her for the first time.

She shrugged and held both hands up as the seething mass of bugs behind her surged forward. They stopped as if hit by a truck.

'Go on, try it,' she said, waving for the bugs to back off.

He pointed it up in the air and pulled the trigger. The faintest of clicks, but nothing else happened.

'You see, Andrew…you're not the only one with what

you call DOVI technology. Your weapon was deactivated before I rounded the corner.'

'You're still not an Ancient though!' he said, placing the pistol back in a soggy holster. 'The Ancients travelled the galaxies spreading the human genome after their planet was destroyed by the star going nova and definitely not trying to wipe them out as you are.'

'How d'you know all this?' she asked, seemingly surprised at his knowledge.

'I've spoken to two Ancients quite recently…that's how I know,' he said, crossing his arms to try and look confident and curtail his shivering.

'Really?' she said, raising her eyebrows. 'And who might they have been?'

'Husband and wife, Neferuptah and Pyriaeus,' he said, nodding.

Her demeanour changed in an instant. Her face went crimson and her mouth twisted in a sneer.

'Pyriaeus?' she hissed. 'I buried that shit alive on Tessamaine and as for that treacherous bitch, Neferuptah…' she continued, almost spitting the name.

Turning on her heel, she marched off the way she'd come so quickly, the bugs struggled to keep out of her way.

'Bring him,' she shouted. 'And get him some dry clothes.'

52

Ed's fighter, Dasos, Prasinos system

ED SCOOTED the mini-me across to the *Arena*, searching for the entrance to the maintenance tunnel.

He'd managed to fit the old freighter in the *Gabriel*'s port hangar, albeit backwards because there wasn't room to go in forwards and turn it around. One of its six landing struts had refused to deploy, so it sat a little lopsided. Cleo wasn't very impressed with the leaky old thing being in her pristine hangar and had to put absorbent pads underneath it to catch its many oily drips, but Ed on the other hand was thrilled.

Finding the entrance, he saw that the tunnel was unlit and dusty. Even with his powerful lights he had to take it easy. Once it cleared, he was able to put the hammer down a bit more and reached the big airlock door soon after. It was closed.

'Hello…anyone home?' he broadcasted on a broad scope of frequencies.

'Who are you?' came the stern reply.

'Edward Virr,' he said. 'Friend of Conor's.'

'You're late…are you looking for Andy?'

'I am, do you know where he is?'

The outer door began opening.

'I sent him to the capital with the other GDA fighters. Don't forget your antigrav drive as you enter like your friend did.'

'Oh, shit,' Ed mumbled, firing it up quickly and entering the airlock.

Exiting on the other side, he saw a couple of faces watching him from a control room set into the sheer rock face. He waved and got a wave back as he wound up the antigrav and ascended the vertical shaft. Emerging a few minutes later through a warehouse and into the artificial daylight, he gained height and squinted around to orientate himself. The high-rises of the capital weren't hard to spot and he headed there as quickly as possible.

The GDA ships were busy and Ed could see the front line of Conor's defenders now able to push back into the city with the help of the air cover. Laser fire crisscrossed in all directions and he was pleased to see the bug body count was vast, especially around the elevator shafts.

'Andy, d'you copy?' he transmitted from the ship's array.

His DOVI was still playing up, so he couldn't try that.

'He went to find the egg layers,' a voice said. 'There was a large explosion shortly after out on the edge of town, so he must have found them. Haven't heard from him since. You can still see the smoke.'

Ed spun his ship around until he saw the thin pillar of smoke in the distance and accelerated in that direction. He picked up a rough line of bugs carrying eggs, although they seemed disorganised and ragged, seemingly unsure of which direction they should now be going.

'Andy, d'you copy?' he asked again, as he reached an industrial area.

The stream of bugs ceased near one of the larger buildings, and as he slowed to inspect where the smoke was coming from, a targeting alarm sounded. Quickly changing course, he pulled a high-G turn and unleashed a missile at the source. He dropped down low as a huge laser bolt flashed within a few metres of his ship.

'That looked like a ship-mounted laser,' he said, as his missile streaked into a large truck parked next to the building where the egg layers were likely to be.

The concussion wave from the massive explosion yanked his ship violently sideways and he had to climb to avoid hitting another building.

'Where the hell did they get one of those?' he shouted, as he checked around for any more suspicious large trucks that might contain another. Turning back, he noticed the debris field had clattered around and over the egg layers' building, but not touched it at all.

'It's got a shield,' he said, before going quiet as behind the adjacent building he caught sight of some wreckage and the reason for the original column of smoke. 'Oh, no,' he mumbled, recognising some of the smouldering components and human bodies lying nearby.

Inspecting the corpses in a slow fly-by and finding neither of them to be Andy, did nothing for the deep sense of dread he felt as he saw the crater that had once been his friend's ship.

If he was in that, there'll be no krypti to find, he thought. Gaining height and turning, he sneered at the shielded building, as tears welled in his eyes.

'Payback time you bastards,' he spat, through clenched teeth.

Selecting the asteri beam he descended to just a few metres and approached the building. He knew from previous experience the beam would drain the power from the shield quicker than any other weapon at his disposal. He stopped around two hundred metres out, set the beam at one and a half metres and unleashed it on the building.

The shield fluoresced through a multitude of colours and as dozens of armed bugs flowed out and engaged him with their hand weapons, he saw something interesting. They'd put a low arch near the main door, just high enough for a bug to pass under where the shield didn't reach the ground. If they hadn't used it, he wouldn't have known it was there.

With his shield coping well against the small arms fire, he swooped over and just skimming the ground for a second he fired two kataligo missiles through the arch. He quickly gained height again and backed away as two huge explosions in the front section of the massive warehouse burst upwards. It was contained initially inside by the shield, but the generator was also inside the building and as all the debris rained down on the rear section it failed and the shield dropped. He stuck another missile in the rear of the building for good measure. The roof burst upwards over a hundred metres before falling back into a cauldron of fire below.

One of the larger egg-laying bugs managed to escape the melee and made a bid for safety behind the adjacent building. Ed made sure it didn't make it using the ship's lasers to disassemble it.

'Fucking have it,' he shouted. 'That's for my friend, you arseholes.'

53

Industrial area, the Arena, *Prasinos system*

THE BUGS HAD SURGED on Andy as soon as Menka had passed by them. They hoisted him up without any consideration for his damaged ankle and carried him off in pursuit of their queen.

'Ow, shit, mind my leg,' he grouched through gritted teeth. 'Clumsy bastards.'

Menka stopped and turned, the mass of bugs following and carrying Andy stopped suddenly too, all comically bumping into each other.

'Easy with our guest,' she said, rolling her eyes. 'Get his ankle strapped up too.'

With Andy griping all the way, they turned the corner and instead of heading right for the egg layer building, they turned left, crossed the double roadway and a vehicle park and entered another smaller carboncrete building. Half a dozen humans greeted the queen and accepted Andy from the bugs. They sat him down, removed his clothes and boots, pumped a couple of injections into his lower leg and dressed him in a set of blue coveralls. Some sort of fracture boot was placed over his foot and ankle. He yelped as it inflated on the inside, repositioning and locking the foot in the correct position. Relief came very quickly, as whatever had been in the injections did its job and the pain washed away.

The building suddenly shook violently, immediately followed by a deep boom. The humans all looked at each other, the worry evident. Then sounds of crashing outside, followed by breaking glass, then shortly after, another boom resonated from the same direction and something heavy fell on the roof above, causing dust and plaster to shower down on them.

While this was going on, Andy noticed the human aids to the queen were having quite an animated but whispered discussion. He couldn't hear what was being said, but the expression on the queen's face was anything but contented.

Finally, she seemed to relent to what they were saying and pointed in his direction.

'Okay, bring him,' she snarled, turning and disappearing down a corridor.

Andy was immediately stood and hustled along in pursuit. He wasn't given time to put the provided sock and boot on his other foot, so he just limped along as best he could.

The corridor they followed the queen and entourage down ended in a garage at the back. Tyre tracks led to a vehicle-sized door that probably opened to a rear roadway.

No vehicle was in residence on this day however, just a row of dark packs laid across the blue hexagonal-tiled floor.

The aids picked one up and began wrapping it around the queen. Before Andy could see exactly what it was, he was dragged over to a similar pack at the far end of the room. As they began doing the same to him, he realised they weren't packs at all, but some sort of armoured sleeveless jacket with a separate wide metal bracelet that clipped on your forearm. The jacket was surprisingly heavy and made from a thick grey canvas type material, with lumpy rectangular panels sewn in front and back.

When the humans began dressing themselves, Andy quickly sat down and slipped the sock and boot on his good leg. The boot proved a bit big, but was better than nothing.

Once they were all similarly garbed, one of the humans grabbed his arm, activated a small touch screen on the bracelet and programmed something into it. Whatever it was, was copied from his own bracelet and when done, he bowed at the queen who nodded in return.

'Send him,' she said.

'Oh, shit,' mumbled Andy, as he realised what it was. The human stood back, touched an icon on his own wrist and with a snap, Andy found himself in complete darkness.

'Did someone turn out the lights?' he asked, trying to use the faint glow from his bracelet screen to see by.

Another loud snap nearby, made him jump and stumble. He yelped as he put too much weight on his bad leg.

More snaps sounded around him, then someone lit a small light and his earlier fears were confirmed.

He'd just jumped.

The space in which he found himself was high ceilinged, so high he couldn't see it. It was about the size of a tennis court with walls of plain carboncrete and he could taste the dust in the air, stirred up by the displacement of the jumps. Grey boxes of machinery filled one end of the room. Connected by wiring and pipes, they hummed and whirred. It was cold, bone-chillingly cold. He shivered, the thin coveralls providing no warmth at all. Several other lights were illuminated and the human who'd dressed him, now removed the jump suit and bracelet. Probably didn't want him jumping off on his own and escaping; not that he had any idea how it worked anyway. Even colder now without the jump suit, he flapped his arms around his body, his breath hanging in clouds around him.

'We need to get you downstairs, My Queen,' one of the humans said. 'We're vulnerable here.'

The party marched off towards a small door at the far end of the room, and Andy was ushered along with them. It opened as they approached and two more humans entered and stood to attention either side of the opening. They both bowed as Menka passed by into a brightly lit stairwell and headed down.

Following behind, Andy reasoned with the carboncrete they must be on one of the bugs' flying rocks, a big one too. That's until he got a glimpse out of a small window on one of the landings. It was only the briefest of glances as he was ushered past.

'Snow?' he murmured. 'How can it be snow…unless?'

The realisation dawned on him. They hadn't jumped onto another ship, they must have jumped onto the surface of Dasos. But where?

On the next landing they exited the stairwell through double doors, emerging into a corridor, one side of which was floor to ceiling glass. He was relieved to find it a lot warmer in here. Able to see outside clearly now, he observed they were in a low-rise building adjacent to a space port. Many ships of all descriptions sat around a wide apron stretching as far as you could see. All were covered in varying thicknesses of snow.

Passing by a row of offices they pushed through another set of double doors into an enormous hangar. Dominating the space was a large commercial ship of some kind. Andy guessed it was some sort of passenger liner, judging by the rows of oval windows along its rather bulbous hull.

Designed more for functionality than elegance, he thought.

A rectangular hatch powered open on its belly next to one of the six huge struts. A set of spiral stairs wound its way down to the hangar floor and a red strip light inside the handrail illuminated the way up.

'HEY, MENKA,' echoed from somewhere in the hangar, somewhere close too, causing the queen to stop dead in her tracks. She scowled and peered around, obviously peeved by the disrespectful use of her old Ancient name.

'Who said that?' she sneered.

A man stepped out from behind the strut nearest the stairway into the ship.

Andy snorted a laugh when he recognised him.

'I did,' said Pyriaeus, leaning casually against the strut and folding his arms.

'PYRIAEUS,' Menka spat. 'So…the treacherous rat lives?'

'Indeed I do,' he said. 'Valiant effort on your part though. I pretty much was dead until Edward and this fine gentleman came by and revived me.'

Menka turned and glowered at Andy.

'If I'd known that, human, I would've let my soldiers rip you to pieces in the reservoir.'

'Love you too,' said Andy, blowing her a kiss.

Baring her teeth, Menka turned back to Pyriaeus, sneered and with a wave of her hand, her human entourage all pulled their weapons and fired at Pyriaeus.

He smiled at her dismayed expression as all the laser bolts passed harmlessly through him and impacted the far hangar wall.

'What is it with this society and fucking holograms,' she snapped and with another wave of her hand, his hologram disappeared. She mounted the stairs and wound her way up, stopping at the top and turning to look down at Andy. 'Leave him here,' she said. 'Well, Andrew. I was going to spare you and take you with me, someone with your obvious talents may have come in useful, but recent news has made me change my mind.'

His escort left him standing at the bottom of the stairway and filed their way up. Before she boarded the ship, she spoke again.

'You have an overdue appointment with some friends

of mine,' she said and with a wave of her hand, a low rumble sounded from the massive main hangar door.

It began to open and Andy's eyes widened as hundreds, maybe thousands of bugs poured in, all turning towards him. He immediately spun around and began running back towards the double doors – well, more fast hobbling really – and looking over his shoulder he realised there was no chance he'd make it. The clattering of their legs on the hangar floor became a deafening roar and just as they were about to envelop him, he dived down on the deck and rolled into a ball.

54

Commercial hangar, Kentro City, Dasos, Prasinos system

'Shiiit,' he bellowed, shutting his eyes as the hoard pounced down on him.

A sudden and complete silence descended on the hangar. Terrified, Andy lay totally still, frozen in place, the coldness of the floor and his ankle complaining bitterly the only sensations he had. No attack. No limbs being ripped off. Just silence.

He tentatively opened one eye. The wall of bugs were two metres from him and slowly backing away as if he had suddenly become toxic. He opened his other eye and lifted his head up. A pair of red lady's high-heeled shoes stepped into his peripheral vision as the bugs continued to back away.

He glanced up, following a pair of shapely legs to find a familiar face smiling down at him.

'Hello, husband,' said Rayl.

'What the fuck?' he stammered

She lifted an arm and pointed at the hangar door.

'You will all exit the building immediately,' she ordered, surprising Andy with an air of authority he hadn't seen in her before.

The bugs all turned tail and as one trotted back towards the door they'd just entered through.

'For fuck's sake, how the hell are you able to do that?' he asked, watching them leave as if nothing had changed. He slowly, with help from Rayl, stood again. She glanced at his leg and raised an eyebrow.

'Walked into a door,' he said, noticing the look.

A low whine sounded from the starship, catching their attention.

'Don't worry,' said Rayl. 'The admiral's got quite a reception for this ship as soon as it's in space.'

They spun around as the main door began closing again.

'Oh, shit,' said Andy, tugging on Rayl's arm and dragging her towards the back door. 'She's not planning on flying out at all.'

They both began running as the starship's jump drive charged. Pyriaeus appeared in front of them, waving his arms for them to get down. As the charging whine reached a crescendo, Andy and Rayl flattened themselves on the ground. Pyriaeus knelt, placed his hands above his head as if holding up a heavy weight and gritted his teeth.

The passenger starship disappeared with an ear-shattering clank, like a large cracked church bell being hit with a sledge hammer. The huge void and displacement of air collapsed in then burst outwards. The entire hangar exploded, sending huge sections of composites and carboncrete spinning hundreds of metres in the air, smashing into and onto many of the ships parked out on the apron. Secondary explosions followed. Lumps of the building and nearby ships crashed into the ground all around them.

Andy hugged Rayl close and once debris had ceased raining down, Pyriaeus dropped the shield he'd held over them and stood again. He glanced ruefully at where the starship had sat moments before.

'Menka hasn't changed in all that time,' he said, with a sigh. 'I'm always the optimist and had hoped she might've seen the error in her ways after so long. To be honest, I think she's worse.'

'You had no idea it was her destroying your world on Tessamaine?' Andy asked, as the two of them stood up.

'I had no clue,' he said, as a flurry of snow blew around their feet.

'You just had a chance to get your revenge, but let her go?' Andy said.

'It's against our accords to take the life of another of the twelve.'

'She was prepared to kill you.'

'Menka always was the odd one out,' he said, staring off into the distance. 'Her ideas about inventing other forms of sentient life went against the accords we set out right at the beginning.'

'What was the betrayal stuff about?'

'Ah…' Pyriaeus sighed. 'At one time we had a bit of a

thing going. We were young. It was before we even left our doomed planet. By the time we left and set off on our voyage it had fizzled out, but when a while later Nefer-uptah and I got together, it suddenly became a big issue and she was the first to go her own way.'

'And holding a grudge by the sound of it,' said Rayl.

'Yeah…' he said, going quiet and sighing again.

'Can we go somewhere warmer?' asked Andy, changing the subject quickly. 'I don't know about you but I'm bloody freezing?. He hugged Rayl close. 'How did you get down here, by the way?'

Almost as he said it, the sound of antigravs in the distance blew in on the breeze and one of the *Gabriel*'s shuttles appeared through the snow clouds, long vortices curling off its winglets.

'Did you really shut yourself in an airlock because of me?' Rayl whispered in his ear.

'Err…yeah,' he replied, a little shamefaced.

She pulled him in even closer.

'You really did love me didn't you?'

'Still do,' he said.

The shuttle screamed in overhead, making further conversation impossible and blowing snow in all direc-tions. Cleo just managed to set it down amongst all the rubble and burning clutter lying around. They hurried over, slipping in the snow and avoiding anything still burning. Andy was very relieved to clamber awkwardly up the steps and into the warmth of the cockpit.'

Cleo grinned at them and closed the airlock doors.

'I love you too,' Rayl whispered in his ear as Cleo

lifted the ship and headed back towards space and the *Gabriel*.

Andy sobbed on her shoulder all the way.

55

Ed's fighter, Capital City, the Arena, *Prasinos system*

ED HAD LANDED near the crater and searched in vain for any trace of his friend. Andy's fighter was completely destroyed, almost completely vaporised in the explosion. He sat on the edge of the reservoir for a few minutes, cradling his rifle. A faint noise from across the road of what he thought sounded like badly timed church bells had him standing on extra alert for a moment. But nothing happened, so he shrugged, took a last look at the crater and went back to his ship.

He had the bit between his teeth now and spent considerable time roaming around, gradually moving back in towards where the other fighters were busy.

He hunted down and despatched dozens of bugs on the way. A strange thing he did notice, was they seemed to gradually lose all purpose. From firing back if they were armed and running and trying to hide, to becoming lethargic and just meandering around as if lost, making them much easier targets.

'We're on our way back out now,' called one of the GDA fighters. 'They say they've got things under control here now since the bugs became strangely passive. They've regained the use of their central control room, so they want us to go around and clear the hangar at the bottom of the elevators.'

'Okay, roger that,' Ed replied.

'Isn't Andy with you?'

'No…his fighter was destroyed.'

'Oh…did he get out?'

'I don't think so.'

'I'm sorry for the loss of your friend.'

'Thank you,' said Ed. 'I need to go and inform the rest of my crew. I'll follow you out.'

Ed had no idea what he was going to say to everyone, especially Rayl, who seemed to be becoming fond of him again. He fretted about it all the way out. He had to queue to use the airlock in the construction tunnel as the admiral was sending in a few hundred marines to aid Conor in clearing out the last of the bugs and bringing aid to the survivors.

When he eventually arrived back at the *Gabriel*, he landed his mini-me back on its cradle, glancing ruefully at the other empty one and sighed.

'It so easily could've been me,' he said as he climbed out and made his way to the bridge.

'Welcome back, boss,' said Phil, as he stepped off the

tube lift. Everyone else smiled and waved as they concentrated on their individual screens.

'Err…could I have everyone's attention for a moment while we're all together,' he said, remaining standing. 'I'm afraid I have some bad news.'

'Hang on,' said Linda, raising a hand. 'Andy's not here.'

'Yes, I know,' he said. 'That's what I wanted…'

'Sorry to interrupt,' said Andy, striding off the tube lift. 'I had a little appointment with the autonurse.'

Ed stood and stared, his eyes wide and a complete look of shock on his face.

'Sorry, Ed…carry on,' Andy said, giving Rayl a grin and sliding into his couch. 'Good to see you back by the way, from wherever it was you disappeared to.'

'Me?…What the fuck are you, you doing here?' was all Ed could get out in a bit of a stutter.

Andy returned a weird look.

'Well…everyone's gotta be somewhere!' he said.

'But you're alive…I saw your ship…what, what was left of it.'

'Ah, right…yeah,' Andy replied, the grin disappearing. 'I got a broken ankle though,' he added hopefully, pointing at his foot.

'A fucking broken ankle,' Ed snapped. 'I've spent the last two hours fretting over how I'm going to tell everyone here you're fucking dead.'

'We didn't know you didn't know,' said Linda.

'How did you get off the *Arena*?' he asked, turning back to glare at Andy again.

'Err…I jumped.'

'In fucking what?'

'A jumping jacket.'

'Are you taking the piss?'

'The queen gave it to me.'

'A giant insect gave you a jacket that can fold space?' he said, throwing his arms in the air. 'D'you think I was born yesterday? D'you really think this is the time and the place for one of your wind-ups? Fuck's sake.'

Ed kicked his couch as he stormed off and disappeared down on the tube lift.

There was a momentary pause on the bridge as everybody glanced around at each other.

'I think Ed's a bit pissed at me,' said Andy, breaking the awkward silence and twiddling his thumbs nervously.

'He's pissed at all of us,' said Linda. 'He'll get over it when he finds out what really happened.'

'I'll go and explain everything,' said Pol, standing. 'Don't blame him…he was just really scared he'd lost a friend.'

She gave Andy's shoulder a squeeze as she passed.

'Just one question,' said Andy. 'What the hell's that heap a shite in the port hangar?'

Linda glanced furtively at Phil.

'You can tell him,' she said, rolling her eyes.

Phil smiled, which made Andy suspicious because he didn't normally do that.

'Erm…it's Ed's new pride and joy,' he said, pulling a pinched expression.

'Did he buy it without seeing it or something?'

Phil sucked air in through clenched teeth.

'I really wouldn't be saying that to him,' Phil replied.

'Especially not at the moment,' said Linda.

Rayl suddenly sat up straight and stared at her screen.

'That's what it meant!' she blurted.

'That's what, what meant?' asked Linda.

'I think I know where the queen went,' said Rayl, sitting back again.

The Gabriel, *orbiting Dasos, Prasinos system*

BACHE LOFTT and another officer were escorted up to the blister on the top deck of the *Gabriel* by Linda. He'd requested the face-to-face meeting after being informed that Rayl might possibly know of Menka's destination.

There, they were greeted by Ed, Andy and Rayl. As this was a formal meeting the greetings were more sombre than usual and they quickly sat in a semicircle on the large round sofa. With the magnificence of Dasos turning slowly above them through the thick diamond glass, they were introduced to Marine Colonel Hallich, whom Bache had tasked with pursuing and eliminating Menka.

'I understand that you have some way of detecting the queen's whereabouts?' Hallich asked Rayl.

'I wouldn't call it detecting,' she said. 'But I can still hear echos of the collective and make sense of some of it.'

'She can have influence over the bugs too,' said Andy.

'Where do you think she is?' the admiral asked.

'I overheard her instructing the flight deck on the liner as she boarded,' said Rayl. 'The numbers didn't mean anything to me as I've never been a navigator, but when I got back here I still remembered them and plugged them into the computer. They were the co-ordinates for a system jumping-in zone.'

'What system?' Hallich asked, bringing out his tablet.

'Somewhere called Gaia in the Helios system,' she said.

'WHAT?' exclaimed Ed, getting a concerned glance from Bache.

'Oh, shit,' said Andy, standing and staring at Rayl. 'You didn't tell me that.'

'Is it somewhere you know?' she asked, recoiling slightly at their reaction. 'I'd never heard of it.'

Bache stared incredulously at Andy.

'Her memories are still coming back,' he explained. 'Although, come to think of it, I don't believe she was on the scene before the name change.'

'It's Earth, our home planet,' Linda said putting her arm around Rayl's shoulder. 'It's not your fault. Before we made first contact, the GDA knew of our planet as Gaia in the Helios system.'

'We need to get under way right now,' said Ed. 'We have to stop her and that ship.'

'How fast is that liner?' Linda asked.

'It's a commercial carrier,' said Bache. 'So nowhere near as fast as this thing. Can the colonel park his assault ships in one of your hangars? otherwise he'll be late to the party,' he asked, looking expectantly at Ed.

'Of course, let's get it done and be on our way,' Ed replied, nodding and standing too.

'I understand the queen is human and is actually an outcast of the Ancients,' said Hallich, as they made their way to the tube lift.

'Yeah,' said Andy. 'A pretty disagreeable one.'

'Does that mean she has the same abilities as that one called Neferuptah?' Bache asked.

'Thankfully, no,' said Ed. 'It seems she hasn't evolved into anything anywhere near as powerful. Neferuptah is unique and very much pro human race.'

'I'll be on the bridge plotting the fastest possible route back to Earth,' said Linda and disappeared off in that direction.

'Can't you persuade her to deal with Menka?' asked Bache. 'She could sort the situation with just a wave of a finger from what I hear.'

'Harming each other is against their accords written in the early days,' said Andy.

'It's down to us then,' said Hallich, as they reached the starboard hangar. 'I'll be back with the teams as quickly as I can.'

'Good luck, guys,' said Bache, shaking hands with all three of them. 'I hope your memory continues to return,' he said nodding to Rayl and disappeared inside the sleek black shuttle.'

Ed and Andy glanced at each other and walked off in opposite directions without saying a word. Rayl sighed and strode quickly to catch up with Andy.

'This has got to stop,' she said, firmly. 'It's like living with two six-year-olds.'

Andy turned and enveloped Rayl in a hug.

'He can be such a twat at times,' he mumbled.

'And you can't?' she whispered back.

The *Gabriel* winked into the Sol system some fourteen hours later. Deliberately avoiding the recognised jump zones, Phil who was piloting at the time had let the starship stretch its legs and cut every corner he safely could. Choosing a spot behind Neptune, he immediately cloaked the ship and brought it up to point nine five light. Pol initiated a system-wide scan as everyone else stared up at the holomap.

'Anything?' Ed asked, as they cleared the huge bulk of the planet.

'Hang on,' said Pol. 'There's a lot of traffic.'

The holomap image of Earth grew bigger and better as they ripped across the Sol system, careful to give the abundance of traffic a wide birth.

'Shit, it's busy these days,' said Andy.

'Jim Rucker told me the space traffic has increased four-fold every year since our first flight,' said Linda.

Everyone on the bridge turned to her with raised eyebrows.

'You and the president on speed dial now?' Andy asked, smirking.

'I had lunch with him and Rebecca a few months ago…you know? Like you do,' she chuckled.

'It's here,' said Pol, bringing the conversation back to the job in hand. 'It's just arrived in the jump zone.'

She pointed up at the holomap as she panned it in on the passenger liner.

'Are you sure it's the same one?' asked Ed. 'It's very late. It should've been here many hours ago and a lot of the galactic cruise lines use similar vessels.'

'Oh yes,' she said. 'But what's strange about it is it appears deserted. There are no life signs at all on the ship.'

'Who's flying it then?' Callon asked, as they watched it move towards Earth.

'Autopilot,' said Andy. 'Must be.'

'Or remotely,' said Callon.

'I have a bad feeling about that ship,' said Phil.

'They could've all jumped off as it arrived, using those jackets they have,' said Linda.

'They're quite noisy though,' said Pol. 'I'd have detected the signatures if they had.'

'It's speeding up,' said Linda. 'It should be slowing to achieve an orbital velocity.'

'Shit,' said Phil. 'It's revenge for what we've done. It's going to impact the planet.'

'Get us there, Phil,' said Ed. 'All weapons online, we have to destroy that ship.'

'We can't,' said Phil. 'We're too far away and already flat out.'

'Jump us there.'

'We're too big. It's already flying through busy space lanes, the odds of jumping into other traffic are almost guaranteed.'

'How long till impact?' Ed asked.

'Thirty-one minutes if it continues to accelerate similarly,' said Pol.

'Ah, crap,' said Linda. 'I've vectored in its entry point to the rotation of Earth, it's going to impact around Rio de Janeiro.'

While everyone had their noses in their screens, Ed slid out of his seat and disappeared on the tube lift. He ran into the hangar and signalled Hallich as he climbed into his mini-me.

'Saddle up, guys…work to do,' he called.

On the bridge, Pol looked up from her screen.

'Hey, where's Ed?' she asked.

They all looked at each other.

'I didn't see him leave, did you?' said Linda, glancing round.

'Cleo, where's Ed?' Phil asked.

'Ed's in the starboard hangar,' she replied.

Almost as she spoke, Ed's mini-me streaked out into space and jumped within seconds, closely followed by the marine ships.

'Oh, fuck,' said Andy. 'What're they going to be able to do with those?'

'If he shoots at the liner, it'll break into several pieces and that'll make the situation even worse,' said Phil.

'Where is he?' asked Linda.

'There,' said Pol, pointing. 'He jumped into the same jump zone and he's playing catch-up now.'

'Ed, d'you copy?' Linda transmitted and got no reply.

'I'll use my DOVI,' said Andy. 'He can't ignore that.'

'His isn't working,' said Pol. 'He took a stun shot in the back and it frazzled it.'

'Then he'd better have a plan,' said Andy. 'Cuz we can't be of any help from here.'

'Ed wouldn't have left without a plan,' said Pol.

57

Ed's mini-me, approaching Earth, Sol system

'WHAT THE HELL am I going to do when I get there?' Ed mumbled to himself. 'I have no plan at all.' He was absolutely fuming with himself and that stupid bloody Menka. How dare she threaten his home.

He peered down at his screen. The liner was dead ahead, still accelerating, and the four marine ships were close behind. His fighter was much quicker than the commercial vessel and he'd reach it in three minutes. But it still wasn't visible to the naked eye.

He could see on his screen, several other ships having to take sudden evasive action and hoped they all managed to avoid each other in the process. He tried his DOVI again, but got the now familiar white noise.

'Shit...think of something,' he raged. 'If you're around, Neferuptah, I could really do with a hand right now.' Then he remembered her words. *There comes a time when you have to face potential extinction events and overcome it yourselves with your own ingenuity.*

'What happens if my ingenuity has buggered off?' he shouted at the cockpit.

He knew if he shot out its alma drive, it would only stop it accelerating and as it was already doing point one five light speed, that really was of no help at all. Blowing it to pieces would only make matters infinitely worse – when all the bits spread out, many of the bigger sections would impact the surface.

'Think, Edward, think.'

Concussion, he thought. 'That just might work,' he muttered. *But the autopilot will counter any influence I induce and set it back on its original course.*

The *Gabriel* hailed him again. He ignored it.

Destroy the array first, then it won't know it's off course.

The liner's drive cones were visible now, glowing blue against the backdrop of stars. Earth was looming bigger every second and the vessel was curving around in an arc to meet it. If he could just nudge the bigger ship a few degrees to starboard, it might be enough for it to bounce off the planet's atmosphere. Leaving it to power away into clear space, where it could be easily destroyed.

He powered in under the liner and slowed to match its speed. It had four larger protrusions on its underside, any one of which could be the main array.

'Hallich, I'm going to destroy its array, can you detonate some missiles off its port side to push it in the opposite direction? On no account hit the ship itself.'

'Roger that, I understand,' Hallich replied. 'Can't we board the ship and divert it?'

'If the autopilot is code locked, which it probably is, we'd run out of time.'

'Roger…one of my men says the forward nacelle under the bow is the main navigation array on that model.'

'Thank you.'

Ed lined it up and using the lasers, put a couple of energy bolts into the array. The covering panels blew away, shattering into a thousand pieces, leaving the internal electronics and the multidirectional detection sphere exposed. Another two bolts and the whole thing exploded outwards with such surprising violence, he had to veer away rapidly as shrapnel peppered his ship. Then a huge flash lit up his cockpit.

'Oh, no…'

Then unconsciousness.

———

'What the fuck was that?' shouted Andy, as everyone on the *Gabriel*'s bridge had to shield their eyes as the liner exploded and lit up the holomap.

'It was wired,' said Phil. 'Any deviation or interference would've done it.'

'Where's Ed's ship?' Pol asked, the concern evident in her tone.

'Two of the marine ships have collided,' said Phil. 'They're spinning out of control.'

'Shit…what a mess,' said Linda.

'I still can't find Ed's ship,' Pol cried, her tone getting more insistent.

'There it is,' said Callon, pointing to a small object spinning away from the planet.

'He's either unconscious or the ship's damaged,' said Phil.

They watched helpless, as several large sections of the liner were now heading for Earth's atmosphere, along with two of the marine ships.

'There's a freighter in trouble too,' said Phil. 'It was the closest commercial vessel to the explosion, must've been hit by debris.'

'This has just got so out of control,' said Linda. 'If only we could get there sooner and use our tractor, we might be able to manipulate some of those larger bits so they miss.'

'Or drop them in an ocean,' said Andy.

'Why don't we jump into the atmosphere and come out to move the troublesome sections?' Callon asked.

Everyone went silent for a moment.

'Didn't think of that,' said Phil. 'Cleo, can you jump us safely into the planet's upper atmosphere?' he asked.

'Underneath the falling debris,' said Linda.

'Give me a moment,' she answered, as the antigravs immediately began spooling up.

'Shit,' said Andy. 'She's doing it.'

'I'll get the tractor up and running,' said Linda. 'Andy, can you spark up the asteri beam and target some of the medium-sized bits?'

'On it,' he said, tapping away earnestly.

'What about Ed?' Pol asked.

'Sorry, Pol,' said Linda. 'Thousands could die if we don't stop those things from impacting the surface. Any one of them will have the same destructive power as a large nuclear warhead.'

'Oh,' Pol grunted, looking like she was about to burst into tears.

'Ed's ship isn't in any danger,' said Phil. 'He'll most likely be unconscious. We'll go grab him as soon as the planet's safe.'

'Okay,' she answered, sounding a little unsure.

The bridge lights dimmed slightly as the huge vessel jumped into a clear area, one hundred thousand feet above Earth's surface. Phil stood the ship on its tail and powered it straight up, taking the screaming motors up to one hundred and eight per cent. They went through the sound barrier in under five seconds and into space some twelve seconds after that.

'There are four sections I'm concerned about,' said Linda, pointing to one of them on the holomap. 'That's the largest, Phil…go there first.'

Phil didn't reply, but brought the ship up to point three light and initiated a wide hundred and eighty degree turn, coming up behind what was a large section of the liner's bow. It was spinning end over end and spewing gasses from multiple locations.

Linda grabbed onto it with the tractor as Phil matched its speed.

'Take us to starboard,' she said. 'Not too quickly, I don't want to lose grip.'

He did as requested and gradually the powerful beam

dragged the spinning lump of death, little by little out of its lethal trajectory.

'That's the next one,' pointed Linda.

Over the next few minutes, they managed to deflect two more ship sections. The fourth, however, was already too close to the atmosphere when they arrived, so Linda manipulated it enough to ensure it fell somewhere in the Pacific Ocean.

The two damaged marine ships had been stabilised and the injured personnel taken to the medical suite on Armstrong Station, Now a very different establishment to when Ed and Andy first visited it a few years ago.

'Let's go get Ed,' said Linda, noticing a huge look of relief on Pol's face.

Phil turned the ship and hit the gas back in the direction where the mini-me would be.

'Can you give me a vector?' he asked.

'Can't find him,' said Pol.

'Weren't you keeping tabs on him while we were busy?' Linda asked.

'I was busy watching what you were doing,' she said.

'Has someone else picked him up?' asked Andy.

'Perhaps he cloaked,' said Callon.

'What would be the point of that?' said Andy.

'I don't know,' she said. 'There's no jump signature and we'd still be able to detect his ship if it was in someone else's hangar.'

'She's right,' said Linda. 'He should be here.'

58

West protection hangar, Rimae base, the Moon, Sol system

ED HAD MADE it inside a pressurised hangar before his cracked canopy finally gave out. After coming round and realising he had a broken leg, one hell of a headache and a damaged front screen on the verge of failing, he had a choice. Go for Armstrong Station or Rimae, the British moon base. They were both about the same distance. He daren't attempt a jump back to the *Gabriel* in case the stresses popped the screen and his array was glitching too.

He only chose the Moon because, one, he could see it and two, he'd never been there before. All the space travelling he'd done over the last few years, all those galaxies, systems and planets visited, and he'd never visited the closest celestial body to his home planet.

Rimae base hangar was small and had been cut into the down slope of a large crater which hid and protected it from above. They didn't need freighters or anything large landing there, as it was a science station and home to around fifty personnel.

He remembered seeing an article on the news a year or so ago, that they'd installed an atmosphere shield and how much easier it had made it for visiting scientists to come and go.

Two Royal Marines ran across to his ship as it settled at a slight angle on the carboncrete floor. He popped the canopy and smiled at the two scowling soldiers. They had their weapons in the shoulder and didn't look too happy at his unscheduled arrival.

'Get out, keeping your hands where we can see them,' one of them demanded.

'I can't,' said Ed, grimacing with the pain. 'I think my leg is broken.'

'Hang on,' said the other one, peering at Ed closely. 'Aren't you Edward Virr?'

'I am he,' he said, nodding.

'Fuck me…what you doing 'ere, mate?'

'I thought I'd pop by for a cuppa and perhaps get your medic to assess my leg,' he said, hopefully.

'Right…don't go anywhere,' the soldier said, lowering his weapon, turning away and chattering on his communicator. His colleague just raised his eyebrows, but kept his rifle up.

Two hours later, Ed was sat in their mess hall, an inflatable leg splint over his fractured tibia and some strong pain killers flowing around his system. Everyone on the base had wanted to come and see him, have a chat and get photos with him. To them, he was the most famous scientist in history and having him in their little science establishment was like all their Christmases coming at once.

'Guys…guys…I really need to call my ship,' he said, for about the third time.

'Is the *Gabriel* going to come here?' someone asked.

'One of our shuttles most likely,' he said.

'Can we meet Cleopatra?' another asked.

'Only if you let me call my ship,' he said, a little more firmly this time as he realised his request had been ignored yet again.

'Wow…Cleopatra's coming,' the same guy enthused. 'I'm told she can manifest herself into anyone.'

'That's completely true,' said the British Prime Minister, Bill McDonold as he strolled through the room, stood next to Ed, placed his hand on his shoulder and smiled at the crowd.

Ed looked up at him suspiciously.

'Cleo, behave,' he said, sighing.

There were gasps of shock as the Prime Minister morphed back into Cleo dressed in her trademark gold-trimmed robes and headdress.

'It's her,' echoed around the room.

Everyone turned as the door slammed open.

'YOU WANKER,' shouted Andy, stumbling into the mess hall and almost falling over in the low gravity. 'WE COULDN'T FIND YOU, we thought you were dead,' he continued, lowering his voice in the sudden silence.

'Err…touché,' Ed replied, pointing poignantly back at Andy.

Andy sighed, puffed out his cheeks and peered around

the room at all the wide-eyed faces staring back at him. A grin slowly formed across his face as he stood just inside the door.

'I think you two need a hug,' said Cleo, helping Ed to his feet.

Andy's grin became wider as he strolled across the room, the crowd moving aside as he passed, and a spontaneous cheer resounded as the two friends enveloped each other.

'Let's not do that again,' whispered Andy.

'Deal,' Ed replied.

A large urn of tea was consumed along with three large Dundee cakes raided from the kitchen, much to everyone's delight.

———

'Where the hell have you two idiots been? And what's that about?' Linda asked, pointing at Ed's crutches as they arrived back on the *Gabriel* an hour later. Pol immediately jumped up and hugged Ed. Rayl gave Andy a wide grin.

'Having our photos taken with our fan club,' said Andy. 'You should have come too, they were asking about you.'

'Meeting a whole room full of scientists,' said Linda, tapping her chin with a forefinger. 'I think I'd rather watch skin form on custard. Spending half my life with the two of you is bad enough.'

'They had cake,' said Andy, with raised eyebrows.

'Did you bring me some?' she asked, looking at the two of them in turn.

'Err…no,' said Ed, with a pinched expression.

'Then why tell me?'

Ed cleared his throat.

'Err…moving swiftly on,' he said. 'Do we have any news from Earth? Andy told me you were able to divert all but one large lump of debris.'

'It went into the South Pacific around two thousand miles east of the Chatham Islands,' said Pol. 'No tsunami warnings issued, they're predicting the islands to have maybe a swell of a couple of feet in a few hours' time.'

'Rio de Janeiro owe us a drink then,' said Andy. 'Oh, by the way, I got this.'

He slid a thick jacket out of a backpack and plonked it on the floor.

'Is that what I think it is?' Ed asked.

'Yeah…a jump jacket. I'm getting Cleo to reverse engineer it, improve it, make it a bit lighter maybe. How useful would these be?'

'Absolutely,' said Ed, stooping awkwardly to pick it up and feeling the weight.'

'Has there been any conjecture about where Menka might be now?'

'It could be anywhere on the route,' said Phil. 'Any navigation evidence was obviously on that ship, so we'll never know.'

'Has anyone informed Bache of the current situation?' Ed asked.

'All done,' said Linda, pointing at the tube lift. 'I sent him a full report on a jump drone. You get yourself into an autonurse, Edward, and sort that leg out.'

Ed hobbled his way back towards the lift, his crutches clicking on the floor. He turned just before he got there.

'The marines?' he said. 'Are they okay? their ships were just as close as me when that thing went up.'

'Two of them are still requiring medical attention and are on Armstrong,' said Linda. 'Their damaged ships are in our hangar. Cleo's fixing them. The other two undamaged ones left for Dasos a couple of hours ago.'

'Why don't we get those two guys into an autonurse?' Ed asked.

Linda sighed and shook her head.

'They don't trust them, they want to heal naturally,' she said, shrugging.

'They think it would make them weak,' said Phil. 'Voodoo medicine,' he added, wiggling his fingers with a smirk.

'Voodoo or not,' said Ed, turning back to the lift. 'I'm not waiting six months for this to heal.'

59

The Masons Arms, South Somerset, England

THE CAMPSITE behind the pub more resembled a space port on this dark November evening. Even the lower overspill carpark was taken up with the old pirate freighter Ed had laid claim to. It was a clear evening, but chilly and the group had gathered in a heated thatched hut in the beer garden. It was discreet and away from the busy bar and restaurant where they would be recognised all the time and never left alone. Both of Ed's black greyhounds, Ripley and Willow, lay on beds in the corner snoring gently and twitching as they ran in their sleep.

'It's my round,' said Andy, giving Callon his tablet and a tray. She could go into the bar and order the drinks as she was relatively unknown.

Ed saw Linda look at her watch.

'He'll be here,' he said. 'He promised and anyway

they're coming with the *K52* to collect the bits of liner you diverted.'

'I hope Grogun's still the captain,' said Linda. 'I'll be having words with Bache if she's not.'

'She is,' said Ed.

'D'you think their forensic teams will find any evidence on them?' Pol asked.

'Unlikely, but it'll be good to get rid of them. They are a navigation nuisance,' said Phil.

The conversation in the hut paused as the unmistakable scream of antigravs swept over the pub.

'Told you he'd be here,' said Ed.

Admiral Bache Loftt arrived at the hut at the same time Callon returned with the drinks. He was alongside Commander Zaphir Mye and Captain Grogun Whipper. A resounding cheer put smiles on their faces as they entered and were greeted by everyone.

'I wish I got that welcome on my own planet,' said Bache, musing.

'Still blaming you for everything?' Ed asked.

Bache nodded.

'And us,' said Zaphir.

'If you're navy, you're to blame for everything,' said Grogun.

'Have I got to go back and get more drinks now?' asked Callon, her shoulders slumping.

'I'll go,' said Zaphir. 'They do accept our credits don't they?'

'I'll have one of those,' said Bache, pointing at Andy's pint of ale.

'Same here,' said Grogun.

While Zaphir disappeared off inside, Bache sat down, exhaled a sigh, leant back, laced his fingers behind his head and closed his eyes.

'What a bloody shit show,' he said. 'It's just one bloody thing after another these days.'

'Wishing you'd stayed retired?' Linda asked.

He opened his eyes and stared at her.

'Hell, yeah…I could've been on a beach somewhere warm without a care for anything except where my next cold drink was coming from.'

'Amen,' said Linda. 'Let's all take the rest of our lives off.'

'Is there somewhere that doesn't have a continuous stream of psychotic aliens, murderers, lunatics, unstable gods and giant roaches with guns?' said Andy. 'Cuz I want to go there.'

'Has anyone seen or heard from our two tame gods recently?' Bache asked, predominantly staring at Ed.

'Err…nothing since she stopped me exiting an airlock,' he said.

'And sending me three rather smelly individuals,' said Bache. 'By the way, is that their old ship in the car park?'

Ed nodded slowly in reply.

'What in the Ancients do you want that shit box for?' he asked.

'It's clandestine,' said Ed. 'No one gives it a second look. The *Gabriel* is big, shiny and attracts attention. That shit box as you call it, doesn't.'

'It stinks inside,' said Andy.

'It goes into Southampton Starship tomorrow for a refit on the inside and to be retrofitted with all the latest kit and hidden weapons,' said Ed. 'It'll be my little secret spy ship.'

'Look at you, going all CIA,' said Linda, sipping her lager and smirking.

'So, does that mean you're not retiring either?' Grogun asked.

'It means, it'll be there if required,' Ed answered.

'I understand you had a little mishap with one of my fighters, Andrew,' Bache said, raising one eyebrow.

'Ah…it'll be fine…it'll buff out,' Andy said hopefully, rolling his eyes.

'Hmm,' grunted Bache, fishing a small piece of jagged blue metal out of a pocket.

'Conor gave me this,' he said.

'Ah,' said Andy. 'I wondered where that bit was.'

'What is it?' asked Rayl.

'His fighter,' said Ed. 'What's left of it.'

Bache nodded and grinned.

'It'll be replaced,' he said, turning to Ed. 'And yours will be repaired too while we're here.'

'Thanks, Admiral,' said Ed. 'Do you guys have any clue where she is?'

Bache shrugged and sighed.

'Unfortunately, there are a multitude of planets, space stations or even an intersect with another vessel en route. The fact the liner was half a day ahead of you and then turned up after you equates to a stop somewhere for several hours. Where, we may never know.'

'I don't like the fact that she's still out there,' said Linda.

'Nobody does,' said Bache. 'But she's an Ancient…

she's been around for three hundred thousand years and taken a very different path to the other two we know. At least we know about her now and if she shows up on any GDA world, flags will be raised. Getting rid of her might prove difficult, but you never know what the future might bring.'

'We need a god gun,' said Andy, leaning back and savouring his pint.

'Are things sorted out on Dasos now?' Linda asked.

'Getting there,' said Bache, taking a deep breath. 'Stathmos Vasi is pretty much clear now. An occasional bug is discovered cowering in a corner somewhere, but the planet is another thing. That will take a while, although, they are quite meek without the collective leadership of the queen. We believe some might have hibernated because they don't like the cold and snow much.'

Zaphir arrived back with drinks for the three of them.

'What've you got there?' Bache asked, eyeing Zaphir's cloudy drink suspiciously.

'It's called Rosie's Pig, a local slider,' she said.

'Cider,' said Andy. 'It's called cider and we're right in the heart of apple country here where a lot of it's made.'

'Looks like dish water,' said Grogun. 'You can keep that.'

Just at that moment, Ripley got off her bed, stretched, sniffed the cider and backed away curling her lip.

'See, even the dog doesn't like it,' laughed Grogun.

Willow, thinking she was missing out on something, jumped up and stuck her nose in the glass, licked her lips and began lapping at the cider.

'Hey,' said Zaphir, snatching the glass away and eyeing it dubiously. 'Yuck.'

Bache laughed with everyone else, stood up and raised his glass.

'Thank you for all your help…*Megáli diárkeia zoís*,' he said.

'Yes,' said Ed. 'Long life…cheers everyone.'

EPILOGUE

Tinmerack Station, orbiting Ferrox VII, Mio system

FERROX VII WAS PREDOMINATELY an industrial manufacturing hub producing smaller parts included in the construction of starships: engines, pumps, airlocks, control systems, arrays, etcetera. If a modern vessel needed it, it would be made somewhere on Ferrox VII.

It comprised three main continents, two almost entirely covered by industrial cities and complexes. The third in the north was completely overlaid by a monstrous mountain range, containing a bottomless supply of raw materials, a hive of gargantuan mines, some opencast, most underground, but all providing the raw materials for the planet's predominantly metallurgical and composite-hungry industries.

Tinmerack Station hanging in orbit above, is over three kilometres long, an ugly conglomeration of mismatched habitation and commercial space engineering units. From a distance it appeared quite pretty against the backdrop of the blue planet. But once you got closer, the unsightly mix of differently shaped and coloured habitats crudely welded together in a completely random manner spoilt the romance. An odd medley of manipulator arms, docking clamps and differing designs of airlock casually littered the outside.

Then there were the ships, dozens of them; some reasonably intact, others stripped to bulkhead skeletons and everything in between, and all crudely attached to various docking clamps distributed haphazardly onto any solid surface. Basically a starship scrapyard. If you couldn't afford a new part for your ship, this is where you came.

Menka scowled at the holomap with an expression of disgust.

'Are you sure this is where the meeting is supposed to be?' she muttered.

The navigator nodded as the pilot released the vessel to the station's automated docking software. The cockpit became gloomy as they crept into the shadow of Tinmerack. Jagged sections of superstructure reached out, threatening to snag the ship as it passed alongside. Menka found it hard not to lean the opposite way, and she gritted her teeth so hard, it made her jaw ache.

The final bang and judder as the docking clamps closed home, almost knocked her off her feet.

'For fuck's sake,' she carped. 'Are they doing this deliberately?'

'No, ma'am,' said the pilot. 'Just old technology.'

'I'm beginning to have major misgivings about this meeting,' she said. 'But, we're here now.'

'Docking tube attached, sealed and pressurised, ma'am.'

She nodded and made her way through and down to the port corridor where two of her staff were waiting by the airlock. One of them gave her a tablet as the other opened the inner door.

'You will remain here,' she said, stepping inside and hitting the cycle icon.

'But, ma'am…'

The inner door closed before he could object too forcibly.

When the outer door slid upwards, it wasn't the grubbiness of the docking tube that repulsed her, it was the smell, a mixture of machine oil and human excrement.

'Delightful,' she muttered, striding the ten metres to the open outer station door.

It cycled as soon as she entered. If she thought the aroma was bad in the tube, it became acutely worse as the station inner door grated to one side, sounding like the bearings hadn't been greased in decades.

Recoiling from the acrid atmosphere, she was greeted by two officious-looking female soldiers wearing full battle armour and carrying modern assault rifles across their chests.

Menka raised her eyebrows as she was scanned with a whirring handheld piece of apparatus. She'd already disabled their weapons, but left the scanner alone. Once they were happy she posed no threat to them, they turned and indicated which way she was intended to go.

Nothing was said, but Menka moved off as indicated, one guard in front and one falling in behind, their amour servos whining as they walked. She noticed a few faces peering out at her from dark corners and anybody they met pinned themselves against the walls at sight of the soldiers.

A small hidden elevator took them up countless levels and when the doors reopened, Menka breathed a sigh of relief. The stink was gone and in its place came fresh filtered air whispering out of vents near the ceiling. The floor in this new wider passageway was carpeted and led to a large entrance hall flanked with huge fluted pillars. Twin staircases led up in semicircles meeting at the top, and an oversize chandelier loomed above them, bathing the hall and stairs in a dim golden hue.

The soldiers led her to the left-hand staircase where a man dressed in a dark suit waited on the first step.

'Good morning,' he said. 'I hope you had a pleasant journey. If you would like to come this way, the lady will see you now.'

Hmm, thought Menka. *Just who the fuck does this woman think she is?*

'Thank you,' she said, hiding her displeasure well, as they left the soldiers and climbed the stairs.

At the top was a rather ostentatious set of ten-foot double doors. Inlaid carvings of ancient warriors fighting strange creatures decorated them, covered in what looked like gold leaf.

Menka rolled her eyes and shook her head, making sure the gesture was unseen by her guide. He meanwhile had reached the door and knocked three times.

It was opened by another female soldier, this one

dressed in a light body armour. She nodded and beckoned Menka inside. The room into which she was ushered was surprisingly small considering the scale of the doors. There was a lot of shades of blue involved. Carpets, furnishings, walls, although for the first time on the station, Menka decided she quite liked the decor. She turned to admire large screens on the walls displaying beautiful planetary scenes, of where Menka could only guess.

'My home planet,' said a voice behind her.

She spun around to meet the arms dealer she'd come all this way to see. She was younger than she'd imagined, slim, long black hair and suspicious blue eyes.

'Can't go back there now,' she added, a veil of sadness washing over her. 'Warrant for my arrest, but then again, there's one of those almost everywhere these days.'

'You're an arms dealer,' said Menka. 'Kinda goes with the territory.'

The girl flinched.

'I prefer, defence facilitator,' she said, strolling over to an ornate dark wooden desk. 'Did you bring the item you wish to trade?'

Menka held up the tablet.

'It's all on there is it?' the girl asked.

Menka turned the tablet on and flicked her hand from the tablet's screen to one of the big screens on the wall. A menu appeared.

The girl held her hand up to face the screen and manipulated her way down the rows of icons, selecting one in particular and spreading her fingers out sharply. The file opened. It displayed a large piece of medical equipment and another list of files specifying its design schematics.

The girl smiled for the first time.

'What's your price for this interesting software?' she asked, turning to Menka, her stern expression returning.

'A ship,' said Menka. 'A fully armed warship, with cloaking and fast…it must be fast.'

'And are you trading that hijacked freighter you arrived in?'

This took Menka by surprise. She hid it, but it reminded her not to take this kid for an idiot. She seemed to conduct herself in a manner beyond her years.

'That can be included in the deal if I get a vessel to my liking,' she said.

The girl sat at her desk and tapped on an inlaid screen for a moment, before pointing up at the ceiling.

'Would something like this be of use?' she asked, leaning back in her chair.

A hologram of an extremely large freighter appeared, turning slowly above them.

'I wanted a fucking warship,' Menka insisted, giving the girl an impatient glare.

'Hmm,' she grunted, pressing another icon.

The holographic ship suddenly began changing shape. Massive sections of its superstructure revolved or opened out to reveal hundreds of weapons pods and missile racks.

'Fucking warshippy enough for you now?' the girl asked, grinning.

'Where the hell did you get that from?' Menka asked, walking around the hologram as it turned in the opposite direction.

'Originally an acquired Klatt battleship, with a minor makeover of my own design. It's now stronger, faster, cloakable, and as you've seen, unassuming when in freighter mode.'

'I like it,' said Menka, turning back to the girl. 'I'll take it.'

She handed the dealer the tablet.

'When do I take delivery?'

'How about this morning?' she said. 'From my personal dock, so you don't have to walk amongst the great unwashed again.'

'My crew?'

'I'll have them escorted along shortly,' she said, standing and signalling the soldier who'd remained on guard by the door.

Menka nodded and turned to leave.

'Thank you for your business,' said the girl, sitting again.

When the door closed and Menka was gone. Ystolion Flast kissed Phil's tablet Menka had given her and placed it almost reverently on her desk.

'Got it all now,' she said, clenching both fists and looking upwards. 'We will soon have revenge, darling... and it will be absolute.'

AFTERWORD

I wanted to say a huge thank you for chosing to read *The Halo Fold*. I sincerely hope you enjoyed the seventh adventure in the *Fold* series.

If you did enjoy this novel, it'd be fantastic if you could write a review. It doesn't have to be long, just a few words, but it is the best way for me to help new readers discover my writing for the first time. I use the best and most imaginative reviews in my marketing too.

If you'd like to stay up to date with what's going on, you're welcome to join my reader group at my website www.nickadamsbooks.com and receive a bi-monthly newsletter, advance notice of new releases and cover reveals. I will never share your email address and you can unsubscribe at any time.

You can also contact me via Facebook, Instagram, or by email. I love hearing from readers – I read every message and try to reply to everyone personally.

Thanks again for your support.
Nick Adams

www.ingramcontent.com/pod-product-compliance
Lightning Source LLC
Chambersburg PA
CBHW011550190726
48287CB00010B/2827